Breakfast with Neruda

Laura Moe

MeritPress

Published by
Merit Press
an imprint of F+W Media, Inc.
10151 Carver Road, Suite 200
Blue Ash, OH 45242. U.S.A.
www.meritpressbooks.com

ISBN 10: 1-4405-9219-5
ISBN 13: 978-1-4405-9219-5
eISBN 10: 1-4405-9220-9
eISBN 13: 978-1-4405-9220-1

Printed in the United States of America.

10 9 8 7 6 5 4 3 2 1

This is a work of fiction. Names, characters, corporations, institutions, organizations, events, or locales in this novel are either the product of the author's imagination or, if real, used fictitiously. The resemblance of any character to actual persons (living or dead) is entirely coincidental.

Many of the designations used by manufacturers and sellers to distinguish their products are claimed as trademarks. Where those designations appear in this book and F+W Media, Inc. was aware of a trademark claim, the designations have been printed with initial capital letters.

Cover design by Frank Rivera.
Cover image © iStockphoto.com/
rudchenko.

This book is available at quantity discounts
for bulk purchases.
For information, please call
1-800-289-0963.

"Daring Enough to Finish" from The Glance: Songs of Soul-Meeting by Rumi, translated by Coleman Barks, translation copyright © 1999 by Coleman Barks, used with permission of Viking Books, an imprint of Penguin, a division of Penguin Random House LLC.

Excerpts from On the Road by Jack Kerouac, used with permission from Penguin Publishing Group, Penguin Random House LLC.

Excerpt from The Shadow of the Wind by Carlos Ruiz Zafón, translated by Lucia Graves, used with permission from Penguin Publishing Group, Penguin Random House LLC.

The first two lines of "Sonnet XL" and third and fourth lines of "Sonnet XVII" from 100 Love Sonnets/Cien sonetos de amor by Pablo Neruda, translated by Stephen Tapscott, copyright © Pablo Neruda, 1959, and Fundación Pablo Neruda, copyright © 1986 by The University of Texas Press. By permission of the publisher.

Dedication

This book is dedicated to all my former students. Your tales are worthy of being told.

CHAPTER ONE

It was green, the silence; the light was moist;
the month of June trembled like a butterfly.

PABLO NERUDA

The hallway is dark and abandoned except for the clanging of metal against tile. Earl, the head custodian, fills a giant bucket near the janitor's closet with water. He looks up at me, nods, and keeps filling the pail.

"How come it's so dark in here?" I ask.

"I look better in the dark," Earl says. He laughs and reveals a gold front tooth. He's a raggedy guy of about sixty who always has a cud of tobacco in his mouth. "Power's still out from the storm."

"Oh yeah," I say, nodding, as if I know anything about the power outage. It had stormed like an apocalypse last night, so yeah, it probably knocked the power off. I hold out my hand. "Michael Flynn, reporting for duty."

"I know who you are," Earl shuts off the hose and looks me over. "Listen, kid, I know what you did to get stuck here all summer, and I don't put up with any crap," he says. "We clear on that?"

"Yes, sir," I respond.

He wheels the bucket into the hallway and I follow. "First thing you're gonna do is start cleaning out the lockers." He snorts. "Kind of ironic for you."

My face reddens, and Earl gestures to the end of the hallway. "Start at that end and work your way back. Take a big trash can with you." He indicates one of the enormous wheeled tubs next to

5

the elevator. "The first thing you'll find is backpacks. When you get a full one, open it up, and if you don't find any explosives," he sneers at me, "take the books out and lay them on the floor, along with the bag. Throw out anything else that's junk, like used notebooks, food, or dirty clothes." Earl reaches for a spray bottle and a wad of rags. "And if you find coats, shoes, or semi-clean clothes, put those on the floor too."

"What do you do with it all?"

"We donate it to the homeless shelter."

I nod.

"Anything else that looks valuable, like calculators, toss on the floor too. We'll separate all that out later."

"Okay."

He hands me the bottle of cleaner and rags. "After you get all the junk out, spray the inside of the locker and wipe it down."

I wait for any more instructions. "Get moving, kid."

I wheel a giant trashcan to the end of the hallway. It's been months since I've been inside the school. It may be the darkened hallways and the lack of students, but I feel like I'm in a whole new universe. I reach out to open the first locker, but it has a lock dangling from its handle. I notice several others do too. "Uh, Earl?" I shout. "This may be a stupid question, but how do I open lockers if they still have locks on them?"

"Oh, hell!" He disappears into the janitor supply room and marches toward me holding bolt cutters. "Hess was supposed to cut these off last week." He snaps the locks off like they're twigs.

I open the first locker and it's stuffed. "Wow. How can people leave all this crap behind?"

"Beats the hell out of me. You kids have no sense of value anymore. My folks would've hog-tied me and hung me from the rafters if I'd left anything valuable at school."

Earl grumbles to himself as he walks back to his end of the hall. I pull out a black book bag. It's like lifting an SUV. I open it up and pull out three textbooks, two library books, a hoodie, and a fairly new pair of shoes. I set them on the floor. Inside the zippered pocket are a calculator and an assortment of pens, pencils, packs of gum, and a full can of Dr Pepper. I shove the pens and gum in my back pocket and stuff the Dr Pepper in the leg pocket of my cargo pants. The rest of what's inside I empty into the bin. I place the bag on top of the hoodie and move on to the next locker. I spot Earl at the opposite end, swabbing the floor, whistling. He's been working here since the Pleistocene. A lot of kids think he's a jerk because he's not exactly a warm fuzzy, but I'm grateful he agreed to let me work off my community service here. Better than wearing a neon orange vest, picking up trash along the freeway or painting rest stop outhouses.

I'm surprised to find book bags in lockers since I heard they were banned after my stunt, and it is kind of ironic I am cleaning the lockers I almost blew up. I didn't mean to blow up the building, only my ex-best friend Rick Shraver's car, but in a moment of freakishly bad judgment, I carried enough explosives in my book bag to detonate the whole west wing of Rooster High.

I got off light, though. I had no criminal record, and had never been in much trouble other than a few detentions. And Rick didn't want to press charges since nothing really happened, so they gave me community service. The judge felt I could be "rehabilitated." I was, however, expelled for the rest of the school year, and I was banned from public school for the rest of the year, so I will be repeating senior year at Rooster High.

It takes all morning to go through the west hallway on the first floor. Hess, the assistant custodian, and another student helper (a.k.a. juvenile delinquent) are working on the second floor. I can hear them clattering and banging above me.

By the time I reach the end of the hallway, I have excavated twenty backpacks, too many books to count, several pieces of jewelry, a pair of glasses, some cash (which I pocket), and an iPod with a charger and earbuds, which I also nab.

I come to a locker I know well, next to what used to be my own. Inside is a leather band jacket. Rick's. I glance down the hall. Earl is clear at the other end. I toss the jacket in the trash, along with the textbooks inside the book bag. Let him have to pay for them. Then I feel kind of guilty and dig it all back out. Rick did kind of half forgive me for trying to incinerate his ride. He didn't want to press charges, but the school did. I set the jacket on the floor, but I keep the Speedway gas card I dug out of one of the pockets.

Earl glances at the mess of stuff on the floor and shakes his head. "You kids act like money grows on trees. You don't know the value of a dollar."

I'm pretty careful with my money, and I don't tell Earl my home is a 1982 Ford LTD station wagon I call the Blue Whale, and the only reason I go to school here is my last known address is in this district.

At 11:15, Earl says, "It's time for lunch, kid."

"How long is the lunch break?"

"Half an hour."

"I guess I'll go home and eat."

"Suit yourself," he says. "Be back at 11:45."

I go out to my car and count the cash I palmed from locker cleanup. A little over eighteen bucks. I pull a plastic grocery bag out from under the passenger side seat and scrounge for some change, which means I now have almost twenty-three bucks to last me for the next five days until pay day. If I plan this right I can get some gas, have enough cash left for a drive-thru lunch, and buy a few groceries.

I stop for gas and get the eleven buck's worth left on Rick's Speedway card and pull into Wendy's drive-thru to order a single cheeseburger, fries, and water. My two-dollar splurge. I park in the lot to eat. I fiddle with the iPod, but the battery is dead.

I finish eating and lob my crumpled wrappers in the trash bin on the way out, but I save my cup.

Back at school I find Earl in the teacher's lounge. I'd never seen the inside of the teachers' hangout. I half expected it to be dark and comfortable like an actual lounge, but it's a miniature version of the school cafeteria. They have the same gray metal tables and plastic chairs.

Hess is there too, along with a girl I don't know, one of those Black-Haired Girls: natural blondes and brunettes who dye their hair black. On most girls it makes them look like they're dead, but on this chick it kind of works. She has navy blue eyes and pale skin, so the hair is an interesting contrast even though she wears zombie eyeliner. She's thin in a not-quite-starving way. Still, she's not my type.

"Hey kid," Earl says. "Have a cookie." A plate of homemade chocolate chip cookies sits on the table.

I never turn down free food. "Thanks."

"My wife makes them."

I take a bite and my endorphins go into overdrive. "This is the best cookie I've ever eaten," I say.

Earl chuckles and slides the plate my way. "Dottie will be glad to hear that. Eat up, kid."

"She keeps us well fed," Hess says. He pats his massive belly. "Wait 'til you try her banana cream pie."

I sit down and take another cookie. I glance at the girl, her long black hair bound in a loose braid halfway down her back. She looks sort of familiar but I can't quite place her.

"Hey," she says. She reaches for a cookie.

"This is Shelly," Hess says to me." Shelly, meet Michael."

"The Unabomber." She bites into the cookie. "Yeah, I've heard about you."

Who hasn't? The YouTube video of my arrest went viral. "I only murdered and ate six people, not ten," I say. "The media exaggerates."

Shelly laughs. "There's nothing to worry about then," she says.

I wonder what she did to spend the summer with the custodians and me.

After I unload all the debris inside the west lockers, I move to the east lockers and clean those out too. After I'm done removing stuff, I start forming piles by separating stuff by category. Around 1:30, Earl brings me a flat cart. "Okay, kid, start stacking the textbooks on this. Try to sort them by subject."

I nod. "What about the other books?"

He wrinkles his brow. "Unless they're library books, just pitch them." He reaches down and picks up a thick book with DISCARD stamped in red on the cover. "Also toss out ones like this that the library no longer wants."

"Can I keep any? I mean, the miscellaneous or discarded ones?"

"Sure, kid. Knock yourself out."

It takes me about half an hour to sort and stack all the books. I start a pile of ones I want to keep and toss the rest in the trashcan. I drop the library books in the drop box outside the library and wheel the textbooks to the loading dock at the back of the school. The rear doors are open and I notice Shelly standing outside, smoking a cigarette. "Hey, you can get in trouble smoking on school grounds," I say.

She turns to look at me. "Ha ha," she says. "I'm already in trouble."

I step outside. "So what did you do to get assigned to Camp Clean Up The School?"

She nods her head at her cigarette. "You're looking at it," she says. "Too many days getting caught smoking on school grounds."

"Irony," I say. "I like that."

"Yeah. Hess doesn't care. He smokes too so he gets it when you just need a cigarette. 'Just don't get caught,' he says."

"Busted."

She inhales deeply and flicks the butt on the cement. "I'm shaking with fear."

We both step back inside. Somehow I know there's more to her story than just smoking, but it's not really my business. "Well, back to the salt mines," I say.

We walk in silence until we reach the staircase.

"See ya," she says.

Earl is loading the clothes on another flat cart when I get back to the hallway. I notice a green book bag next to my stack of books. "Figured you might need something to carry them in," he grumbles. "Seeing how the cops took your other bag away."

"Thanks," I say.

"Let's gather up the rest of this crap and call it a day."

We box up the homeless shelter stuff and wheel it out to the loading dock. Earl slaps me on the back. "Okay, kid. Tomorrow we start working on the rooms. See you at eight."

I shove my new books inside the bag, and head out to the Blue Whale.

I get in the car and realize I should have taken a shower. "Shit," I mutter. I pull out my Tracfone and punch in Annie's number. She answers on the third ring. "Hey, is there a clear path to the bathroom?"

"Yeah, pretty much."

"Okay. I'll be over soon," I say. "I need a shower before work."

I drive toward my family's townhouse. It's kind of a crappy place, a rented two-story with a fenced-in back porch. I rap on the front door and my sister yells, "It's open!"

I take a deep breath and shove at the door, and it opens just enough for me to sidle my way inside. The place reeks of stale cigarettes, rotting food, and dead mice. I cough and hold my nose.

There is so much stuff in here I have to climb into what was once the living room. The blinds are open, but it's always dark in here.

"Hey!" I hear my sister say.

"Where are you?" I ask.

"In the kitchen."

I shuffle, carefully clutching my bag, to the narrow path leading to the kitchen. I expel my breath and take another breath. It doesn't smell much better in here.

Annie stands at the counter, making a peanut butter and jelly sandwich. "Want one?"

I glance at the stacks of dirty pots and plates cluttering the counter. But I notice a spray bottle of Windex and see Annie has cleaned off a space for making sandwiches. "Sure."

My younger siblings and I all have different fathers. My brother, Jeff Nolan, is a pasty-faced blond with hazel eyes, and my sister, Annie Durant, is biracial. She's small and dark with deep, cocoa eyes. My sister and I have dark hair, but I'm tall and have green eyes. To strangers we look like three random kids, not siblings who used to curl together like puppies in strange beds every night.

We're all close in age. Jeff and I will both be seniors together now that I have to repeat, and Annie will be a sophomore.

"You working tonight?" she asks.

"Yeah. I have to be there in an hour, so that's why I need a shower."

She grins. "You're a poet and you don't know it."

I roll my eyes at her and dig through my pack. My shirt is a wrinkled mess but if I shake it enough times it won't look too bad. It's just the movie theater. I wear a vest over it anyway. "So what are you up to today?"

She sets my sandwich on a napkin and hands it to me. "Scott and I are going to a concert."

"Cool." She's been dating Scott, a fellow band member, since they were in eighth grade. He's an okay guy for a tuba player.

I notice a Timbits box on the counter. "I see Jeff has been by recently." He works at Tim Hortons, and sometimes brings work with him when he visits.

Annie passes the box to me and I fish out a couple. I hand her back the carton, but she waves them away. "Keep 'em," she says. "You need them more than we do."

"Thanks." I pop the donut bits in my mouth. "Mom home?"

Annie sighs. "She's out at a flea market."

"Jesus," I say. I finish my sandwich and donut pieces and take a drink of water directly from the tap. I don't trust the cleanliness of any of their glasses. I wipe my mouth, and say, "Hey, wait 'til you see what I got today." I unzip my bag and pull out the iPod. "Look."

Annie's face lights up. "Wow. Where'd you get that?"

"It was inside one of the book bags. Earl said I could keep some of the stuff." I had planned on keeping the iPod, but how would I keep it charged up? I hand it to my sister. "It's for you."

"Seriously?"

"Yeah, and I got you something else too."

She raises her eyebrows. I can almost hear her mind screaming not more stuff!

"Don't worry," I say. "It doesn't take up much space, and you can throw it out." I pull out one of the books I earned from the lockers and pass it to my sister.

Her face breaks into a grin. "*The Arabian Nights!*"

When my sister's dad, Bob, was still alive he used to read stories from *The Arabian Nights* to get us to sleep.

"Sorry it's kind of beat up, but it was a freebie from the school lockers."

She holds the book against her chest. "Thank you for this. I won't throw it away. I'll toss out something of Mom's to make room for it."

Our mom's stuff has accumulated enough to start spilling inside my sister's room. And Mom freaks if you throw anything out. Oddly enough, as much crap as is in the house, she notices when things are missing. It wasn't always like this. We used to move every few months, but about five years ago, when Mom married Tomas, we moved here. He's long gone, but the junk multiplies.

Jeff got lucky. He lives with his dad and his new family. Since they live nearby, Annie and I see Jeff at school all the time. Rooster, Ohio, is a small enough place, and everyone goes to one of three high schools in the county. Jeff's dad gave me my car. Not that he knows I live in it. At the time I just needed a car to get to work and back. I moved out even before I got expelled because Mom's piles of crap had buried my bedroom.

Annie started keeping her clothes in a dresser drawer on the back porch about a year ago so she won't smell like the inside of the townhouse. Even in cold weather she changes clothes behind a curtain she devised from a blanket.

"I started sleeping out back," she tells me. We walk to the back door and I see Annie has rigged up a folding lawn chair with some cushions. "I can't breathe inside this house."

"You're always welcome to sleep in the backseat of my car," I say.

"I might take you up on that if things get any worse."

I give her a quick hug. "Thanks for the sandwich." I pick up my bag and carefully trek my way up to the bathroom. Keeping a usable bathroom and a somewhat functional kitchen were the sole triumphs my sister had negotiated with our mother. So far. I just wonder when Annie will be shoved completely out the door too.

I drape the shirt over the shower door, hoping the steam straightens it out.

When I get back downstairs, Annie is sitting on the porch reading from the book. She looks up when I step outside. "Remember *The Fisherman and the Genie?*"

The Fisherman and the Genie was one of our favorites as kids, probably because it was Bob's favorite.

"Thanks again for the book," Annie says.

"No problem."

She picks up the iPod and charger and hands them to me. "Here. You don't have any way to listen to music," she says. "I have the radio or my stereo. Plus I already have an MP3 player."

"Are you sure?" I say.

"Yeah. I'm sure."

***

I get off work around 10:30 and stop at Kroger to buy a box of crackers (bread molds too quickly in this summer heat), a jar of Jif peanut butter, and a squirt bottle of honey. In the school library I read an article in *Outdoor Life* about surviving hikes and getting lost in the woods. It said peanut butter and honey are perfect foods because they're nutritious and don't spoil when they get too hot or cold. According to the article, a jar of honey can last 3,000 years, so I've been pretty much living on peanut butter and honey and fast-food dollar menus since I moved out of Mom's house. I buy a couple bananas and apples. I almost never eat salads or vegetables because they spoil quickly.

I count my leftover money: $13.12. Hopefully I'll find some more cash in the east wing lockers tomorrow.

I drive around the Graham Park neighborhood close to the school, but not so close I'm actually on the lot. I have to wait for the night custodians to leave at eleven; usually the school parking lot is empty by 11:15. The few minutes I charged the iPod at Mom's didn't last, and my phone is also dead, so I still don't know what time it is.

I sometimes sleep near my mom's, but now that I have to be at school so early, I park the car on or close to the school grounds to make sure I get there on time. I don't want to screw up this community service gig.

I could park the car anywhere I guess, but there are parts of town where I don't want to be seen, and also parts of town that scare the crap out of me. It's so hot inside the car I won't sleep for long stretches anyway. Tonight I settle in a dark spot near the football field, behind the training room. The heat forces me to sleep with the windows and the tailgate open.

CHAPTER TWO

The first thing that wakes me is the light. The sun rises early in summer and hits me in waves. Next thing I notice, of course, is the heat. My T-shirt and boxers are stuck to me. The third thing is the smell of something burning. A cigarette. But I don't smoke. What the hell? I jolt upright.

"Morning, sunshine." Shelly is sitting in the open tailgate of my car, smoking. "Nice place you have here," she says. "And such a good neighborhood."

I run a hand through my hair and wipe my eyes. I grab a pair of shorts and slide them on over my boxers.

Shelly laughs. "Don't be embarrassed. I know about morning wood."

I'm actually more embarrassed that she found me sleeping in the car. "What time is it?" I ask.

"Six-thirty or so."

I try to conjure the reason that my car is parked behind the school at 6:30 in the morning when our sentences don't begin until eight. "I worked really late last night," I say, "and I didn't want to be late and have Earl turn me in to the court."

"Oh," she says. She glances at the stacks of clothes and stuff everywhere. "Sure," she says, as if she sees through my lie.

I slide out of the back of the car. "I work right after school, so I change clothes in here a lot." *Good cover, Michael*, I tell myself. I turn away from her and pee along the back fence.

She reaches into her purse and pulls out a twenty. "How about breakfast?" she says. "Steak 'n Shake?"

"You're buying?"

"Technically my dad is buying. But you're driving."

I envy her money. I'm also envious that she has a father, especially one who will give her a twenty with no questions asked. I clean the debris off the passenger seat and toss it all in the back. The door groans as she opens it and gets in. She glances around at the stuff littering the backseat.

"I am way overdue for going to the Laundromat," I say. Piles of my dirty shirts and pants are tossed on the seat next to my columns of books.

We drive in silence for a couple minutes, and then she fiddles with my radio. "It only gets AM," I say.

"Why?"

"It's old, and it didn't come with FM. The antenna broke off a long time ago, so even what I do get is scratchy."

She snaps off the radio. "That's okay. I'll just let you tell me why the hell you're living in your car."

My face grows hot. I barely know this chick who, like me, lives on the south side of the law. "First, you tell me what the hell you did to get sentenced to community service."

"I already told you. Got caught smoking."

"That only gets you a few detentions or Saturday schools," I say. I shoot her a glance. "I mean, look what I did. And it's a lot worse than inhaling too many packs of Kools."

She crosses her arms. "I smoke Marlboros."

"Whatever. I know what you did is at least as bad, if not worse, than me almost accidently annihilating the school building."

She fumbles through her enormous purse. "It's kind of a long, boring story," she says.

I give her a charming grin. "The radio doesn't work, and I'm not very interesting, so . . ."

"Fine. We'll flip for who has to spill their guts first." We pull into the restaurant parking lot. I glance in the window and see a few kids from school, including my ex-best friend sitting next to my ex-girlfriend. "Not here," I say, and back out of the parking space.

"Frenemies?" she asks.

"Something like that."

She glances at her phone. "I guess we don't really have time to get waited on anyway. It's like ten after seven already." I drive down Rocket Road and pull into the drive-thru at McDonald's.

I order the Big Breakfast Platter with extra butter, an extra biscuit, a large Diet Coke, and an apple pie. Shelly glances at me. "Sure you don't want a side of beef with that? Wouldn't want you to starve."

I stifle a laugh. "If I'm telling you my life story, you have to feed me first."

Shelly just orders an Egg McMuffin and small mocha latte. She hands me the twenty, and I pay the girl at the window. It's Krissy Jones from my AP English class last year. She acts friendly enough, but her eyes dart between the two of us as if she's a little afraid. I take the change and am tempted to pocket it, but Shelly holds out her hand. I smirk, and dribble the coins in her palm and place the bills in her lap.

"Shall we flip now?" she asks.

"Can we eat first?"

We pull around and park by the exit lane. I open the bags. The uncommon smell of hot breakfast food fills me with glee. Normally all I eat in the morning is a few handfuls of dry cereal and a banana. I hold the Styrofoam plate in my hands like it's a silver platter and take a giant whiff. Shelly snickers and shakes her head as I stab at the eggs with the plastic fork and practically inhale them.

Shelly watches me as she slowly nibbles at her sandwich. She waits until I have finished the eggs, sausage, and hash browns and start to butter my biscuit before she says, "Heads or tails?"

With my mouth full of biscuit, I say, "Heads."

She flips one of her quarters. "It's tails." She smiles. "Okay, buddy. Spill the story. Why the hell did you want to blow us to smithereens? And why do you live in your car?"

I glance at her. I wonder how much of the truth I want to share. She already knows how I got in trouble, which doesn't really relate to how I left home.

"First of all," I say, "you are not allowed to say you're sorry for me, or about anything I plan to tell you. Is that clear?"

She chuckles. "Okay."

"Okay." I cram the second biscuit inside my mouth and wash it down with a big gulp of Diet Coke. I belch. "Tell me what you think you know about me," I say.

"Well, not much, except they actually found enough firecrackers in your book bag to burn down a chunk of the building."

"True so far."

"Why did you do that?"

I stare out the windshield, half watching the morning traffic build up on Rocket Road. "I wasn't planning to blow up the school."

"Why the firecrackers then?"

"It's complicated," I say.

"Did getting expelled get you booted out of your house?"

I shrug. "Yeah. Kinda." I let the lie linger. I don't want to tell her about my mom's hoarding. Nobody knows about that except Annie and Jeff and me, and none of us is talking. I think Rick suspected too, because I stopped inviting him to my house.

"Isn't there some other relative you could live with?" Shelly asks.

I could have stayed with my grandmother for a while, but she's crazy too in her three-pack-a-day bottle-of-whiskey way, though at least her apartment isn't filled with useless junk. Grandma Barb lives in a senior apartment facility and has just the one bedroom. I could probably go there in an emergency, like if we get a blizzard this winter, but I can't live there since I'm not fifty-five-plus.

"No."

"What about your dad?"

"He's not in the picture," I snap. Unlike Jeff, who actually lives with his dad, and saw him every weekend before he moved in with him, I have never met my own father. I don't even know his name. Flynn is my mother's maiden name.

"But you still haven't told me why you had explosives in your book bag," she says.

I slump back in the seat and take a breath. "Do you know Rick Shraver?"

"Marginally."

"Yeah, well, he was my target. Not him, exactly. I was just going to blow up his car."

I glance at her but I can't read her reaction. "Anyway, he and I used to be friends. Since grade school we were tight. But junior year I started seeing Ashley Anders . . ." It's hard to think about her now. Ashley Anders, with her butter-colored hair and ocean-colored eyes.

"Go on," Shelly says.

"I never should have let Rick get to know her. I started seeing Ashley year before last, and we also hung around Rick sometimes. We'd go to the movies and stuff. A couple times when I had to work, the two of them got together and hung out. He was my best friend, right? I mean, shouldn't he be the one guy I trusted with my girlfriend? "

"You'd think."

"Yeah. Well, I couldn't get off work on prom night last March. And by then . . ." I was about to say I had been living in my car for several months, but I wanted Shelly to think my moving out had to do with the bomb disaster. "I needed money for my car insurance and couldn't afford to risk getting fired, and nobody would trade with me."

"Sucks," she says.

I nod. "Ashley and Rick stopped by the theater before dinner so she could show me her prom dress. And those two looked really good together, you know? At ease and in sync, yet nothing odd clicked in me. Yet.

"I remember she wore this cobalt blue gown and her normally pale skin was sprayed with a fake tan. Not a gross fakey one, but just enough color to make it look more like the beginning of June instead of the end of March. People in line at the concession stand all stared at her, as if she had just come from the Academy Awards."

I shift in my seat and look at Shelly. "Have you ever had one of those ESP kind of moments, like it's the best time in your life, but you know this is the last best moment of your life, and soon everything will turn to shit?"

She nods.

"Well, this was one of those times. I mean, Rick didn't hold her hand or anything, and they didn't appear to be acting like a couple, but there was this invisible energy between them, something that maybe even they weren't aware of. Maybe he was, but Ashley came up and kissed me, which right there in front of all those people made me look damn good. Anyway, somehow I knew that kiss was the last one. I had this unspoken dread, and that dread followed me through the rest of my shift. When I got off, I was supposed to meet them at the after prom at Main Lanes Bowling, but they weren't there. I drove around, and didn't find them at his house or her house. And I'm wondering, what the hell?

"So I cruised around all night, worrying, thinking. I stopped and slept for a couple of hours, and drove around again. I woke at seven in the morning and I drove past the Red Roof Inn, and that's when I saw them, coming out of a room." I picture it now:

Ashley's hair all messed up in a knot on top her head, she and Rick holding hands.

"And something in me just snapped. I feel sick remembering it all now. How I wanted to mash my foot on the accelerator and crush them with my car. The only thing that stopped me was a little kid who came out of the adjoining room, so I just sped off."

"And you plotted your revenge?" Shelly says.

I nod. "Yeah, I guess."

"Wow," Shelly says. "Sorry about that."

"You said you weren't going to feel sorry for me."

"I'm not sorry *for* you, I'm sorry with you." She lights a cigarette. "One question, though."

"Yeah?"

"How did you get caught? Did you tell someone what you planned to do?"

"No. When I was stuffing my bag in my locker before homeroom, one of the firecrackers, an M-80, which looks like dynamite, fell on the floor and a group of girls freaked out and started screaming, "OMG, he has dynamite! He's going to blow up the school!" A couple teachers ran out of their rooms, and the rest, they say, is history."

"How were you planning on blowing up his car?"

"I was going to skip study hall and plant the fireworks," I say. "Funny thing is I hadn't brought any matches, which kind of helped my case."

Shelly laughs and shakes her head. "I'm surprised you didn't make 'Morons in the News' on *Bob & Sheri*."

"I made the national news, though." All the networks ran the story. And the YouTube clips of my arrest will live online forever.

"So what did you do with your time off after they booted you out of school?" she asked.

"Worked at the theater. Read a lot of books."

Shelly glances at her phone. "We better go."

"Wait. You have to tell me your story."

"We'll save it for lunch."

We get back to the school with enough time for me take what my sister calls a "whore bath" in the men's room, and report for duty. Earl has brought in a plate of peanut butter cookies. I'm liking him more and more.

By lunchtime, Shelly has evaporated. Hess tells me she had a court date. That sneaky bitch. She knew all along she wouldn't be here.

***

It reaches 100 degrees today, which means my car is 250 degrees inside when I get off work. Or rather, work detail. The AC in the Blue Whale hasn't worked since the beginning of time, so I soak my hands in water from the outside spigot so the dark blue plastic steering wheel doesn't char my skin. I start the Whale up and use my 4-70 air-conditioning: which is where I open all four windows and fly down the freeway at seventy miles an hour to cool her off.

My phone buzzes just as I pull off at a rest area. Mitch has texted and wants me to come in early. One good thing about this weather is the movie theaters are crowded. I text back, *give me an hour.*

There is no way I can close the windows and lock the car in this heat, so I haul my whole pack into the men's room. I take another sink bath, shampoo my hair, put on deodorant, and rummage through my bag for one of the cologne samples I ripped out of *GQ* magazines at the public library. I have Guess or Montblanc. I choose Guess, deciding to save the other in case I ever get a date again. I also change my shirt. My cargo pants are filthy. All I have left is a pair of jeans, and the theater has a dress code: khaki or olive green pants only. No shorts. Hell. I text my brother Jeff.

-Got any long pants I can borrow?

-Yeah

-Can I come by?

-Meet me at TH in 30

-Need to b khaki or green

-K

I hand wash my cargo pants in the sink. The hand soap will make them stiff, but at least I won't smell like a Rottweiler that rolled in cow shit next time I wear them.

I put on the jeans, stash my shampoo and other crap in the bag, wring out the pants, and go back out to my car. Nothing's missing. It's too hot to commit crimes.

I clip the wet pants to a line I rigged up in the back seat. The 4-70 air will help dry them.

At Tim Hortons, I sit at a booth and wait for my brother. They know me in here so I know they won't throw me out for loitering. In fact, Lexie, who's working the counter, brings me a cup of water. I thank her and read while I wait for Jeff.

A few minutes later, Jeff slides into my booth. "Hey, bro," he says. "What do you know?" He is freshly showered, wearing his brown Tim Hortons uniform. His short blond hair is still damp from a shower. He hands me a pair of khaki pants.

"Thanks."

"Want something to eat?"

"Sure. I can always eat." Jeff chuckles and gets me a box of Timbits and cup of chicken noodle soup.

***

One bad thing about working in the only movie theater in town is I know too many people who come here. I am standing behind the concession counter when I spot Rick and Ashley in line at the ticket booth. I feign a stomach cramp and tell Mitch I need to take a quick break. "It must be the tacos I had at lunch," I say. I'm not ready to face either of them. I spend about ten minutes in the employee restroom, plenty of time to avoid a confrontation.

I work until midnight. My pants are not stolen (thank you!) but not completely dry, either. The humidity clings to everything like spider webs.

The good thing about living in a relatively safe side of town is I can sleep with the car windows open without getting murdered. But tonight it storms again, a mega-special effects show of rock concert lightning and thunder, and I am trapped in a mobile greenhouse. Sleep will be rough, if it comes at all.

I try to listen to music to drown out the storm. I had remembered to charge up the iPod at work, but the music on it sucks. Taylor Swift and Justin Bieber-ish boy band shit. Once I get paid I'll buy an iTunes card and download something decent like some jazz or blues.

The rain clatters as if a herd of buffalo is stampeding on my roof, and the wind rocks the Blue Whale back and forth like a boat. If it weren't a hurricane out there, the rocking motion would be relaxing.

The storm dies down after an hour or so, and I manage to get a fistful of sleep. I wake up all clammy and my clothes are stuck to my skin.

CHAPTER THREE

I feel like road kill, but I squirm up and extricate my weary body from the Blue Whale to piss in the bushes. I stumble back to my car and Shelly is sitting on the open tailgate, inhaling a Marlboro.

"Hey," I say.

"I see you survived the latest tornado," she says.

"Really? So that *was* a tornado."

"Yeah. A small one hit the north end of town," she says. "The power's out at our house again."

"Same here," I say.

"Ha ha."

We drive around, trying to find a place to eat that has power. Rocket Road looks like a missile hit it. Trees lie on their sides, roots exposed like tangled wires. The Burger King sign and Speedway signs have blown down. Neither place has electricity. "This looks like a war zone," Shelly says.

"Creepy."

We drive further. "Look! Tim Hortons has power!" she says.

We pull into the lot. It's crowded, and Jeff is working. When we finally get to the front of the line, I say, "You're here early."

"Yeah. Nobody has power but us, so we've been real busy," Jeff said.

"Hey Nolan," Shelly says. "I didn't know you worked here."

"Yeah. Been here since December," Jeff says.

"Cool." She looks at me. "We'll have to get this to go." She orders a glazed donut, a breakfast panini, a mocha latte, and a bottle of water.

"So much for my anorexia theory," I say.

She shrugs. "I'm naturally thin."

"Large oatmeal, an apple, and a coffee," I tell my brother. Jeff gives me a cross-eyed grin. "I need the fiber," I say.

He chuckles. "Actually we're out of oatmeal, but I can give you a couple bran muffins."

Shelly pays for breakfast again with another fresh twenty. When Jeff goes to retrieve our order, I ask Shelly, "Do you guys have a tree full of twenties in your yard?"

"Something like that," she says.

Jeff hands us our order. He asks Shelly, "How do you know my mangy brother?"

She laughs. "We're serving the community together at school all summer."

Jeff raises his eyebrows and shakes his head. "Have fun."

I should feel guilty letting her pay, I guess, but it's not like she's my girlfriend. Hell, until two days ago I didn't even know her name. Besides, she has a money tree in her yard.

Back in the car, she says, "I can't believe you wanted oatmeal. That's baby food."

"I love oatmeal. It's a super food. I may turn into a hulking pile of muscle any second now." I flex for effect. She laughs, and her face morphs into a thing of beauty, and I kind of regret not buying her at least a cup of coffee. But then again I can't afford a cup of coffee.

"So you know my story," I say. "Your turn now, buddy."

She snorts and chomps on her sandwich. She wipes her mouth, and says, "I told you, I have a nicotine addiction. Seriously. My mom smoked like a chimney when she was pregnant with me, and I came out smoking. I've been smoking since I was ten."

"That's probably not good for your health."

"No shit, Sherlock."

"So have you tried to quit?"

"Only about 4,000 times. I can smoke with a patch on each arm." She sips her coffee. "Nicotine loves me."

"Wow."

"Yeah, it's a wowie." She picks her donut apart and offers me half. I don't refuse, so she stuffs it in my mouth as I drive. "It helps keep me skinny, though."

"I wouldn't call you skinny," I say. "Thin, but you've got curves where a girl needs them."

She looks down at herself. "Yeah, I am smokin' hot."

I laugh. "Okay," I say. "I get the smoking thing, but there's part of the story you're not telling me."

"Yeah, but you're not telling me everything either," she says. "So we're kind of even, aren't we?"

I park the car under some partial shade in the front lot at school. "If a time comes when I trust you," she says, "I'll fill in the details of my debacle, and you'll tell me the real reason you live in your car."

"Agreed." I nod, and open my car door. We start to walk into the building together. "So how do you know my brother?"

"We were lab partners in biology last year," she says.

"He's good people," I say.

The building is clammy and dark when we get inside. "The generator's not working right," Earl says, "so it's going to be a hot one."

"Where's Hess?" Shelly asks.

"He's gonna be late. He's got trees blocking his driveway."

"Our electricity is out as well," Shelly says. "And Michael . . . he doesn't have any power, either." She winks at me.

Earl tells us it's too damn hot to clean upstairs, so he has us wiping counters in first-floor rooms. By lunchtime it's possibly hotter inside than out. Earl sweats so much his shirt is soaked.

"Maybe we ought to call it a day," Earl says. "We have all summer." He smiles, and says, "And this time I have two full-time slaves."

Shelly and I walk outside together. She is texting. I notice my car and Earl's pickup are the only ones left in the lot. The school administrators only work in the mornings during summer, and none of them bothered to come in today. "Don't you drive?" I ask.

"Used to."

"How'd you get here?"

"My dad drops me off every day. My mom picks me up." Her phone emits a bloodcurdling scream.

"Nice ring tone," I say.

"It's my mom's." She glances at her text. "Shit. My mom is just starting her Pilates class. I have to wait here for another hour and a half."

"I can take you home," I say.

"Okay. Thanks." She texts her mom, and stashes the phone in her bag.

In the car she says, "I'm in no hurry to get home. Wanna just drive around? Look at storm damage?"

I check my gas gauge. "This thing only gets about eight miles to a gallon," I say. "And I've got just enough gas to last me 'til next payday."

"I'm not allowed to drive, but you are," she says. "We can take one of my parents' cars."

There are neighborhoods in Rooster where average families live, and then there are trailer parks, apartments, and townhouses, like where my mom and sister live. A select group in this town lives in houses like Shelly's: a three-story brick mansion with a three-car garage. I park my ride on the street. "You can pull it in the driveway," she says.

"No way. This thing leaks fluids."

We get out and walk up the long driveway to her front door. "I'm going to stay outside," I say. "I smell like a cat box."

"Don't be stupid. Nobody else is home."

I look down at my wrinkled, sweaty self. I have never felt more like white trash than I do now.

"Besides, we won't actually be going in the house," she says. "We'll go through the kitchen." She grabs my shirtsleeve and tugs me inside with her. Her house is also without power, but I can hear a generator running in the backyard. The ceiling fans run slowly, just enough to make the inside slightly less hot than the outside. The kitchen is all white and aluminum, like something out of a magazine.

"So are you guys rich or something?" I ask.

She shrugs. "My dad's a lawyer. I guess he does okay."

"What does your mom do?"

"Teaches yoga and Pilates."

"I thought you said . . ." I realize I have caught her in a lie. Her mother didn't smoke. What yoga teacher smokes? "Never mind."

Shelly dumps her purse on the counter and tries to flip on the TV. The screen does not respond. "Cable must still be out."

"Or the power," I say.

"Shit. I forgot." She places the remote back on the counter and picks up her bag. We step out into the garage. It's the size of a football field. A black Mercedes SL and a blue Miata rest on the sparkling clean concrete. No motor oil stains or power steering fluids here. "Which one do you want to drive?" she asks.

The Miata is a stick shift, and it's been awhile since I've driven a stick, but I calculate the sports car will cost me less jail time if I total it. "Miata."

"Good choice," she says. She grabs a set of keys from a hook and tosses them to me. "Top down of course."

Much of Rooster looks like Rocket Road with trees and power lines lying in or along the road. "It looks like news footage from Kabul," I say, "not Southeastern Ohio."

"It's like a preview of the end of the world," Shelly says.

My phone rings. It's Mitch. "What?" I say.

"Is that any way to talk to your boss?" he says. He's like a year or two older than me, and not at all a bossy type. "Hey, I need you this afternoon if you can make it in," he says. "I had two people call off because they're stuck on streets with trees in the road."

Hell yes. Air-conditioning! "Yeah, okay. Give me an hour or so." I jam my phone back in my pocket and tell Shelly, "I got called into work, so I need to take you home."

I pull the Miata back into its parking space, put it in gear, and shut off the motor. I hand her the keys. "That was fun," I say. "I like driving a stick."

"Listen, if you want to take a shower, you're welcome to," Shelly says. "We have hot water. And I can give you some of my brother's clothes."

A shower and fresh clothes sound like heaven. "Won't he notice a few things missing?"

"Josh has enough clothes to clothe a small African nation," she says. "He's got stuff he's never worn. And he's in Europe all summer. He'll forget what clothes he owns by the time he comes home."

"Aren't you afraid a criminal like me will steal all the silverware?"

She laughs. "You have nowhere to put it. Besides, we're partners in crime."

I slide off my shoes and leave them in the garage. I had noticed the white carpet in the living room. Those shoes have crawled inside dumpsters. She leads me inside the palatial living room with its whole wall of windows. They overlook a tree-lined lake. "Wow, this place is like something out of a reality show," I say.

"It's just stuff," she says. "Come on." She pushes me toward the mosaic-tiled staircase and walks me to a large bedroom with a queen-sized bed. "This is Josh's room." The bed is unmade, and tennis balls, golf clubs, and shoes are strewn everywhere. His closet door hangs open, and a mountain of clothes forms a peak on the floor. She pulls a couple brand new Izod shirts off hangers and hands them to me. "He got these a year ago and has never worn them."

"What if he asks about them?"

"He won't. Besides, my parents can buy him new ones."

Shelly pulls out an armful of clothes from the back of closet. "He's got some Dockers and shorts too." She dumps them all on the bed. "Take what you want. And there are socks and boxers in the drawers."

"You have no idea how much I appreciate this."

"I'll make you earn it somehow." She winks at me, and closes the bedroom door behind her on the way out.

I grin as I take off my clothes. I mean yeah, she's not my type, but I'd do her.

After I shower and dress, I feel like a new person wearing clothes not bought at Goodwill. They fit as if made for me. I look at my reflection in the mirror. The rabid dog who entered this house is replaced by a clean, lean, heartbreaking machine.

I don't want to be greedy, so I only take two each of the shirts, pants, shorts, boxers, and pairs of socks. Besides, I don't have room for much.

Shelly stands at the kitchen sink texting when I walk in. She whistles. "Wow, you clean up pretty good for a homeless guy."

I snort, and set the clothes on the counter. "Are you sure it's okay if I take this stuff?

"Yeah. Let me get you a bag." She rustles through a cabinet and pulls out a plastic Kroger bag and hands it to me.

"Thanks," I say. "This matches the rest of my luggage."

"Here," she hands me another. "Don't put the skanky ones in with the clean ones."

"Yeah, good thinking."

"Do you want something to eat before you go?"

"Okay."

"What do you want? I can nuke up some leftover steak, or chicken. Any of the carnivore's delights."

"I'd really like a salad," I say. "I hardly ever get fresh food. It won't keep in my massive refrigerator."

She goes to the fridge and pulls out an armful of vegetables. "What kind of dressing?"

"Ranch." She pulls a bunch of bottles and plastic containers out of the fridge. She slices open a bag of salad and dumps half the bag on my plate, and the rest on hers. We assemble our salads. I choose tomatoes, carrots, celery, and cucumber slices. The first bite is the second most heavenly thing that's happened to me today.

"Will your parents adopt me?" I say.

Shelly stabs at her plate, and I feel something in her shift. "Doubt it," she says.

***

I end up working a double. The theater is packed since the mall has fully functioning air-conditioning. I get off work at two, and drive around to cool off, then head for my spot behind the football field. As soon as I get comfortable, the thunder starts again. Shit. Just what we need. More storms.

I roll up the windows and close the tailgate, and get almost no sleep while Hurricane Motherfucker swirls around me. I figure it's about four when I finally doze off. The next thing I know, I hear tapping on my tailgate window. Shelly presses a $20 bill against the window, and says, "Breakfast is served!"

By ten o'clock or so the lack of sleep catches up with me. I move a bunch of desks back into Mrs. Fine's room and sit down at one. I don't remember setting my head down, and I don't know how long I slept. A half-hour maybe.

"Hey kid, get your ass up!" Earl bangs on the desk.

I wipe my face. "Sorry. It's been rough sleeping weather."

"Yeah, I hear you on that. You folks don't have a generator?"

"No."

He pauses. Thinks. "Go wash your face in cold water, and move on to Mr. Cox's room."

It's another day of intense heat, possibly worse than yesterday. Even though the temperature only reaches 95, the humidity is also about 95. "God, it's so sticky out here," Shelly says, as she and I walk out to my car to drive to lunch. "It's like wearing gum."

"Yeah, I'm looking forward to my shift again tonight," I say. "I'm exhausted, but the air-conditioning makes me feel less like an amoeba."

We sit inside Wendy's and bask in its full-fledged air-conditioning. "Do you think Earl and Hess would notice if we don't go back?" she says.

"Yeah. They'd probably call the cops."

"The jails have AC don't they?"

I smirk, and stuff a bite of my double cheeseburger in my mouth. I glance at the wall-mounted TV and read the news banner. "AEP says some power may not come on for another week."

"Bummer," she says. "The generator helps, though. I can run a fan on my face all night. And our food is cold, so I guess we're sort of lucky."

"I haven't noticed any difference," I say.

She laughs. "You're probably the one guy in this town who could survive this apocalypse." She steals one of my french fries

After we get in the car, she asks, "So how come you, Jeff, and Annie all have different last names?"

"My siblings and I have different fathers."

"Hmm. I see that a lot around here," she says.

We pull out onto Rocket Road and head back toward school. "Okay, this has been bugging me since we moved here," she says.

"What's that?"

"How come it's called Rocket Road? We're nowhere near NASA."

"I thought everyone knew about the story."

"My family has only lived here like three years," she says.

"It used to be called Second Avenue, but got changed to Rocket Road when astronaut Jed Rogers died."

"I've never heard of him."

"He didn't do anything spectacular like walk on the moon," I say, "but the town felt slighted when John Glenn had a highway and high school named after him. So we renamed Second Avenue in Rogers's honor after he died."

She considers this a moment. "Why is it most people get recognition only after they're dead?" she says. "I want my glory when I can still hear the shouts and taunts."

"What do you want to be remembered for?" I ask.

"I don't know. But I want it to be spectacular."

Some of the traffic lights don't work and traffic is slow. "We're going to be late," I say.

"Earl might skin us alive," she says.

I chuckle. "So where did you live before moving here?"

"Where do you think I'm from?"

"Possibly another planet," I say. "But I sense you lived in a city."

"Why?" she asks.

"You don't seem to be afraid of anything."

"What's there to be scared of here? It's a cow town."

"Cows can be scary if they chase you."

"Ha ha," she says.

"Besides, we have meth labs and devil worshippers all over, so there's plenty to be scared of here."

"Hmm," she says. She lights a cigarette. Normally I hate when people smoke in my car, but she opens her window to let out the fumes. "So explain about the different fathers."

I nod, take a gulp of pop, and rest it between my legs. "If you look in the dictionary under 'white trash' there's a picture of my family."

"So why do you live in your car?"

"I told you, my mom tossed me out."

She nods. "Does Jeff live in his car too?"

"No. He lives with his dad. Which is why Jeff is almost normal."

"What about your sister?"

"Annie still lives with our mom."

"Does she see her dad?"

"No," I say. "He died."

"Oh. I'm sorry," she says.

"Yeah, Bob was kind of cool," I say. I steer the conversation away from me. "Hey, you never said where you used to live."

"Cleveland."

"Why'd you move here?"

"Dad made chief partner at the Columbus office of his firm."

"Do you miss Cleveland?"

"Sometimes," she says. "I miss living near the lake and having access to a bookstore."

"Yeah, we haven't had one here for five years now," I say. "But why Rooster? Why not Columbus?"

"My parents wanted to live in a suburb rather than the city."

"Rooster's more than a suburb," I say. "It's the boondocks."

I pull into the school lot five minutes late. "Shit will hit the fan," I say.

Earl surprises us by not seeming to notice our tardiness. An hour later he sends us home.

It's like walking through bathwater outside, and even hotter in my car. I spread a bed sheet over the vinyl seats, but the sheet keeps slipping. Maybe I could duct tape it down.

On my way to work I stop at Walgreen's to get some duct tape and end up buying the best thing ever invented: a battery-operated fan with a mister. I buy a ten-pack of AA batteries too since they're on sale.

I leave work around one in the morning. It's still muggy out, but now that I have my new fan, I am able to sort of sleep.

***

Shelly wakes me up by tickling my feet. "Hey, the power came on at our house."

I snap my feet away and pull off my damp T-shirt. "Bully for you."

"Well good morning to you too, Mr. Cranky Pants." She picks up my fan, whose battery died some time ago. "What is this?"

"The best thing ever invented," I say. "Whoever came up with this deserves a Nobel Prize."

"Is it a fan?"

"It's a mister and a fan. I can spritz myself with water, then aim the fan at my head. It lets me sleep for about four hours before the batteries run out."

"Cool."

As we drive in search of breakfast I notice something missing. "What, no cigarette this morning?"

"I'm trying to quit. My court-ordered therapist kind of recommended it."

"So you see a therapist. Is it because you're crazy?"

"Yeah, something like that," she says.

"You're a story with a chunk of pages missing," I say. "I mean, you wear this hard shell on the outside, but the Shelly I know is generous and sort of nice."

She punches me. Kind of hard too. "If you ever call me nice again I'll kill you."

I rub my shoulder. "Sorry, bitch."

She grins. "That's better." She looks at her empty cigarette case and sighs. "Some of your pages have been ripped out too."

"It's because my pages are printed on cheap paper."

She laughs. "You're lacking entire chapters."

"Yeah. And the rest of the pages are stuck together with generic pancake syrup."

"Ooh, now I'm in the mood for pancakes," she says. "Let's go to Eat'n Park. Get the breakfast bar."

"I guess that confirms you're not bulimic," I say.

"No way. I like food too much. That whole vomiting thing." She sticks a finger in her mouth to fake vomiting. "Ugh. I hate hurling," she sighs. "I just hope I don't get fat by giving up cigarettes."

We have to get our pancakes to go since Eat'n Park is almost ten miles from the school. Shelly dips them in syrup and feeds them to me in small bites as I drive.

Today we clean one of the art rooms. Before I got booted out, art had been one of my favorite classes. While we were sculpting busts out of clay, Miss Frame, the art teacher, said, "Remember to leave room for the brain."

I wish I had taken her advice before I accidentally tried to blow up the school.

CHAPTER FOUR

Sometimes when I am totally broke I drive around and dumpster dive at restaurants and grocery stores. I find entire loaves of bread still in their wrappers and unopened bags of one-day expired carrots and fruits.

It's almost as if the managers of Dan's Donuts expect people to pick through their trash because their donuts are thrown away inside boxes, not just tossed in the dumpster behind the building. I buy donuts there when I do have money, just to say thank you for feeding hungry vagrants like me.

I often find decent meals inside restaurant dumpsters too. Last night I drove by Olive Garden after work and watched as a guy tossed out a large aluminum pan. It was covered, and when I lifted the lid, the gates of heaven opened up. Lasagna! I also found a bag of salad. It was warm, soaked in dressing, but still edible.

Shelly notices the empty pan when she stands by my car this morning. "So what was in this?"

"Lasagna," I say. "I went dumpster diving last night at Olive Garden." I collect the food containers and wrap them in a Kroger bag to toss out.

"I know a little something about that," she says.

I give her a quizzical look. "Why does a rich girl like you need to crawl through dumpsters?"

"I was sort of on my own for awhile."

"And you'll tell me when we have that long conversation some day," I say.

She crosses her arms and leans against the rear fender. "Something like that."

"You know, the more you don't tell me, the wilder my imagination gets about your story."

She laughs. "I hope it's an amazing adventure."

"Oh it is." I walk over to the dumpster behind the building and toss the Olive Garden remains inside. It suddenly occurs to me it's Saturday, and we don't have to clean the school today. "You do know it's Saturday."

She shrugs. "I thought we could just hang out. You know, cruise around." She digs into her bag and pulls out a Speedway card. "And I'll pay for the gas."

I chuckle. "I'm starting to feel like your platonic gigolo."

"Be sure to put that on your college applications."

I scratch through my rumpled hair. "I don't have to work later today, so, yeah. Let's go driving. I had to cover so many hours last week that Mitch forced me to take the weekend off so that he didn't have to pay me overtime."

Shelly looks different today, but I can't figure out why. She's wearing her usual shorts and T-shirt. Haircut? I don't know. She looks better than usual.

I fill up the tank and we get coffee and donuts at Dan's Donuts after I explain to Shelly how they feed vagabonds like me. Shelly leaves the counter girl a $2 tip. We get back to the car, and Shelly says, "Let's just drive."

It's a nice day out. Warm, but not the toxic heat of the past week. The humidity is low, and the 4-70 air feels almost cold. We drive around in comfortable silence. I glance at her, and it hits me; she isn't wearing the raccoon eye makeup. Her eyes look bigger, and bluer. I almost compliment her, but I'm afraid it might piss her off, so we just drive. After about an hour Shelly says she's hungry for real food.

Since we are in no hurry, we go to Bob Evans and get waited on where I order the Farmer's Breakfast. It comes with eggs, sausage, home fries, and unlimited pancakes. When my mountain of food arrives, Shelly says, "Are you planning on plowing a field today?"

I grin. "Maybe." I chomp on some home fries. "Since you don't drive, how did you get to the school this morning?" I ask.

"My mom dropped me off," she says. "I told her I was meeting a friend."

"How did you know I'd be there?"

She shrugs. "You're always there."

"So, we're friends?"

"Yeah," she says. She sips her coffee. "I could do worse."

I nod and chew. "What do you want to do all day, friend?"

She shrugs. "I know we just ate, but maybe we can have a picnic somewhere later since it's so nice out."

It is a spectacular day. I couldn't have asked for finer weather on a day off.

We stop by the theater to pick up my check and drive to the bank branch inside Kroger so I can cash it. The lot is nearly full since it's Saturday morning. "Sorry to have to park so far," I say.

"I don't mind," she says. "It's so pretty out, and you need to walk off that giant breakfast."

After I get my money, I say, "Hey, since I have cash, the picnic is my treat. Cheaply, though. No caviar and *foie gras*."

She links her arm in mine. "Okay."

We graze the aisles, and I pick out a baguette, some grapes, and a hunk of cheddar cheese.

"How very French of you," she says.

"*Oui, oui, mademoiselle.*" I had three years of French, but don't remember a lot of it other than food names. Funny, but our French teacher is named Mr. German, and our Spanish teacher is Mrs. French.

"Let's get a bottle of wine too," she says.

I chuckle. "Nice try. We're not old enough."

"According to my sources I'm a twenty-two-year-old grad student." We go to the wine aisle and Shelly browses through the wine bottles.

"How do you know the difference?" I ask.

"Some wines are sweet, some are mellow, and some are tart. Do you have any preferences?" she asks.

I shrug. "The only time I had wine was when my brother and I tried some Mad Dog 20/20 one of my mom's boyfriends left on the kitchen counter. It was like drinking battery acid."

She scrunches her face. "Mad Dog is not wine."

"You're the expert. Or as they say *en français, tu es un sommelier.*"

"Reds are good for picnics because you're supposed to drink them warm." She reaches up and pulls down a bottle of Pinot noir. I notice the price. Twenty-eight bucks. If I were buying, I'd choose the one below it on sale for $5.99.

Amazingly, we make it through the line with Shelly's fake ID. We walk a few paces out the door when I hear a man and a boy behind me, laughing. I glance back and notice a boy of about six standing inside the grocery cart, the man pushing it. They roar past us. The dad growls like a motor, and the kid screeches in laughter all the way to their minivan. I feel something inside me rip open as I set the groceries in the backseat. I stand up and watch them.

"What's the matter?" Shelly asks.

I shake my head and get in the car.

She sets her bag on the floor and snaps her seatbelt. "Why were you staring at them?" she asks. "Do you know them?"

"No."

"Then what is it?" she asks.

I stare out the windshield and watch the van drive out of the parking lot. "I just wonder what it's like to have a dad."

Shelly places a hand on my arm. "You don't have a dad?"

"Not my own." I click my seatbelt. "Jeff's dad sometimes played with all of us when we were young. A couple of my mom's boyfriends did too. But none of them was my father."

Shelly asks, "So what happened to him?"

"I don't know. My mom says he moved away before I was born."

"So he doesn't even know about you?"

"No, I guess not," I say. I start the car and back out of the space.

"Parents lie, you know," she says.

"What do you mean?"

"Your dad may be living right here in Rooster, walking around, and you don't even know it." Shelly reaches for her cigarette case, remembers it's empty, and stuffs it back in her bag. She chews on a piece of cinnamon gum. "Have you tried looking for him?" she asks.

I look for him every day, I think, every time I see a tall, dark-haired guy. "I wouldn't know where to start."

"You have his last name, don't you?"

"No. Flynn is my mom's maiden name."

"So how come she didn't give Jeff and Annie her name?"

"They know who their dads are. My mom won't tell me his name." What I don't want to say is she may not know his name. When I was small I used to ask at least once a year, and every time I got a different story. Sometimes I was a king's son who had been left on her doorstep, or she bought me at a flea market. My favorite tale was that I had been born a baby dragon, but somehow morphed into a boy. Eventually, I stopped asking. Any number of men in Rooster or Columbus could be my dad. I look for guys I resemble since I don't look much like my mother. She has blond hair and brown eyes, like Jeff, and my hair is dark, almost black, and my eyes are green. Jeff looks like her, and Annie resembles her father. Me? I'm a broken pencil in a box of felt-tip markers.

I don't tell Shelly any of this, though. I divert the attention back to her. "So in what ways have your parents lied to you?" I ask.

She holds out empty fingers and pretends to puff on a cigarette. "That's another long conversation for another day." She takes an imaginary puff. "Just drive."

We head south of town on a two-lane highway, one of those unevenly paved country roads common in this part of Ohio, roads that seem to lead to nowhere, where you can drive for hours and not see a soul, and suddenly you come to an intersection and there's a four-lane highway zipping with traffic. We come to a fork, where we can choose east or south.

"Which way?" I ask.

"South."

"Aren't you afraid we'll run into a meth lab?"

She shrugs. "We'll take our chances."

I shake my head. "You know, we have all day. Don't you want to share some of that long conversation with me?"

She bites her nail and ignores my question. She reaches into her purse for a stick of gum. "I've gone from being a chain-smoker to a chain chewer," she says.

At one intersection we spot a farmer's market stand. We stop and buy a bag of fresh peaches and a sack of tomatoes. As we drive, she reaches for a tomato and bites into it like she's eating an apple.

"I've never seen anyone eat a tomato like that," I say.

"What do you mean?"

"I eat tomatoes on salads and stuff, but never, like, you know, just bite into it."

She holds the tomato close to my mouth. "Taste it," she says.

I do, and its sweet earthiness envelops me. The juice runs down my chin. "That is good," I say.

"Have I steered you wrong yet?"

"Not so far."

She slides her flip-flops off and places her feet on the dashboard. The wind whips through our hair. It's such a great moment; time can stop now and I will die happy.

We keep driving south, probably close to forty miles from town, when we spot a sign that reads "Hardin–Essex Family Reunion 1 mile."

"Wanna crash it?" she asks.

"But we're not Hardins or Essexes."

"Free food!"

I laugh at the idea. "Hell, I could be a Hardin or an Essex for all I know. Why not?"

Another sign a half-mile up says, "Hardin–Essex Family! Watch for balloons," and a few moments later, on the left-hand side I see a mailbox draped in orange and blue balloons. I notice a large open patch already teeming with cars. I park close to the highway in case we get chased out and need to make a quick getaway. My beat-up station wagon makes me look like the white trash distant cousin I hope they think I am.

"So are we Hardins? Or Essexes?" I ask.

She thinks. "I will be an Essex, and you're my boyfriend from college. I am, after all, a graduate student at Ohio State."

I laugh. As I get out of the car, I notice others are carrying food with them. "Should we share some of what we bought?"

"Yeah, probably," she says. "Not the peaches or tomatoes, though. Or the wine."

"The bread, grapes, and cheese?"

"Sure." I pick up the Kroger bag. We walk uphill and notice a gathering of several dozen people ranging in age from newborns to old people. I glance at Shelly, and she glances back at me. We smile. "What's our cover story?"

"I've been away at college at Ohio State and you're my boyfriend from Columbus. My name is Wanda."

"And I'm Jim."

There is enough food to feed half of Rooster, and the aromas are overpowering. It looks like there are a hundred or so people here. Who would know if we were meant to be here or not? I wonder if we're the only interlopers. We brought food, though, so I don't feel too bad about crashing.

Shelly and I move toward the food tables, and a chubby woman with iron-colored, spiky hair says, "Breads go over here, hon." She indicates a long table covered in a checked tablecloth. I notice she wears a badge claiming her as a Hardin. Not everyone is wearing a badge, but many are. Blue for Hardin, orange for Essex.

"We brought grapes and cheese too," Shelly says.

"You can put that next to the meats, and the grapes can go on the salad table," the woman says. "Grab a plate and help yourselves." She smiles at us and walks away.

We lay our parcels in the appropriate spots and search for the plate table. "Man, everything smells so good," I say. Even though Shelly and I ate only a couple hours before, this is good food. Baked beans, ham, hamburgers, hot dogs, pickles, chicken casserole, homemade macaroni and cheese, biscuits, fresh vegetables, sliced meats, fried chicken, potato salad, green salad, deviled eggs, fresh noodles, potato chips, fruit, and an endless array of desserts.

I'd love a beer, but since I'm driving, and not really sure where we are, I opt for a Pepsi instead. Shelly drinks a Diet Coke.

Shelly and I find a spot in the shade and settle onto the grass. My plate is overloaded with as much as I could put on it. I notice Shelly has also not scrimped on her servings. "I know we just ate," I say, "but, damn, everything looks and smells incredible." I take a forkful of macaroni and cheese, something I have not eaten in years. It's pure joy. I make a mental note to get seconds.

We eat and watch the Hardin–Essex families intermingle. After I vacuum up all my food, I have no room for any more. Neither does Shelly. "Maybe we should walk around a bit and digest."

We toss our plates and napkins in the trash bin. There is a recycle bin for the plastic ware, and we place our forks and spoons in it.

"Let's go toss horseshoes with a group of kids," Shelly says.

"Never done that before," I say.

"Neither have I." She grabs my hand. It's been ages since I felt a girl touch me, and her fingers feel soft against mine. I let her lead me toward the other kids.

We spend a couple hours tossing horseshoes and playing corn hole. Enough time to develop appetites to try trash can dinner.

"It's sort of like a giant vat of beef stew," says a blond woman wearing an Essex badge. "You take meat, like sausage and beef, and add your vegetables and cook it all day over an open fire."

I taste a forkful. "This is one of the best things I have ever eaten."

"You must be one of Lee's people," the blonde says to me. "You look just like him when he was young, may he rest in peace."

I feel a stab inside. I notice her badge says she's an Essex. Could Lee be my dad? I glance at Shelly, and as if she reads my mind, she asks, "Wasn't he from Rooster?"

"No, hon. I don't think he ever went there," the blonde says. "He pretty much stayed in Cincinnati."

Someone in the background calls the woman's name. "Be right there!" she yells. She turns back to me. "Well, it was nice talking to you," she says. "Enjoy!"

"You, too," I say. When the woman is out of earshot, I ask Shelly, "Wouldn't that be wild if I really was an Essex?"

Shelly glances at her phone. "It's only two o'clock," she says. "We could head back into town and look up Lee Essex from Cincinnati on one of the library computers?"

On the drive back toward Rooster she hands me a peach. I drive one-handed, savoring the crisp sweetness of the peach.

"There is nothing like summer fruit," I say. "Too bad it's not always summer."

"It is in Hawaii."

"Maybe I'll move there someday," I say, knowing the odds of my leaving Rooster are about a million to one.

As I drive I try not to get too excited, but I can't help thinking I may have found a new clue to my identity.

"Can you call your mom and ask her if she knows someone named Lee Essex?"

"No," I say. "She gets mad every time I bring up the subject of my father." I notice a sign for a hiking trail. "I don't know about you, but I could use a walk. Get rid of some of this food."

"That sounds good."

I pull up next to a couple parked cars. "I can't lock the car, so take your bag with you."

She stows the peaches and tomatoes under her seat. "Precious objects."

The trail is short, only a mile each way, but any movement will help. We climb out of the car and I notice Shelly is wearing flip-flops. "You can't hike in those."

"I'll be fine."

"I'm a runner," I say. "You can't take your feet for granted."

She sighs. "How about if we just do a half-mile then turn back?"

The trail is paved and shady. What I really want to do is take off and run, get lost in these woods. Too many times I have discovered false clues to my identity. Why should today be any different? But you never know. Shelly might be the good luck charm I need.

"Hey Wanda," I say, after we finish our mile. "Thanks for being with me today."

"No problem, Jim."

No one bothered my car while we walked. It's too nice out to commit crimes. Or maybe the car looks too crappy to bother with.

***

Shelly logs into the library computer with her library card and types in Lee Essex AND Cincinnati. There are multiple listings. "How old would he be?" she asks.

"Probably around forty or so," I say.

She Googles Lee Essex AND Cincinnati. We find a Lee Essex who looks to be around seventy, a black guy with the same name, and a blond guy younger than me. She checks Facebook, LinkedIn, and Tumblr. We cross-reference Lee Hardin, but come up empty. Shelly also checks his name with cities and towns surrounding Cincinnati and Rooster.

"This is a shot in the dark," I say. "The woman said this Lee guy never came around here. As far as I know my mom's never been to Cincinnati."

We continue searching until we hear, "the library will be closing in fifteen minutes," from the loudspeaker.

It's after five by the time I pull up to Shelly's house. "Shit," she says. "I totally forgot to call or text my parents." She pulls her phone out of her bag and texts.

-Sorry. Forgot. Home Now. See you in a couple.

She starts to bundle up her stuff.

"Thanks," I say.

"For what?"

"For being my friend."

I'm a block away from her house when my phone rings. It's Shelly. "Did you forget something?"

"Yes," she says, "but that's not why I called. My mom invited you to have dinner with us."

"You're not sick of me?"

"I *am*, but I know how much you like a free meal."

I laugh. "Okay. I'll be right back."

Shelly meets me in the driveway, and we enter the house through the garage to the kitchen. Her mom is slim and blond, wearing shorts and flips-flops. She's about the same size as Shelly and could pass for her older, blond sister.

"Hi." She extends her hand. "I'm Claire."

"Michael," I say.

"I understand you're a friend from school."

"Yes ma'am." I don't think Shelly has shared that I'm a fellow criminal element, and I don't volunteer the information.

"I'm glad to meet you. You're more than welcome to stay for dinner. We're just doing salads and chicken on the grill."

"Thank you, I will."

"Do you need to call your folks and let them know?"

"No. My mom is working. She won't care."

Shelly grabs my arm, and tells her mother, "We'll be in the family room."

We go downstairs to a vast, finished basement. The furniture in most basements I've been in is castoffs from old living rooms, but everything in here looks brand new. The giant TV covers half the wall, and there's a pool table, gym equipment, and a game table.

"We also have a sauna and a guest suite down here," she says. "I know; it's all pretty bourgeois."

I look around. "This is nice."

She shrugs. "Want to take a swim before dinner?"

"You have a pool down here too?"

She laughs. "No, that's outside." We plunk down on the massive black leather couch. Shelly picks up a remote. "Let's see what's on TV."

I have not watched television for almost a year. Between work and living, TV is the last thing on my mind. Shelly flips through the channels, and squeals as a program starts. "Oh! *The Big Hoard!* I love this show."

I feel waves of nausea crash into me. Is she shitting me? How much does Shelly know about me? "There's a show about hoarding?" The word "hoarding" catches on my tongue, as if saying it takes me one step closer to telling Shelly about my home life.

"Yeah," she says, "I watch it all the time, and it always freaks me out."

"What's the point of the show?" I say.

"They find people who hoard stuff, and their friends and family try to convince them to clean up their houses," Shelly says. "They bring in a psychologist and a cleaning crew."

"Does it work?"

"Sometimes," Shelly says.

"What happens when it doesn't?" I ask.

Shelly shrugs. "The people get evicted by the health department or the fire marshal makes them move."

I focus on the screen as the camera pans to a room that could be inside my mother's house. A banner comes across the screen, and warns, "This program contains material not suitable for young children." The voiceover says, "Hoarders are people whose lives are consumed with possessions. Their excessive acquiring of things creates massive amounts of clutter and causes impairment of reality."

They introduce the hoarder, a woman in San Francisco named Connie, and her daughter Pam, who is trying to convince her mother to clean her house so the health department doesn't force her from her home.

I feel chills run through me as I watch Pam try to convince her mother to throw something out. "No, I can still wear that," Connie whines.

"When is the last time you actually wore it?" Pam says. She holds the blouse up. "And look. It's all stained."

Connie grabs the blouse from her daughter and mumbles she's keeping it.

Pam gestures to the mess in the room. "Mom, you can't keep all this stuff. It's ruining your life."

Shit. This could me or Annie or Jeff having this very same argument with our mom.

The camera cuts away to the kitchen, and the daughter talks directly to the camera. "There is not one clean surface in this house," Pam says. "Mom was always a little messy, but after Dad died, she buried herself with stuff."

In the living room the only place to sit is the couch, which Connie uses as her bed. The camera pans to Connie's bedroom. "There's a bed buried under there somewhere," Pam says. "I think it's been three years since she slept in it."

The next scene shows another family; the voiceover says, "This is a Category Five hoard, the worst kind. The cleaning crew must sort through nearly 5,000 pounds of junk. The smell of rotting food permeates the house, which is infested with fleas and roaches." A gloved cleaning crew member holds up what was once a cat. "Two fossilized bodies of cats were found in the rubble," the announcer says, "along with countless roaches and rats."

"Oh, man," I say.

"Yeah, it can get pretty gross."

A teenaged kid named Todd tells the camera, "When my mom buys pop and puts it in the fridge, it quickly tastes like rotting food," he says. "Everything we eat or drink tastes rotten."

I run to the bathroom. I am shaking, trying to process this. That kid on the screen could be me. My dirtiest secret is out there on a TV show. Millions know what my siblings and I live with.

As I walk back from the bathroom, I hear someone on screen say, "Hoarding goes beyond getting emotionally attached to items.

Hoarders just can't let go. They get overwhelmed, not about the clutter itself, but with the decision of what to do with the clutter."

I slouch next to Shelly on the sofa. "I didn't take you for being squeamish," she says, laughing.

"I'm okay," I lie. "I just needed to pee." I don't want to watch this show anymore, but I need to watch it. It's a living train wreck.

After the commercial break, I am riveted as Todd's sister tells the camera, "We're kind of used to living like this, but we get doorbell dread." The girl sighs. "Usually if someone comes to the door, I crack it just enough to say my mom is asleep or something."

"We never bring friends over," Todd says. Man, I have been there. My life is unfolding on Shelly's TV screen.

"If Madeline does not clean up the junk within two weeks," the psychologist, who is a hoarding specialist, tells the camera, "she will lose her children to Children's Services." That's been one of Annie's and my biggest fears, and that's why we haven't told anyone about mom.

I watch as the cleaning crew tosses bags of garbage in an industrial-sized trash bin. "So far Madeline has been cooperative," the psychologist says, "but we never know what will make a hoarder reverse his or her decision to let go of something."

The camera cuts back to the first hoarder, Connie. The daughter is standing in the messy living room and throws her hands up. "I'm done here, Mom. If you won't let anything go, I can't stand here and be part of it."

The daughter drives away in her blue pickup truck as the psychologist tries to convince Connie to get rid of a box of blank cassette tapes. "No, those are still good," Connie says. "Someone can use them."

"Then why don't we put those in the donation pile?" the psychologist says.

"You won't throw them out?" Connie says.

"No, we will donate them somewhere, and someone who has space can use them."

Connie agrees.

"Progress has been made," the announcer says.

The screen cuts to two weeks later. "While there is still a long way to go," the announcer says, "Connie has made tremendous progress in reducing her hoard." Boxes of stuff still line the walls, but the living room looks almost livable. "The kitchen has clean counters, and the sink is fixed."

The camera moves to the bedroom. "Connie is still working on making the rest of her room livable, but as you can see, she has made tremendous strides."

After another commercial, the focus is back on the family with doorbell dread. The psychologist says, "The morning began well, but Madeline got upset when the cleanup crew tried to throw away a broken chair." On screen Madeline is ordering the crew to take everything out of the trash and put it back in the house. "Hoarders believe everything is useful," the psychologist says.

That's my mother up there on the television. I think of the day she screeched at me for tossing out an empty potato chip bag. "I was going to use that!" she said.

"For what?" I yelled.

"To store something in."

"It's trash, Mom."

"Everything has a use."

Madeline also refuses to let go of the garbage in the kitchen. "It's not that bad," Madeline says, as she walks out of the room. The psychologist says this is typical of clutter blindness. "She doesn't see the clutter. She sees wonderful things that give her pleasure."

Todd, her son, says he is scared. He wipes tears from his eyes. "If Mom won't clean this up, Sara and I will end up in foster care."

The psychologist adds, "There is a huge potential for fatality in these situations. Inhabitants of houses like Madeline's can get diseases from vermin, mold, and food poisoning. And if a fire breaks out, the family either can't get out, or the rescuers can't reach them."

In the end, Madeline loses custody of her children, and the house is condemned.

"This show always makes me feel dirty," Shelly says, "like I need a shower." She dusts herself off as if wiping away imaginary filth, and I know in that moment, I can never, ever tell Shelly the truth about my mother.

Shelly shuts off the TV and pops up. "Let's go for a swim."

I raise my eyebrows. "Okay, but I'd have to skinny dip."

"Yeah, my parents might frown on that," she says. "Let's go see if Josh left a suit behind."

Upstairs Shelly rummages through her brother's closet and dresser. "He doesn't care when you go through his stuff?" I ask.

"No. Anything forbidden he would have taken with him to Europe or buried it somewhere. Unlike me, Josh is pretty transparent."

"You're about as transparent as Sheetrock," I say.

She sticks her tongue out at me and opens the bottom dresser drawer where she finds a couple pairs of swim trunks. Shelly holds them up. "Red or olive green?"

"You choose."

She tosses me the green ones. "They match your eyes." She walks to the door. "I'll meet you down by the pool."

I change quickly, and carry my clothes with me. Shelly is already in the pool when I step outside.

"You look like such a dork," she says.

"Are the trunks too big?"

"No. You're holding onto your clothes like a homeless vagrant," she says. "Oh wait, you are one." She splashes water at me and I step back.

"You'll pay for that." I dump my bundle on the concrete and dive into the pool near her. When I surface I swoosh her with a wave of water and she squeals, and wooshes water back at me. She tries to dunk me, but I'm stronger and easily sink her underwater. She's slippery as a fish, though, and pops away. By the time I find her she has swum to the other side of the pool.

She leans against the side and splashes her feet. I swim beside her and paddle my feet too.

"This is great," I say. "If I lived here I'd never leave home."

She sloshes water at me. "A swimming pool isn't a reason to keep someone from running away."

I give her a long look. "So you took off?"

She is silent, so I know it's true. I have figured out that Shelly is like a hunted animal, and one cannot prod her too quickly with questions. I have to let her tell me when she wants to. There's more to the story than just running away.

Around seven, Shelly walks me out to my car. "Your parents are nice," I say.

She shrugs. "Yeah. I could do worse."

I open my car door.

"Hey, thanks again for today."

"It was fun."

I'm not sure what I am supposed to do now. Shake her hand? Kiss her? We're friends, and I liked when she held my hand, but if I kiss her she might just kick me in the nads.

I reach inside my car and pick up the bags of peaches and tomatoes and her bottle of wine. "Don't forget these."

She grips the wine and pulls out a peach. She passes the sacks back to me. "Keep the rest."

"Are you sure?"

"You need them more than I do."

"Thanks."

She starts to walk up the driveway. She turns. "See you at the salt mines Monday."

Inside the bag are two peaches and the last tomato. I eat them after I have found a parking spot at the rest stop just outside of town. I park on the side with the semis, figuring I have less of a chance of getting murdered in the night. It's cool enough for me to close the windows most of the way. I never really got the whole 'sleeping weather' thing until I started living in my car. This is one of the best nights of sleep I have had in ages. It gets so chilly at one point I have to wrap up in a blanket.

CHAPTER FIVE

I am sitting at McDonald's around 9:00 A.M. when my phone
buzzes. It's a text from Shelly.

-What R U doing?

-At McDs. Having coffee.

-CALL ME.

-Cant. almost out of minutes.

-JUST CALL ME!!!!!

-OK!

I hit call, and she says in a rush, "My-dad-says-we-can-borrow-
his-Miata-and-drive-to-Columbus-to-celebrate-your-birthday."

"But my birthday is . . ."

"Today! I know! Happy birthday! And he gave me one of
his credit cards so I can buy you lunch somewhere nice, so wear
something not awful."

I laugh. "Okay."

"Half an hour." She hangs up.

I wash my face in the McDonald's bathroom and wet down
my unruly hair. Hopefully Annie can give me a haircut soon. She's
planning to study cosmetology at the vocational school next year
and likes to practice haircuts. Sometimes she massacres me, but
hey, the haircut is free.

I rummage through my clothes. I don't want to wear any of
Josh's castoffs in case Shelly's folks recognize them. The nicest shirt
I own is a short sleeve Hawaiian print. Rick gave it to me last
Christmas. Last year flowered shirts were sort of a fad at school.
Since I've never worn it, it qualifies as my "not awful shirt." My
best pants are a pair of jeans Jeff gave to me on my actual birthday

in May, and I have not yet worn them either. I had planned to wear the jeans on the first day of my second try at senior year. But hey, it's my birthday again, and who am I to turn down a free lunch?

I rub the sample of Chrome cologne I found in a *Sports Illustrated* magazine on my chest and neck. I check my look in the car window. I look like a dork, but this is the best I can do.

I park on the curb in front of Shelly's house. The blue Miata sits in the driveway, and the top is already down. Shelly stands next to the open door of the passenger side wearing ginormous sunglasses, sandals, and a raspberry-colored sundress. Her black hair is neatly braided and she is wearing lipstick.

"You clean up nicely," I say.

She hands me the keys. "So do you." She touches the fabric of my floral shirt. "Nice shirt." The compliment seems genuine.

I slide into the driver's side and Shelly sits down and closes her door.

"Dad says don't touch the radio. He has satellite." She opens the glove compartment and pulls out two pairs of sunglasses. One is blue mirrored and the other is plain black. "Choose."

I try them each on separately. "Which one makes me look more like an international man of mystery?"

She laughs and I try them on again. "The mirrored ones."

She stashes the black pair back in the glove compartment and I start the car. As I back down the driveway, I notice the tank is full.

"You're lucky my parents like you," she says. "Dad only lets Josh drive this car."

"He doesn't know we took it the other day?"

"No," she says. "And he never will."

It's a little intimidating driving such a tiny car on the freeway, like being a midget in a land of giants, but I quickly find my pace and feel comfortable. I glance over and notice Shelly has donned a pink-and-green scarf over her hair. "Very retro chic," I say.

"And practical."

We don't talk much on the way to Columbus. The wind and the traffic make it too loud to do anything but shout, but I enjoy the feel of the car, and the adventure of heading into an unknown. I've driven to Columbus many times, but never in a sports car with a girl.

As we approach the outskirts of Columbus, I shout, "Where are we going?"

"Since it's your birthday I'll let you choose," she says. "If you like Italian, we could go to Buca di Beppo. That's in Worthington. Good food, but no patio."

"And my other choice?"

"Lindey's in German Village. We can eat outside there."

"Lindey's," I say.

I head straight into the city on I-70, get off at Fourth Street, and follow the signs toward German Village, just south of downtown. We drive around to find a parking spot a couple blocks up.

"Should we put the top up and lock it?" I ask.

"There's nothing in it but a pair of sunglasses," she says. She stashes the scarf in her purse and checks her look in the rearview mirror. I go around and hold the door for her. "Look at you being the gentleman."

"Given it's my birthday, I'm demonstrating my increased maturity." As we walk, I say, "So what made you want to see me today?"

She shrugs. "I had nothing better to do."

"Gee, thanks, I think."

We stand at the entrance of the restaurant and Shelly points to a sign that reads Free Valet Parking.

"That's okay," I say. "The walk felt nice."

There are still a couple tables available outdoors. We settle into our seats and a waiter brings us water glasses and a basket of rolls.

I order iced tea and Shelly orders a glass of white wine with some Italian sounding name.

I open my menu and see an array of food I'd never be able to afford. Some of the terms I recognize from French class.

"I could order a burger," I say, "but I don't want to be *gauche*."

"Order something unique, something you have never eaten before. You eat burgers all the time."

"What do you recommend?"

"I'm getting quiche," she says. The waiter sets down our beverages. "It's your birthday. Live it up. Get something decadent."

I order the quiche as well.

"Sorry," I say, after the waiter walks away. "I'm not very imaginative when it comes to food. I was raised on canned pork and beans and corn dogs. The most exotic thing I've ever eaten is Gouda cheese in French class."

"I keep forgetting you're a homeless hick."

My face reddens. I take a gulp of tea.

"I meant that as a compliment," she says. "You don't seem like an ignoramus like so many of the guys at school. You have untapped potential."

"If this were a story," I say, "I'm not sure if you'd be the hero or the villain."

"That's what I mean," she says. "Your sentences are grammatically correct. Most of those guys at school say crap like, 'where you at?' and 'I seen that.' You actually use verbs correctly."

"I have went there," I say. "And I seen it."

She covers her ears in mock horror. "Stop! You're murdering me."

I laugh. "Maybe I'm just naturally brilliant."

"No, that's not it."

"You're just full of the compliments today. Is that any way to treat the birthday boy?"

She grins. "I guess not."

I rip into a piece of bread from the basket. "One of my mom's husbands was a literature teacher. Annie's dad. He read to us all the time, so I grew up reading and listening to stories."

"What happened to him?"

"Annie's dad?" I take a long breath. This is one of the stories I don't want to tell. It kind of serves as the beginning of our troubles. "I didn't always live in Rooster either," I say. "Before that, we lived here in Columbus, where Annie's dad was teaching at Ohio State."

"He was a professor?"

"A graduate student, working on his doctorate, and he taught classes there. That's how my mom met him. When Jeff and I were small, I guess she wanted to better herself, and since we were poor, she got to take classes for free."

I rip another hunk of bread from the basket. "We lived in this one-bedroom apartment. I was three and Jeff was two. We all slept on a mattress on the floor. My mother had wanted to be something more than a breakfast waitress in a Tee Jaye's. Plus she sometimes worked nights at 7-Eleven."

"So who took care of you when your mother worked?"

"I don't remember a lot of the details about when I was a kid. My earliest memories are of being woken in the middle of the night and shifted from one location to another. Sometimes Jeff and I slept in the back of the car while she worked. In fact, I think we lived in mom's car for awhile, so I guess my lifestyle is not new to me. It's just not my first choice of addresses."

"How did your mom have time to take a class?"

"I don't know, but she took this class taught by a cute, young guy named Bob, and back then, my mom was still hot, even though she'd had two babies."

"So they started dating?"

I nodded. "I remember the first time we went to his house for dinner. He was funny and nice. It was winter, and it snowed, so we spent the night at his house. He had a place near campus. I don't think he owned it. Rented it maybe. We moved in with him shortly after that. It was on California Street. I remember that because I loved that we lived on California Street. I thought that made us closer to Hollywood. Bob used to say 'if we can't live in California, we can live on California.' There were a lot of students who lived in the area in big, old two-story houses with lots of room. Our house had three bedrooms so Jeff and I each had our own room until Annie came along."

"So living with him was an improvement."

"Big time," I say. "And mom must be as fertile as a rainforest because she immediately got pregnant with Annie, so she and Bob got married." I drink some tea. "My mom quit working once Annie was born, and for awhile she was a housewife. Bob didn't make a lot, but enough to rent a house, and Jeff's dad sent support checks, so we didn't starve."

"How old were you when he died?"

"Six or seven I think. Annie was like three."

"Did you like him?"

"Oh, yeah," I say. "Bob was a great guy." Bob and Paul were both good stepdads. My mom may be nuts, but she chooses her men well. Most of them anyway, so I think my own father might be an okay guy. "Bob was smart, and we had books all over the place. We lived like a Norman Rockwell painting. Mom was home, the house was clean, and she cooked for us. Bob helped us with homework and we read stories. I even wrote a few."

"Do you still have them?"

I chew on another hunk of bread. "I don't have anything from that time."

"Because you live in your car?"

I look down at the table. "No, because of what happened to Bob."

The waiter brings our lunches. A big pie-shaped yellow slab of eggs inside a crust with some fruit on the side. He refills my iced tea and Shelly's water glass. We bite into our meals. I don't know what to expect. The thing on my plate looks weird, but when I take a bite, my taste buds go into overdrive.

"Wow, this is really good," I say.

"Told ya." Shelly takes a sip of her wine.

I want to devour it all at once, yet also take my time savoring the eggs and cheese and whatever else is in this quiche thing.

"So what happened to Bob?" Shelly asks.

I take a big bite and swallow. "He and my mom were saving to buy a house, so Bob started working a second job a couple nights a week. He tended bar at a place downtown." I take a drink from my water, not wanting to tell this story. "Bob didn't go in until nine or so, so he always read us stories before bed. Back then I went to bed around 7:30. He often read us tales from *The Arabian Nights*. He said those had been his favorite when he was a kid."

I chug some tea and wipe my mouth. "Anyway, one night he didn't come home. When I got up the next morning my mom was in the kitchen sobbing her eyes out. Bob had been shot in a drive-by after work while walking to his car."

"Oh that's terrible."

"Yeah. He got caught in the crossfire between gangs," I say. "Things kind of headed downhill fast after that. Bob had only taught part-time, and didn't have life insurance. We had to move out of the house since we couldn't afford rent. Mom sold what she could and we ended up back in Rooster, where Mom came from. We lived with her mom for a while. But her mother threw us out."

"Why?"

I grab Shelly's wine and take a big swig. I set the glass back on the table, leaving my fingers around the base. "My mom, she was, well . . . she kind of went through a phase where she had a different guy every night." I finish Shelly's wine. "It may be how she made her living for awhile."

"Oh."

"Yeah." I can't believe I'm telling her this. I don't think anyone outside the family knows. "She finally found another husband, though. Tomas. We moved in with him in the townhouse where she lives now."

"So is your stepdad the reason you got tossed out?"

"No. He's been out of the picture for awhile. Tomas was the total opposite of Bob. He drank, smoked pot, lived on welfare, and was an all-around asshole."

"Why did she marry him?"

I shrug. "Who knows? Loneliness? Money? The bad thing is my mom drank with him, and the two of them just sat around the house drunk and stoned, so Jeff's dad took him to live with him."

"How come he didn't take you and Annie as well?"

"He already had a whole family with his new wife."

"Oh."

"But Jeff has had it okay. His life is somewhat normal."

"So how bad was it for you and Annie?"

"Kind of bad." I suck down my tea until it's just ice and set the glass down. "Tomas would take off for days, sometimes weeks at a time. Then he'd come back and act like it was normal for a husband to just disappear. If she yelled at him about it, he hit her."

"Did he ever abuse you or your sister?"

"He came at me a couple of times, but I fought back. Tomas wasn't a big guy, and by then I could almost kick his ass, especially when he was loaded."

"How long was he in the picture?"

"He moved out at the end of my eighth-grade year."

It was shortly after that I started noticing the accumulation of things. The house was always a mess, but things got worse. Piles of crap just grew. There were days my mom didn't leave the house, but I am never telling Shelly this part of my story.

"Eventually Tomas left for good," I say. "He could be dead for all we know."

"Wow," she says.

"Yeah. I've had kind of a shaky history with dads, none of which was my own."

The waiter fills my tea and sets a chocolate cupcake in front of me with a candle in it. "A pretty little bird told me it was your birthday," he says.

After lunch, Shelly suggests we walk over to The Book Loft. "I can get you a birthday present."

"I thought lunch was my present."

"The Book Loft is also part of your gift."

"Is it a bookstore?"

"Yeah, and it has thirty-two rooms."

"That sounds cool. Let's go."

We walk about three blocks. It's a nice walk through an old neighborhood where the streets are made of cobblestone. "It's a lot different here than Rooster," I say.

I spot a strip of shops in an old brick storefront. I notice a Cup O Joe coffee shop. Next to it is a neon sign and a giant red banner identifying The Book Loft. We stop at the entrance, which has a couple benches and planters. "It looks like someone's house," I say. We walk further in and there are several tables loaded with books. "This is awesome."

"This is just the beginning," Shelly says. "Don't forget the thirty-two rooms inside."

Outside the store entrance Shelly glances at the announcements of authors who will be coming for book signings.

"Ugh," she says. "Pelee Peugeot."

"Never heard of her."

"She's this pretentious, ghastly, self-absorbed bitch who writes chick lit," Shelly says. "My mom loves her stuff."

"How do you know she's ghastly?"

"And self-absorbed and pretentious," she says. "She came to Columbus around Christmastime a couple years ago and did a reading at the Barnes & Noble at Easton. Josh and I drove up to get Mom an autographed copy of her latest bestseller. We got there kind of late because Josh has no concept of time. So we had to park clear over by Macy's and hike to the store in a mini-blizzard. Anyway, we get there an hour before the store is closing. Pelee Peugeot is still there sitting next to a stack of hardback books of all her titles. The line is kind of long, so I stand in line to wait while Josh hurriedly buys her latest book."

Shelly picks up a copy of Vonnegut's *Slaughterhouse-Five*. "Five ninety-nine," she says. "Not bad." She picks up a copy to buy and wanders away from me.

"So what happens next?" I ask.

"So I stand there and I start listening as this Pelee chick does her thing. Any time a man wants an autograph, even if he has a woman with him, she swings her long, flaming hair and reaches out to touch him, calling him darling or sweetie. But I notice if it is just a woman, she uses this flat tone, and says, 'Who should I make this out to?' So when Josh comes back, I tell him to be the one to get her signature. 'Seriously?' he whines. 'It's a chick book.' Which it kind of is. She writes these cheesy mysteries about a jaded female detective who looks amazingly like a younger version of herself. 'Trust me,' I tell Josh. 'The performance will be worth it.' So he shrugs, and I get out of line. I stand at a rack of books nearby so I'm in both eye and ear shot of her. Josh is the last one in line, and when he gets to her, she looks up and gushes, "I love to meet my male readers," she says. She grabs his hand and strokes it. 'Especially ones so handsome.' And my brother is good-looking. Kind of like a young Brad Pitt. Anyway, Josh glances at me with this horrified look on his face as Pelee flips her hair at him. It's no doubt dyed because she's like 500 years old, but you can tell she tries to look twenty-five. She's had so much Botox her face looks she's caught in the headlights. And her lips puff up like a blowfish. She bats her false eyelashes at my then eighteen-year-old brother, and opens the book to sign it. 'So what's your name, sweetheart?' She talks like Kathie Lee Gifford with that gushy, East Coast accent. Anyway, Josh just says, "It's for my mom." Pelee's Botoxed face freezes, and she says, 'Oh.' There's this uncomfortable moment where she is sitting there, the book open on the table in front of her, and waiting. Finally, I yell, 'Her name is Claire.' Pelee Peugeot glances my way, and I can see meanness in her eyes, as if the devil has sent her here to sign his books. She turns back to my brother, and with a frigid smile full of teeth, she says, 'Is that with a C or a K?' Josh told me later she creeped him out big time."

"Maybe she was just weird that day." I open the door to the bookstore.

"No," Shelly says. "I Googled her, and I found out her real name is Anne Smith. She's had five husbands, all younger. She has a kid by Number Three, but she left him with his father so she could go off to Greece and start writing. That's where she met Number Four."

"So how did she get the name?"

Shelly shrugs. "I saw this YouTube interview where she had some bullshit story about once having been rescued by some guy driving a Peugeot."

"It's kind of a cool name," I say.

Shelly shrugs. "I guess. But she's still a bitch."

We step inside the store. "Smells like paper," I say.

"Duh."

A bearded guy wearing a Book Loft T-shirt asks if he can help us. "He needs a map," Shelly tells him, and the guy hands me a photocopy of the store layout.

"I don't know where to start," I say. "It's like a book museum."

We step up to the first level where current bestsellers are displayed. I spot a Pelee Peugeot book on the *New York Times* bestseller shelf.

"That bitch," Shelly whispers. She reaches for the book. She leans in to me and whispers, "Normally I bend a few pages of her books every time I go to Barnes & Noble. That way it will get remaindered, and Pewee Pissant can't make any money off it." She sets the book back on the shelf unharmed. "But this is an independent bookstore, so I'll be nice."

"Remind me not to piss you off," I say.

"Don't worry," she says. "Your pages are already bent."

We thread our way up and down various staircases and rooms. Each room is unique, and I notice the music changes every few paces. In one room we hear Patsy Cline. A few steps away, Coltrane wails on sax, and yet another room plays John Lee Hooker. It reminds me of Bob. He was into music, and he's the reason I know something about jazz and blues.

The shelves are filled to capacity in each room. "It's almost too much," I say. "Overwhelming."

"Pick out whatever you want," she says.

"I want it all."

"Well, my dad's rich, but he's not that rich."

"I could live here," I say. Is this where it starts? This tendency to want to hold on to everything? To keep all the books of the world within reach? "This store reminds me of the Cemetery of Forgotten Books." Shelly gives me a quizzical look. "In a book I read a couple years ago called *The Shadow of the Wind*, there was this secret hideaway where they stashed old books," I say, "The Cemetery of Forgotten Books."

"What's the book about?"

"It's about this boy's possession of a rare book he picked out from the cemetery. It houses the last copies of all the books that have gone out of print."

"It's a book about a book?"

"Yeah, it's kind of hard to explain . . . part mystery, part love story. The kid picks out a book that leads into all sorts of intrigue."

"Let's see if we can find it," she says. She looks on the map. "Fiction is in rooms eight, nine, and ten."

Even with a map, the rooms are hard to figure out. If we were in a hurry, I'd ask for help, but I like the adventure of finding things. Like Daniel Sempere and his father, we move through the labyrinth of books and search through the fiction section.

"Who's it by?" she asks.

"Carlos Ruiz Zafón."

We find it under Zafón, along with his other books. "I liked *The Angel's Game* too," I say, "but not as much as *The Shadow of the Wind. The Angel's Game* is more of a ghost story. *The Shadow of the Wind* has more layers."

"You talk like someone in AP English."

I blush. "I *am* in AP English. Or I was before, you know."

"Yeah." She nods. "Before the shit hit the fan."

"Just because I live in my car doesn't mean I don't have a brain."

"I didn't mean that. It's just . . . I don't know what I meant."

"It's okay," I say. "It's my birthday, you're allowed to insult my intelligence." But I realize I am kind of trying to impress her with my vocabulary. She has money and two parents and lives in a big fancy house. Words are all I have.

She swats me with the book. I take it from her hands, open to page five, and read from the last paragraph. "Every book, every volume you see here, has a soul. The soul of the person who wrote it and of those who have read it and lived and dreamed with it. Every time a book changes hands, every time someone runs his eyes down its pages, its spirit grows and strengthens."

"Books do have souls," she says.

"What's your favorite book?" I ask. "And don't say *Little Women* or *Twilight* or I will steal your father's car and leave you here."

She laughs. "You really don't know me very well at all. *Little Women*? Hardly. And I may look Goth, but the vampire book thing doesn't turn me on."

"That's a relief. But seriously, if you were being evacuated to a planet and could take only one book, what would it be?" I say.

"Like in *The Green Book*?"

"Never heard of it."

"It's a kid's book," she says, "where this girl can only take one book with her to a new planet, so she chooses a blank book so she can write her own stories."

"Cool," I say. "Is that your book?"

"No. I like that one, but there are others I like more." She thinks for a minute. "I can only choose one?"

"Yep."

As usual, she turns the question back to me. "So what's your go-to book?"

"No, I asked you first, and since it's my not birthday, you have to tell me."

She unravels her black hair from the braid and shakes her head. Her hair cascades across her shoulder in wavy dents.

"Nice delaying tactic," I tell her.

"I can't think with my hair in a knot."

I laugh and smooth a strand of hair out her face, and my hand brushes her skin. We stare at one another for a long second. "It used to be *The Catcher in the Rye*," she says.

"What is it now?" I ask.

I want to kiss her, but am afraid to spoil the moment. Besides, she hasn't answered my question.

"Promise you won't laugh or make a sound of derision?"

"Nice vocab word," I say. "Seriously. Tell me."

She takes a breath. "It's a toss up between *On the Road* by Jack Kerouac and *100 Love Sonnets* by Pablo Neruda."

"I *love* Neruda," I say. "I have a battered copy of his *Selected Poems*."

"The one with a picture of him on front? Clasping his hands together?" I nod. "I have that book, too," she says. "In fact I took it with me when I . . ." She does not finish. Instead she quotes from one of Neruda's sonnets. "I love you as certain dark things are to be loved . . ."

"In secret, between the shadow and the soul," I add.

She smiles. "You're not a total ignoramus." She reaches up and caresses my cheek, pulls me to her, and our lips meet. The world evaporates around us. It's been so long since I kissed a girl a lingering thirst fills me, making me feel robust and alive. But our moment is broken by a toddler who grabs at my pant leg. I look down, and a round-faced boy giggles.

"Hey, buddy," I ask. "Are you lost?"

He shakes his head.

"Bernard!" a woman of around thirty says. She reaches for the boy and hoists him onto her hip. "Sorry."

"No problem," I say. But the spell is broken. Shelly has already moved on to peruse the shelves again. "Let's go find the poetry room," she says. "I'll show you my favorite sonnet."

She hands me the stack of books she plans to buy, takes my hand, and leads me toward the poetry. On the way, I notice a poster with a quote by Edmund Wilson: "No two persons ever read the same book."

We end up in room thirteen. I pick up a book. "Look," I say, holding it out. "A book called *Making Out in Chinese*." I want to make out with Shelly in any language.

She laughs. "They must do it differently than the rest of us." Shelly scans the shelves and finds the book she was looking for, a bubble-gum pink paperback of Pablo Neruda's *100 Love Sonnets*. "Here it is. Sonnet 89." She looks up at me. "This poem always makes me cry."

This makes me curious, and I glance over her shoulder as we read the poem together. I think it's the most wonderful poem I have ever read.

She closes the book and her eyes are wet. "This is what we all want, isn't it?" She says, her voice a whisper. "To love and be loved by someone so completely that we are unbroken."

I don't know how to react, but I know not to ruin the moment by speaking. I pull her into my arms. It's one of those times when words won't do, one of those inexplicable moments where the door to what makes Shelly tick has opened. Not far. But she has let me into the foyer, and I want to linger there awhile longer before she either tosses me out, or takes my hand and draws me inside. I stroke her silky hair, and she weeps softly into my chest.

When we finally pull apart the book's pink cover and some of its pages are crushed between us. "I guess we're buying this one," I say.

She smiles and says, "Happy Not Really Your Birthday."

CHAPTER SIX

After leaving The Book Loft we sit side by side outdoors at Cup O Joe, sipping cold mocha lattes. We sit close together without touching. Our silence is easy and necessary. Shelly and I shared something powerful, and I wonder what she feels right now, but I'm afraid to break our chain. I want to know her fully, to step inside her skin and burrow around. Like a hunter who waits for the fawn to become comfortable enough to let down her guard, I will wait. Our time together is fragile as butterfly wings, bright and beautiful, yet easily damaged.

Shelly begins reading *The Shadow of the Wind*. I pull the mangled poetry book out of the bag and smooth its cover. "Thanks for the book," I say. "I first heard of Neruda in Honors 10 English."

"Which poems?"

"'Ode to Tomatoes' and 'Tonight I Can Write the Saddest Lines.'"

"Hmm," she mutters. "We read some Neruda in Mrs. Silver's class." Shelly leans her head on my shoulder. We take turns reading poems aloud to one another.

She takes my hand and lets it linger on her lap as she rests her head on my shoulder. The afternoon leans into laziness, and we linger, just being. I am content, like a cat in a sunny window, and this is another moment where the world can explode and I can die happy.

Then Shelly's phone screams that *Psycho* shower scene scream.

"Crap." She sighs, and looks at the text. "Yes, we are still alive," she says out loud, as she pecks out her message. She glances at her screen, and stashes her phone in her bag. "We have to go."

I expect an explanation, but she offers none. We walk back to the car, hand in hand, in no hurry. I regret we didn't park farther away. I almost wish the car were stolen, out of gas, or not able to start. I want to extend this day with Shelly indefinitely. But we cannot stop time, nor can we repeat it. No moment can ever be duplicated. Copied maybe, but the original will always be its own entity.

I hold Shelly's door for her, and she climbs in, places her shades over her eyes, and wraps her hair back into a braid. I put on the mirrored sunglasses and start the car. "Buckle up."

She grins and snaps her seatbelt across her lap. Before I pull out of the parking space, I look at her, and say, "This has been the best un-birthday ever."

We talk very little on the way back. Shelly tries to read her book, but the pages flap in the wind, so she stuffs it under the seat and leans her head back. She has not put the scarf back on, and the shorter pieces of hair in the front fly around her face like nets.

The ride home moves by too quickly. I pull the little blue car into Shelly's driveway and feel a heaviness in my chest. I take a deep breath and hand her the sunglasses. I feel something between us shift.

"What's the matter?" she asks.

"I hate to give up the car. I don't want to go back to my own pitiful mobile home."

She laughs. The real truth is I don't want to separate from Shelly and our fragile bond. I fear that string might break as soon as she enters her house, and she will not look back.

She leans over and kisses me, and the world is righted again. I think.

"See you tomorrow," she says.

I stay up late reading Neruda's poems, marking my favorites with ripped flags of paper. I wonder which ones are Shelly's favorites. Will she decide I'm a dork if we don't like the same poems?

Ashley used to tease me, calling me a "word nerd" whenever I tried to talk to her about books. Her idea of literature was *Twilight* and *The Notebook*. I loaned her *The Shadow of the Wind*, but she said she couldn't get into it. "Too many descriptions," she had said. She tried to get me to read *Twilight*, and I couldn't get past the first page.

But Shelly has some reading chops, so maybe she will like *The Shadow of the Wind*. Is she even thinking about me as much as I am thinking about her?

***

I wake on my own, and glance at my phone. Seven forty-five. Shit! I scramble into my clothes and piss along the fence. Inside the building I rinse my face in the water fountain just inside the door. I make it to the custodial office just in time to hear Earl bark at me, "The day starts at eight, not eight oh five!"

"Sorry. Overslept."

I'm rumpled and hungry, but most of all worried. Why didn't Shelly wake me?

Earl says today we will be working in the library. "We need to pull the tables and chairs out into the hall."

"Do the books stay in?"

"Now what do you think? That we're going to stack up shelves and shelves of books in the hallway? Mrs. Morgan would kill me if we did that."

"Yeah, I guess that's a dumb question."

"And you're a senior again this year?" He shakes his head. "Woe to the world when we release you."

I want to ask him where Shelly is, but I don't want Earl to ask me why I am asking about her.

He unlocks the library and flips the lights on with a key. The school replaced all the light switches in the hallways, gym, cafeteria, and library with key locks because too many kids played with the lights at random.

"We'll leave the computers where they are. Our main function in here is to clean the carpets and fix anything on Mrs. Morgan's work order." He slips his glasses out of his front pocket and reads a sheaf of papers. "Fix the broken lock on the AV storage door, change the bulbs in her office, and mend a couple broken chairs." He folds the papers. "Let's get started, kid."

Being inside the school library always reminds me of Rick. I first met him ages ago in the elementary school library. Back then we were in sixth grade at the old 4–6 school, and he was a dorky red-haired new kid with braces, and I was a dorky semi-new kid who wore secondhand, sometimes smelly clothes. Among our classmates we were odd ducks. It was bad enough Billy Meeks and his cadre of bullies tormented me. They'd done it since I moved here a few months before, and I heard Michael Faggot, or Faggot Flynn yelled as I passed by them in the hallways. Physically, they never touched me, though. Not since I kicked Billy in the balls after he spit on my brother on the playground. But he and his friends burned with animosity toward me, and anyone else they knew they could pick on: poor kids, nerdy kids, and new kids. One day this skinny redheaded kid with a mouthful of braces walked into Mrs. Peterson's fourth-period sixth-grade language arts class. I noticed the look Billy Meeks shot to Jason Stoddard, as if they were marking him as their territory. I knew the new kid was a goner as soon as I saw him, and Meeks and Stoddard had him in their sights, aiming their rifles at him from the deer stand.

Mrs. Peterson told us to line up to go to the library for our biweekly visit. Every two weeks on Friday before lunch, one of the secretaries opened the doors to the library, and she snapped at us to sit down and stay quiet. If we wanted to check out a book, we had to wait for the secretary to boot up the computer at the desk. The school once had a librarian, but when she retired, the school didn't replace her. The only time we got to use the library was on rainy days after lunch or when Mrs. Peterson insisted they let her class visit. I was secretly in love with Mrs. Peterson.

I sidled up to the new kid in line, and said, "Hey, I'm Michael."

"Rick," he said. He shook my hand.

Just then Billy purposely shoved me against Rick with his shoulder, knocking us both against the wall. "Oh, so sorry, your major Faggotism," Billy said. He leered at Rick, then me. "I see you finally found a boyfriend."

On the way down the steps, Rick asked, "Who is that?"

"The school asshole. Or at least the biggest asshole in sixth grade."

We purposely sat away from them in the library, but Billy and Jason shot us looks the whole time. I sat with Rick at lunch at the table where other misfits sat: a couple of gamer guys, a boy who always picked his nose, and two girls from band who only talked to each other. None of us were friends, per se, but in the lunchroom, if we sat together, the sheer number of us somehow protected our group. We were safe until we got released to the dreaded playground. Every day I prayed for rain so we would be allowed to either go to the library or the gym.

I never went to the gym; it was an open savanna for bully targets. The other geeks and I always opted for the library, and those twenty minutes were kind of a slice of heaven for me. Even though the magazines were old and the pages of the paperbacks yellowed, being in the company of the printed word made me feel whole. It still does. So even though I suck at science and math, my English teachers have always loved me.

But this day was not one of those lucky rainy days. The new kid and I were relegated to meet our dooms on the playground with the other losers. Somehow I knew Rick the Redhead would be the chief target today. He was new, a distraction, new blood. Like on the savanna, fresh blood provided temptation.

"Listen," I told Rick, "these kids are going to mess with you."

"Yeah, I kind of figured that," he said. "It's the redhead thing. And the braces."

"And you don't weigh much more than a sack of potatoes."

He laughed. "You're one to talk."

"Too bad we don't have superpowers." I said. "Or swords or laser beams."

"True, but I have a better weapon," he said. "Just watch."

As if on cue, Billy and his tribe sauntered over to the edge of the building where Rick and I stood. They were careful to watch for the teacher on duty, made sure she was not watching. "Hey, Ugly," Billy said to me. "Aren't you going to introduce us to your new faggot friend?"

We both ignored him, and he shoved me into the wall. I expected to feel a fist in my face, but as soon as Billy lifted his arm to punch me, Rick let out a bloodcurdling scream that could have been on the soundtrack of *Nightmare on Elm Street*. He wailed so loud, the entire playground stopped, and everyone looked. I put my hands over my ears. I was surprised the screeching didn't break glass. Billy and his friends also covered their ears and backed way, but the teacher on duty caught Billy's arm and asked what was going on.

"N . . . nothing," Billy said. "He just started screaming."

"Billy, I am not unfamiliar with your reputation," she said. "Are you bothering these boys?"

"No ma'am," he said.

Rick had meanwhile stopped wailing. How could such a small guy make such a big sound?

As he and I walked back inside the building, I asked him how he did it. "It's easy. You just push the air up through your diaphragm, in your stomach. You don't use your throat at all."

"Where did you learn that?"

"Singing lessons," he said. "It's how singers and stage actors project their voices." It turned out Rick had a variety of sound effects he knew how to use. He could mimic livestock and sirens. He was also quickly snatched up to be the chief tenor in the school choir.

Billy stopped picking on Rick and me after that, and once we moved on to the big Junior/Senior High building, where kids from three elementary schools filtered into the 7–12 school, Billy had a whole new crop of nerds to pick on. He himself got bullied by high school kids.

Rick and I made friends with Mrs. Morgan, the head librarian, and her assistant Mrs. Beale, and we worked as library aides during our lunch periods and study halls until we started high school. Miraculously, Rick and I outgrew our skinny dorkiness. By high school, we had started to look like humans instead of pogo sticks with hair.

I still visited the library a lot during study hall, but Rick kind of moved on. He used his extra time in the band and choir rooms, honing his music skills, and later, scamming me out of a girlfriend.

***

For the next couple hours Earl and I stack chairs on a flat cart, move them into the hall, clear the cart, and reload. Every time I go to the hallway I look for signs of Shelly. Is she even here today? Is she avoiding me?

I picture her sitting at home, laughing about what an idiot I am to her parents. "He quotes poetry. Can he be any more lame?" Or maybe she calls a friend and tells her, "Let me tell you about my worst day ever. Remember that idiot guy who tried to blow up the school? Well, I went out with him a couple times, and he is such a dork."

"Hey kid," Earl says, "get your head out of your ass, and help me move this furniture." The tables and chairs are heavy and wooden. Together we lift the tables and carry them one by one out to the hallway. "Sons of bitches weigh more than we do," Earl grumbles.

After twenty tables and eighty chairs, Earl wipes his brow and says it's time for a coffee break. We saunter down to the lounge and I see a plate of peanut butter cookies. I don't want to appear greedy, but this is my breakfast, so I grab three and practically inhale them.

Earl hands me a steaming cup of coffee in a Styrofoam cup.

"Thanks," I say.

"Didn't want you to choke on all them cookies."

"Yeah, I uh, didn't have time for breakfast."

I take one more, and Hess walks in, trailed by Shelly. "Hey," she says.

I want to shout at her, yell that I spent the morning imagining the worst possible scenarios, but she sits next to me, smiles, and all is right in the world again.

"I figured out why you like *The Shadow of the Wind* so much," she says.

"Yeah?" I bite into a cookie and pretend her presence isn't playing a beat box in my chest.

Besides the wonderful writing, engaging characters, and the shroud of mystery, *you're* Julián Carax."

"What do you mean?"

"The character Julian Carax in Zafón's *The Shadow of the Wind* is a boy who never knew his father, and he spends his life trying to find him. Carax writes a book he calls *The Shadow of the Wind*, which Daniel Sempere discovers in the Cemetery of Forgotten Books," she says. Shelly touches my arm. "In a way, Carlos Ruiz Zafón wrote your story, too."

Her fingers send electric currents through my skin. "Huh," I say. "I never thought of that."

Shelly and I drive to Burger King for lunch. She has started smoking again, but as a healthy diversion, she orders the veggie burger, which she claims does not taste like a Nike insole. I still opt for a double cheeseburger. We share a large order of fries.

"I think we should try to find your father," she says.

"I don't even have a name," I say. "I wouldn't know where to start."

"Have you ever seen your birth certificate?"

"No."

"Where were you born?"

"In Columbus, I think." The thought of going through my mother's house, rummaging through the stacks of crap to find my birth certificate makes me lose my appetite. "I think my mom lost it in one of our moves," I say.

"Well, even if your mom doesn't have your certificate, we can get a copy of it online from the records office."

"Don't I need an adult's permission?"

She tweaks her brow at me. "I can get anything. If I can't, I know people who can."

I give her a doubtful look.

"My dad's a lawyer," she says. "I know about this stuff. All we need is your full name, date of birth, and city where you were born." She ruffles through her giant purse and pulls out a pocket-sized notebook and pen. "Do you have to work after school today?"

"Yeah."

"Give me your info and I'll look it up for you." I write down my name, date of birth, and Social Security number for her. "Good thing I'm not worth anything, or I'd worry about you stealing my identity."

She snorts. "You're probably some eccentric millionaire like Howard Hughes who lives in squalor."

"I wish."

She looks over what I had written. "I'll have to give an actual address," she says. "Not the parking lot of Rooster High School."

"Very funny," I say, and write my mother's address. "I use my mom's address for mail," I say. "I'd better tell my sister so she can intercept the mail. My mom might freak if she knows I'm looking for my dad."

"Parents are freak shows."

"That they are," I say. I stop writing. "Listen, can we wait until tomorrow to do this? I'd kind of like to be the one to do the search. It's not that I don't trust you. It's just . . . I've waited a long time. This is kind of important."

She considers this for a second. "I totally get that."

I park in a shady spot behind the building. Shelly gets out and runs toward the fence separating the football field from the parking lot. She grasps the barbed wire and stares out at the field. "Look," she says.

I follow Shelly down to the fence, and ask, "What are you looking at?"

She points at the ducks walking on the tarmac. I lean my elbows over the fence and gaze at the pair of ducks tottering across the AstroTurf.

"Odd," I say. "The school pond is way out on the other side of the school property. They walked a long way to get here."

"You and I are kind of like those ducks," she says. "An odd pair of misfits, way out of our leagues, but without enough sense to know it."

"I think we know it, we just don't know enough to care."

She leans against me. "Caring what inconsequential people think of you is a ginormous waste of a life."

"Am I a person of consequence?"

"Right now, you're the person of consequence."

I slide an arm around her and hold her closer. "Ditto," I say.

"We're two halves of some ancient coin," she says. "Money that no longer has any value, but contains a long and ragged history."

CHAPTER SEVEN

Annie calls as I walk back into the building and asks me to stop by the townhouse as soon as possible. "Mom bought you something," she says, "and I'm afraid if you don't come get it right away, she'll find a place for it inside the house."

"How big is it?"

"It's a bunch of small stuff, but if she puts one more thing in here I think I'll suffocate."

I worry about my sister. Last year she had bronchitis twice, and I know it has to do with whatever bacteria are simmering under the filth. "What is it? Does Mom remember I live in a car?"

She laughs. "She knows that. She got you some camping equipment."

"Oh. Actually, that may come in handy," I say. "I'll be over right after school."

"It's still in her car, but if she tries to bring it in the house I'll keep it on the back porch. That way you won't have to come inside."

"Thank you. You're my favorite sister."

I miss living with my siblings. I don't miss the crazy days of spending the nights in strangers' homes, or the revolving door of my mother's husbands and lovers. But I miss the camaraderie between Jeff, Annie, and me. We squabbled as kids, tried to get one another in trouble, and called each other some of the most foul words not in the dictionary, but nobody else was allowed to call us names. Once when Jeff and I were walking back home from playing softball down the street, we came upon a group of girls taunting Annie, yelling things at her like, "a half-breed jababbi."

One girl reached out and yanked Annie's hair. Jeff and I glanced at one another, ran full speed, and knocked those brats down. One of the girls' mothers scrambled over and split us all up. The girls claimed we started it. Annie was crying too hard to say much. Jeff and I stuck to our story. Mom just shrugged it off, and told the woman to keep her damn kids the hell away from us. As fractured as we are as a family, I would kill for each of them.

***

At the end of the day, Shelly asks, "What's up? Wanna do anything?"

"I have to work later, but first I need to stop by my mom's and pick up something."

"Want company?"

"No!"

She gives me a questioning glance.

"I mean, it won't take long." Some secrets are best left unearthed. Shelly likes me now, but one false move will send her running. Besides, I have other layers of secrets she can scavenge over. "I wouldn't have time to get you home and get to work on time."

"Okay. Maybe next time."

"Yeah," I say, meaning never.

We head out the door, and as I walk to my car, Shelly looks at my grimy pants and says, "You can't wear those to work."

I shrug. "It's okay for the theater. Khaki and olive are okay. Just no jeans."

"That's not what I meant," she says. "You can't go into work looking like something on the bottom of the laundry basket."

I shrug. "I don't have time to worry about it now. I don't have any clean pants." I glance at my filthy cargo pants. "This is all I have. I'll change my shirt when I get there."

"Give me your dirty clothes. I'll take them home and wash them."

"You've already done more than enough for me."

"We're friends, right?"

"Yeah, I guess we are."

"Friends take care of each other. Someday you'll repay the favor." She winks, and I give her a grin. I hand her my pillowcase full of wadded up clothes. "Give me those pants too."

I've learned it's easier not to argue with Shelly. I crawl into the back of my station wagon. The only other clean thing I have is a pair of cargo shorts. I shuck off my trousers and slide into the shorts.

Shelly holds on to my filthy ones like they're nuclear waste and dumps them inside the pillowcase. She kisses me quickly on the lips and says she will see me in the morning. "Don't forget, we have an important date tomorrow."

I stop by Tim Hortons on the way to the townhouse and get a box of Timbits with Jeff's discount. He tells me to say hi to Mom for him. I park behind my mom's wreck of a car in front of the townhouse and walk to the back porch. Annie is sitting in her lawn chair with her feet propped on top of an inverted plastic bucket, reading from *The Arabian Nights*. Annie's legs have grown long and lean, and today her hair is woven into a thick braid down her back. When she wears her hair down it's wavy and wild. Even though her dad was black, Annie resembles Mom in her features.

"Hey," I say.

"Hey." She sets the book next to her. "Did you know some of those stories are pretty racy?"

"Really? Your dad never read those to us," I say.

"Or if he did, we didn't understand what they meant."

The cushions my sister sleeps on are put away, the sheets and blankets tucked inside a duffle bag. The dresser where Annie keeps her clothes is free of anything on top. The condition of the porch would not alert neighbors or authorities that there is a problem inside the home.

I hand her the donuts. "Ooh, my favorite." She opens the box and pops one in her mouth and hands me the box.

I pick out two chocolate ones. "Mom home?" The back door opens and my mother steps outside. She is dressed in her nurse's aide uniform, her long blond hair pinned up in back. She works in a nursing home and the old folks adore her. For all her foibles, our mom is a good listener and a gentle soul.

She still resembles the young bleached blonde from old pictures, but now her face is lined from cigarettes and life. Mom walks over and squeezes me into her, and I squeeze her back. She holds me out at arm's length. "You look good, son. You must be eating regularly."

"It's all that free popcorn."

She studies my face. "Are you in love?"

I blush. "Mom!"

"You're embarrassed, so it must be true. What's her name?"

"We've only gone out a couple times."

"Jeff told me he saw you with some Goth chick the other day," Annie says. "Who is it?"

"I . . . uh . . . don't think you'd know her." I'm embarrassed to say I don't know Shelly's last name. Did she tell me and I don't remember? "Jeff says hello."

My mom touches my cheek. "Did Annie tell you I got you something?"

"Yeah," I say. "That's why I stopped by. I can't stay long, though. I'm due at the theater in a like thirty minutes."

"It's still in my car," Mom says. She steps off the porch and walks toward the front of the house.

I give Annie a quick hug, say, "See ya," and follow my mother to the street. Her car is not that old—a five-year-old Taurus—but it looks worse than mine. I don't think it's been washed since she bought it from Paul three years ago. Like the house, her car is stuffed with objects, and she has just enough room to see out the back window and the passenger side front window.

"One of my patients is cleaning out his house," she says. "He asked if I needed any camping gear, and I told him I have a boy who likes to camp." She glances at me. "I didn't tell him you camp out in your car. But anyway, he gave me all this equipment I thought you might be able to use."

Inside my mom's trunk is a pop-up tent, a camp stove, two lanterns, a flashlight, a sleeping bag, some camp dishes, and a thick jacket. "Wow, Mom, this is great. He just gave it to you?"

She sighs. "Yeah, poor guy. He's not even that old, sixty something, but he won't be walking in the woods anymore. He had one leg amputated, and looks like he may lose the other. Sweet thing. He calls me Julie because he says I remind him of the girl on *The Mod Squad.*"

"The *what* squad?"

"Some old TV show from the sixties."

As much as I don't want to clutter up my car, this acquisition actually makes sense even though it reeks of musty basement. I put my arm around her shoulder. "Thanks, Mom."

I haul it over to my car and dump the stuff in the back. The odor stinks up the car, but I can set it all outside tonight after work. Maybe I'll buy some Febreze and spray it.

We stand by the driver's side of my car. "You need any money, hon?" she asks.

"No, I'm good," I say. "But thanks." I hug her quickly and get in my car. As I drive away, I feel my face grow hot and my breath quiver. I miss my mom so much. I miss who she used to be, before her life revolved around the accumulation of things.

I pull into the mall parking lot and change my shirt. I hope Mitch doesn't notice I'm wearing cargo shorts rather than pants. I grab my pack and hoist it over my shoulder, cracking the windows an inch all around, and hope nobody steals the camp gear. Maybe the odor will keep thieves at bay.

In the break room I stash my bag in my locker and pin my nametag on my chest. I don't have time to freshen up, so I smear some deodorant under my pits and splash some AXE cologne on my face. It's the world's worst aftershave, but I found a small pocket-sized bottle of it on the floor of Theater 6 one night and use it in emergencies. Like today.

Mitch frowns when he notices my shorts.

"Sorry," I say. "We didn't have time to wash clothes with the power being out and all. Then we went camping."

"You'll have to work the ticket booth," he says, "where nobody can see your hairy spider legs."

He's killing me. I hate working the ticket booth, and Mitch knows it. I'd rather sweep floors and clean restrooms. Direct customer contact gives me the willies. When shows get sold out, or people arrive late to a movie, or we don't honor discounts on hot films, somehow it's my fault. If I take too long getting change some people go ape shit. Then there are the scammers who claim they gave me a twenty when they really gave me a ten. Mitch had warned me about those types on the first day. "Always keep the money they gave you in front of you until after you have confirmed their change. That way they can't question it." Guys try that trick more than chicks, especially if they have a date with them. If guys don't bring enough cash to buy popcorn, they think they can fake out the idiot in the ticket booth. I want to tell them I'm not as dumb as I look, asshole.

The worst thing about working the ticket booth is seeing kids from school, guys on the football team who treat me like shit because I'm cross-country, which they think is a sissy sport, and kids who don't have to work, the kind of kids who live in Shelly's neighborhood. Maybe the type of guys she should be going out with instead of scumbags like me.

But as she said, she and I are those lost ducks who strayed too far from the pool, too far from our kind, and maybe we need to find our way around this spiny world. It's as if the world is made of porcupine hide, and we need to tread lightly.

As soon as I open my door after work, my car emits a moldy stench, so I roll all the windows down as I drive down Rocket Road. Maybe it would have been better if someone had robbed me. The camp gear reeks of dirty cat box, and it makes me wonder if cleaning it up is going to take more than Febreze and a day in the sun. I park the car near the football field and grab the whole mess and toss it all on the ground.

Hunkered in my car, I can't sleep. It's not the lingering smell from the camp gear or the heat. The night is cool and pleasant, and I know later I will need a blanket on top of my sheet. My mind is revving over the possibility of finding out who I am tomorrow.

My whole life I have searched for him in the shadows and the bright sun, searched for him in coffee shops and bookstores and gas stations. I conjured him in the black-haired dishwasher at Bob Evans's restaurant, and believed I saw him in the spaghetti aisle of the grocery store. Scenarios of our meetings roll through my head like a film where I imagine him lumbering toward me with the slightly askew gait I inherited (I don't walk like Jeff or my mother), his arms spread out to welcome his long-lost son. At the pool he taught me how to dive and swim, and later, on vacations, we went to the beach where he taught me how to body surf. I envisioned meeting him at the circus, where he took my hand and bought me a bunch of balloons. In another film, he carried me on his shoulders at a county fair. He and I bowled together at Main Lanes and ate ice cream in Graham Park. My father played catch with me in the backyard of his sprawling home, the one with the pool and a pair of well-behaved Golden Retrievers. He bought me Christmas presents and threw birthday parties for me, sparing no expense. My father introduced me to his coworkers, saying proudly, "Here's my boy. Someday he'll be running this company." He told me bawdy jokes and said I was going to be a "lady-killer," and showed me how to shave without cutting myself. He instructed me on how to treat a lady on a date, and how to tie my tie and wear cologne. He coached me in softball and football, and cheered at every game.

But none of this is true, and in every film, he has no face. He has no name. Because I have no name. I am not who I imagine I am. I am nobody.

That's my biography: the boy with no name.

I am teeming inside, and throw the sheet off me. Maybe Shelly is wrong; I don't need to find my father. I just need to accept he will never be a part of my life.

CHAPTER EIGHT

After a restless night's sleep, I rise early. It's a splendid morning, and it's been awhile since I have run, so I rummage through my clothes and find my running shoes and track shorts. I had charged up the iPod and the MP3 I found in the lockers. The iPod music sucks, but the MP3 player has some good music on it. Blues and some classic rock like Steppenwolf and The Doors. I plug the ear-buds in my ears, turn on Steppenwolf's "Born to Be Wild," and run on the track. When I reach the end of three miles, I'm a little winded and very sweaty. "Me and the Devil" by Gil Scott-Heron plays in my ears as I do a cool-down walk. I heave my sweaty self uphill back to my car, and Earl is parked next to me in his battered pickup. He's leaning against my rear fender, puffing on a pipe. Shit! Does he know I have been parking here all night?

"You're up early, kid," he says as I approach.

"I needed a run."

"I see your car here sometimes before I get here," he says. "You come in early a lot?"

"Yeah," I say, half out of breath. "I try to stay in shape for cross-country. Training starts in July."

"Uh-huh." He nods slowly. I don't know how to read that nod. Does he believe me? I almost wish he'd come out and ask me if I'm living in my car. He scans the camping equipment strewn near my car. "Camping out here?"

I flushed. "I brought this stuff in to see if I can freshen it up," I say. "Our cat peed all over it, and my brother and I want to go camping this weekend. I was hoping to maybe scrub it up during lunch."

"Sure, kid. We have some stuff that will get the stink out."

"Thanks."

Earl takes another look at the gear. "That camping gear is good quality. Old, but quality stuff."

"Yeah, it's not bad."

"You need a shower." He glances at his watch. "You've got time. See ya inside, kid." He gets in his truck and drives to his usual parking spot by the rear doors.

I rustle through the backseat and gather some semi-clean clothes and a towel. I also grab my travel-size shampoo and soap, toothbrush and toothpaste. I glance at my phone. Seven-fifteen. Shelly will be here soon. I leave a note to tell her I'm in the shower and to wait for me. I half expect her to join me in the boy's locker room. Not that I'd mind.

When I come back out she's sitting on the open tailgate of the car, smoking. I know better than to comment.

I spread my damp towel across the back of my seat. "That shower felt good," I say, as I finger through my wet hair. "It's rare I get a total body shower."

"You live like a Frenchman."

"*Oui, oui, mademoiselle.*"

"Except you smell a little better. They don't wear deodorant."

I nestle the MP3 player in the zipper pocket of my backpack and shove my sweaty shorts in the back of the car. I notice a pile of laundered and folded clothes resting on the seat. "Thanks for doing my laundry," I say, as I sit down next to her and sling an arm around her. I pull her close and kiss her.

She shrugs. "It's no big deal."

"To you, maybe."

"I have something else for you," she says. She tosses a plastic bag at me.

It contains one of her brother's shirts, a pair of olive-green Dockers, and a half-bottle of Guess Seductive Homme Blue. "This way you won't smell like you've been sleeping in a sewer," she says.

"Isn't this your brother's?"

"I bought him a new bottle," she says. "I'll tell him I broke the old one by accident."

"Thanks," I say. "If it weren't for lies, you and I wouldn't survive." I splash on some of the cologne and place it in the bag. "I think Earl suspects something."

"About you living here?"

"Yeah. He was parked next to my car waiting for me when I came back from a morning run."

"What did he say?"

"Just that he's noticed my car here early in the morning sometimes before he gets here."

"Oh shit," she says.

"Yeah. My thinking exactly."

She laughs and slides off the tailgate. Shelly unwraps a piece of cinnamon gum and chews it. "Even though I'm smoking again, I'm still trying to cut back." She looks at the football field. "I think I'll go see if our ducks are out there today."

I dress quickly in a pair of clean shorts and the T-shirt Shelly brought me and finger comb my hair. I swish some mouthwash around and spit it to the side of the car, and I slide on my secondhand Nikes.

Shelly whistles when she sees me. "You clean up pretty well for a vagrant."

"Thanks. Were the ducks there?" I ask.

She shakes her head. "What's the story with the stinky camping gear?"

"My mom found it in the basement," I tell her. "She thought I could use it. I didn't realize how bad it smelled until I put it in my car."

"I guess it's not a bad idea."

She spits her gum out on the ground. "What are we hungry for today?"

"Let's live dangerously," I say. "Burger King."

Before we get into the car, Shelly makes me pose for a picture. "Why?" I ask.

"Because you don't look like a rabid dog for once."

"Gee thanks."

"Stand still and look human." She holds up her iPhone and snaps a pic.

I try to pay for my own breakfast to thank her for the clothes and cologne, but Shelly pushes my money away. "My parents hemorrhage money," she says. The counter girl laughs and looks at us curiously. We both order ham-and-cheese croissants, large coffees, and hash browns.

I lift the tray. "Heart attack on a plate."

"Let's hope you don't keel over before you find your father," she says.

We sit near the window so I can keep an eye on the car. Not that anyone would steal it.

"If you could have breakfast with anyone in the world," Shelly says, "living or dead, who would you choose?"

"Besides you?"

She nods. I think for a second. "I don't know. Elvis, Einstein, Marie Curie, or . . ."

"You can only choose one."

"Oh man." I consider again. "Probably Pablo Neruda. How about you?"

Shelly stirs sugar in her coffee and takes a sip. "Jack Kerouac."

I laugh. "Breakfast with him would be beer in a tavern at four o'clock in the afternoon."

"Can you imagine the four of us in here together?" she asks.

"Neruda and Kerouac in Burger King? That would be freaky."

We eat in silence for a few seconds. "Today is the day you find out who you really are," Shelly says.

"I'm not sure I want to know."

"There is always a risk. You could find out your dad is a pedophile or a circus clown."

I recall my dreams of the faceless men and I think of the kind of men my mother is attracted to now. She had chosen good mates in Bob and Paul, so there may be hope I am the son of a decent man. Lately, though, my mother's boyfriends and husbands have all been losers, users, and abusers.

If I have learned anything from my mother's string of men, it's how not to be a schmuck. "What if I find out my dad is a serial killer?" I ask. "And what happens once I find him?"

Shelly takes a deep breath and steals one of my potato triangles. "Let's just find him first. Then we'll worry about the details."

We arrive back at school a few minutes before eight. Earl and Hess are bent in conversation in the teacher's lounge. They glance up when Shelly and I step inside.

"Where are you planning to camp?" Hess asks.

"We haven't decided yet," I say.

"My wife and I like Spring Valley near Cambridge," he says.

"Thanks," I say. "We might check it out." I hate lying to Hess and Earl. They're good guys.

CHAPTER NINE

At lunchtime, Hess offers to go to a drive-thru for everyone. Shelly and I use the time to scrub the grime off the tent, which really did have cat piss on it. We scour and rinse the tent and pop it open to let it dry in the sun. While we work, Shelly plaits her hair in a long braid draped to one side.

"Very fetching," I say.

She shrugs. "It's cooler."

The sleeping bag turns out to be down filled, which will come in handy this winter if we can get the odor out. I guess if I get cold enough the stink won't matter.

It feels good to be outside, scrubbing and rinsing alongside Shelly. The stove and the dishes clean up easily with the hose, but the fabrics have absorbed a foul stench. We soak the jacket and the sleeping bag in a cleaning solution Hess concocted and hang it to dry over one of the railings by the back door. The wet feathers make it heavy, but I hope the sun and breeze will dry it. I hang the jacket on the opposite railing.

"How long was this stuff in your basement?" Shelly asks.

"Long enough," I say.

"Your cat must be a piece of work. Maybe the smell of other animals from nature made him use it as a litter box," she says. "To mark his territory."

"Maybe.

She studies me. "You don't really have a cat, do you? And you and Jeff never go camping."

"No," I admit. "My mom thought I'd be able to use this old stuff."

"So even though you tried to blow up the school, and she tossed you out, she still loves you?"

"Something like that," I say. "No matter what we do, our parents still care about us. Look at you. Whatever you did to be my co-criminal, your parents still love you."

"Nice try, but I'm not ready for that conversation."

"I can wait." I point a finger at her. "Someday, though."

"And someday you'll tell me the real reason you live in your car."

By the end of our workday, most of the camp gear is almost dry. Earl lets me hang the damp sleeping bag and jacket inside the school. I drape them over some chairs in the custodial storage room. The tent is dry, though, and I stash the now fresh-smelling tent and other gear in the back of my car. It all smells like industrial cleaner, but that's a whole lot better than cat urine and mold.

Shelly glances at the pile of dirty clothes and sheets littering the backseat of my car. "We can wash the rest of those at my house while we look up your birth certificate."

As I drive, every time I turn a corner the camping stuff rolls around. "It sounds like you have a body in the back," Shelly says.

"Yeah, I'm going to have to organize it better."

"Or store it somewhere."

"Maybe I can leave it in Jeff's basement until winter."

I grab the duffle, fill it with the rest of my dirty clothes, sling it over my shoulder, and haul it up her driveway.

"I'll show you how to work the washer, and then I'm going to change clothes."

She dumps in a capful of detergent and sets the load on high. I lift the duffle and start shoving clothes inside the washer.

"Don't you separate lights and darks?" she asks.

"Huh?"

She shakes her head. "You're supposed to wash dark clothes separately from lighter-colored ones. It keeps your underwear from turning gray."

"Oh. I never thought of that." I shrug. "I guess that makes sense." I look at my now wet pile of clothes inside the washer. "Too late now."

She picks up my duffle with two fingers and holds it out like it's a stinky fish. "Might as well throw this in as well."

I cram it in the washer. "Thanks for letting me do this."

"How did you live without me before?"

"Obviously I was dangling on the edge of a cliff."

"I'm going to change clothes," she says. "Give me five minutes, then come up to my room."

"Will you be naked?"

"You wish," she says.

A few minutes later we sit in front of her laptop, and a fully clothed Shelly powers it up. "The moment of truth," Shelly says. "Are you ready?"

"Yes and no." This feels too easy. "In a few minutes I find out if I'm half Mexican or Amish or Italian."

"You're probably the spawn of alien life forms," she says.

I laugh, and swing my arm around her shoulder. I say in my best cheesy French accent, "Perhaps I am a Frenchman after all."

She feigns a British accent. "Or perhaps you're a royal, the long lost bastard child of Prince Charles."

"Oh, do behave."

She types Ohio vital records in the search bar and the website appears on screen.

The first thing I notice is the time frame to get the certificate. "It takes twenty to thirty-five business days," I say.

"That's just a rough estimate."

"And it costs eighty-five bucks! Plus shipping," I say.

"Don't worry about it," she says. "I have open access to a credit card."

"Are you sure your dad is okay with you spending money like this?"

"He wheezes money," she says. "Don't worry about it. What's your full name?"

"Michael Gillam Flynn."

"Gillam?"

"I'm named after my dead uncle," I say.

Shelly types in my name, date of birth, and Columbus, Ohio. The screen takes its time spooling.

"Why is it taking so long?" I ask.

"There's a lot of people in Ohio."

Finally the screen shows a hit. My name's there, as is my mother's, but my father's name is a giant blank space.

"What the hell?" I shout.

I want to hit something. "Every damn time I get close, I hit a brick wall. Damn it!" I slam my fist on the top of her desk. I stalk out of her room and run down the steps. I fling the front door open and pace on her front lawn.

Shelly follows me out. "Michael!"

I wave my fists and shout, "What the hell do I do now?" I walk back and forth on the lawn. "Why is she keeping this such a big fucking secret? Is my father a Cuban spy? Or a Middle Eastern terrorist? I mean, what the hell? Why can't she just tell me? Was I hatched instead of born? Am I a goddamned alien, or just a figment of your wild imagination?" I pinch my own flesh and it stings, so I know I am real.

Shelly lets me rant some more. When I am finally quiet, she touches my arm, says, "I'm really sorry, Michael." She reaches out to caress my face. "I guess the good news is you're not Amish."

"No, I'm a damned alien from Mars."

"Your skin isn't green enough."

I grimace. I know she's trying to make me feel better, but I'm not really in a joking mood. I want to be mad a little longer. But it's not Shelly I'm mad at. I'm mad at my life.

"Maybe we should take a drive so you can think behind the wheel," she says. "We can go back to The Book Loft if you want."

"All those words will be a distraction right now," I say.

"Let's put the top down on the Miata and just take a drive then," she says. "It will clear your head."

"Aren't you afraid I'll do something crazy like ram us into a wall?"

She shrugs. "And if you did, I might be okay with that."

I shoot her a look.

"I'm kidding," she says. "Come on."

Shifting gears on the Miata feels cathartic, as if I have control of at least one thing in my life. By the time we get to the entrance ramp to I-70, I have calmed down a little. I rev the car down the freeway ramp and head west toward Columbus. When we reach sixty miles an hour, Shelly flips her side braid behind her and wipes her neck. "I feel like I'm wearing a ferret."

I laugh, and drive, navigating through the brink of rush hour. In the freeway din, Shelly yells. "I'm hungry again. Let's stop at Panera on 256."

"What's Panera?"

"Kind of a coffee shop."

"Okay. I could use a cup of coffee."

"Yeah, that'll relax you right up."

"Shut up." I smile at her. "I'll get decaf, okay?"

She guides me to Panera, which sits next to T.G.I. Friday's. I've never been to either place before but I have seen them from the freeway. I park the little car in a space near the entrance. "Is this place fancy dancy?"

"Hell no. It's a dressed-up version of fast food with good pastries." We walk in and I notice two counters. "You can order on either side," Shelly says. "The pastries are here on the left, and the food is on the right."

From the food menu I order a big bowl of cheddar-broccoli soup and some exotic sounding sandwich with Asiago cheese. The kid at the counter swears it's good. Shelly orders a bowl of pasta with pesto and a salad.

"That smells wonderful," I say as we sit down.

"Take a bite." She gives me a forkful of the best pasta I have ever eaten. "It has pesto in it."

I have no idea what pesto is, but I nod and pretend I know what the hell she's talking about.

Shelly's phone buzzes. She looks at the number. "Jeez, how do these creeps get my cell number?"

"Who is it?"

"Some telemarketer. I like messing with them." She punches Accept and places the phone on speaker on our table.

"Good afternoon," a slightly Indian-sounding voice says. "Is this Mrs. Miller?"

"Uh-huh," Shelly says. So her last name is Miller. Noted.

"My name is Dave, and I am calling from Visa Bank Trust. And I want to tell you about this one-time opportunity to reduce the rate of interest on your Visa card." He goes through his long spiel.

After a moment of silence, Shelly says, "I have a question."

"Yes?"

"Are you naked?" she says in a breathy seductive tone.

"Wh . . . what?"

She picks up the phone and whispers, "What are you wearing, Dave? Do you need help removing your clothes so I can ravage every inch of your dark-skinned, Delhi body?"

Whoever "Dave" is hangs up. I laugh. "You are way too good at that," I say. "I'm a little turned on right now."

She shoves her phone in her bag and sips her coffee. "You men are so easy," she says. "It's harder to rattle the women callers."

We get back to her house around six-thirty. Neither of her parents is home yet. Shelly puts my clothes and duffle in the dryer and gets us each a bottle of beer from the fridge. We sit by the pool and dangle our feet in the water. She unravels her hair from the braid and fluffs it out with her hands, letting it fall over her shoulders in wrinkled waves. She leans her head against my shoulder, and I wrap my arms around her.

"If we had a soundtrack for this moment," I say, "it would have to be Tom Waits singing 'Blue Valentine.'" In my scratchiest voice, I mangle the lyrics to the song.

Shelly and I fold and stack my laundry back into the now clean duffle. "Thanks for everything you've done for me," I say.

She rolls her eyes, folds a T-shirt, and carefully stashes it in the duffle. "I wouldn't do it if I didn't like having you around," she says. "Dork."

"Freak."

"Moron," she says.

I pull her close and kiss her deeply. My hands wander over her body, and I get hard. I reach my hand under her skirt, and she pulls back, and whispers, "My parents will be home soon. You'd better hit the road."

"Oh. Okay."

I stuff the rest of my clothes in the canvas bag and tie it shut. I hoist the duffle over my shoulder.

"You seem pissed," she says.

"No, I'm just . . . I'm just kind of confused. I thought you were attracted to me."

"I am attracted to you," she says. "I'm just not ready to take this to the next level."

"Okay."

"Listen, despite what you may have heard about me, I'm not some tramp who does it anywhere and everywhere," she says.

"I never thought that about you."

"Who do you think I am?"

I set the duffle down. "I'm not sure. I know you're bold and adventurous."

She touches my chest. "We have a good thing, but I don't want to rush things," she says. "Listen, you've had a tough day, and you probably deserve a little physical reward, but I just can't help you right now."

"I didn't expect sex as a reward. I would never be happy forcing myself on you."

"And that's one of the things I like about you."

I kiss her quickly and open the door. "I'll see you tomorrow."

"Wait," she says. She scurries to the kitchen and comes back with a plastic Kroger bag. Inside are half a loaf of French bread, a jar of peanut butter, a banana, and an orange. "I can't do breakfast in the morning, and I don't want you to starve."

I smile. "Thanks." I grasp the bag by the handles. "Are you coming to school at all tomorrow?"

"Yeah, but I'll be a little late."

I wait for her to tell me why, but I know she won't.

CHAPTER TEN

At the end of the work detail today, Annie texts me and asks me to stop by. She wants me to help keep Mom from going to a flea market. Sometimes one or both of us can talk her out of buying more stuff, but mostly, it's a huge waste of time. I text back, "OK."

"Do you work tonight?" Shelly asks.

"No, I have to go see my sister."

"Need company?"

"No. My mom might be sleeping." Shelly accepts my reason and kisses me goodbye. "See you in the A.M.," she says.

Annie is sweeping the porch when I approach. "Keeping your room clean, I see."

She rolls her eyes at me. "What's up, big bro?"

"Mom up yet?"

"I think she's in the shower. She worked late last night, but you know lack of sleep won't keep her from another flea market."

"Unfortunately."

I glance at the title of the book sitting on Annie's chair. "*The Hunger Games*? Are you the last person on the planet who hasn't read that book yet?"

She laughs. "I saw the movie, but the book is better."

"Duh." I sit on the steps, and Annie sets the broom aside and plops down beside me.

"How is life treating you?" she asks.

I wave my palm up and down. "So-so."

"Are things still working out with the Goth girl?"

I blush. "What do you mean?"

"Jeff told me he saw you with her again the other day."

"Things are fine," I say. "So what's going on with you?"

Annie's shoulders droop. "Mom went to Goodwill yesterday alone. She got mad when I tried to talk her out of going, so she made me stay behind."

"Shit."

"Yeah." Sometimes Annie goes along just to talk Mom out of buying more crap none of us needs. Occasionally this works, depending on our mom's mood. But if she's really bothered by something, nobody gets through to her. When our mother gets upset, or when she's in a great mood, she buys lots of useless junk.

I hug my sister. "Want me to go inside and find something to throw away while she's in the shower?"

She grins. "Yeah. The stairs are getting too cluttered."

I dig through the bottom of a layer and end up taking away a box containing a used laser toner cartridge and a broken clock. I hide them under some boxes in the apartment complex Dumpster and go back and sit on the porch steps.

"I'm at band camp next week," Annie says. "A week to breathe and be normal." We both know a week's worth of crap will be added to the piles inside the house.

"I'll stop by and make sure your porch stays clean," I say.

She wraps an arm around my shoulder. "Thanks. You're a good brother."

The white cat meanders across the lawn. He's sort of a neighborhood cat, so his flesh is full and well cared for. He comes here often enough Annie named him Mr. White, and he often nestles in with her at night. He approaches us, and I hold out my hand for him to sniff. The cat rubs his head against my palm, and I pet the top of his head. "Hey, Mr. White," I say.

"Will you remember to bring him some food while I'm away? Mom will forget."

"Sure," I say. "Is there anything you need to buy for camp? I can take you shopping."

"Yeah. I need some junk food."

"Let's go." We have plenty of time before Mom leaves for the flea market. It takes her at least an hour after she gets up to get ready.

We head over to Walmart. Mom has given Annie twenty bucks to spend, so we load up on bags of chips, some Little Debbie cakes, and a giant box of Cheez-Its. Annie tosses a bag of Hershey's Kisses in the grocery cart."

"Aren't you afraid these will melt?" I ask.

"Yeah, you're right," she says. "Last year the dorms were like an oven."

"Get M&M's instead," I tell her. "Melts in your mouth, not all over your underwear."

It comes to sixteen bucks. Annie wants to spend the change on gum, but I talk her out of it. "Keep the rest in case you want to buy pop or anything at Kenyon." I slip her a five on the way out the door. "And get something on me."

"I can't take your money," she says.

"Sure you can. I get a regular check, and I live cheaply." I don't tell her my Goth girl is also my sugar mama.

"So what are you looking forward to most about band camp?" I ask as we walk to the car. It's her second time going there. It's held on the Kenyon College campus, and I'm insanely jealous. They have an awesome bookstore I discovered when I drove my sister up last year. This year I won't have time to go, and Annie will have to ride the band bus.

"Not being home," Annie says.

Mom is showered, dressed, and smoking a cigarette in the front yard when I pull up in my car. She is studying her ratty looking rosebushes. "They might actually grow if you water them," I say.

"I've been working nights all week," my mom says. "By the time I get home, it's too dark." She gives me a quick hug. "Where have you two been?"

Annie holds up the Walmart bag. "Getting band camp supplies."

"That reminds me," Mom says, "Can you pick her up and take her to school with you in the morning? I'm working a five-to-three shift again tonight and don't know what time I'll get up."

"What time does she have to be there?"

"I think around nine or ten," Annie says.

"I have to be at school by eight," I say. "Can you be ready by 7:45?"

"I guess," she says, with a sigh. Annie is not a morning person. She ambles to the back porch carrying her bag of junk food.

Mom holds her Kool in one hand and digs at the weeds with the other. There is never a good time to ask this, so I just blurt it out. "Mom, who is my father? What's his name?"

She inhales deeply on her cigarette, and smoke spumes around her like fog. "Why do you keep asking me that?"

"I need to know," I say. "I need to know who I am."

"It was a long time ago," she says. "I don't even remember."

"Well according to the records office I don't have one."

"When did you go to the Hall of Records?"

"I got on the Internet to look for a copy of my birth certificate. There was no name listed under father."

She points at me with her cigarette hand. "You have no right," she sputters. "Just . . . you just stop it right now."

I stomp to the back of the townhouse and find Annie sitting on the steps, cleaning her horn. I groan and plop down next to her.

She glances at me. "What's the matter?"

"Another brick wall," I say. I lean my elbows against the upper step. "Annie, has Mom ever talked to you about my real dad?"

"No," she says. "Every time I ask, I get a different answer. Either she doesn't know, or it's too awful to talk about."

"Yeah, she won't tell me either." I rest my head in my hands behind my head and scrutinize my half-sister. "You know I'm insanely jealous of you and Jeff."

"Why? My dad's dead."

"But at least you knew him, and you know who you are."

"It would be the same if you were adopted."

"That would be different," I say. "Only the state would know my true identity. Nobody seems to know who I am except Mom, and she won't tell me." I fill Annie in on going online and coming away with nothing.

"Maybe Mom's trying to protect you."

"From what?"

"Like maybe he's a serial killer or an animal abuser or a Russian Mafia dude."

I lean back and rest my elbows on the top step. "But wouldn't I have crazy urges too?"

"You are crazy," she says. "You tried to blow up the school."

"No, just a locker. And that was supposed to be Rick's car, so I'm crazy and stupid."

Annie does a final swipe on her trumpet and sets it inside the case. "Maybe your dad is a spy, and she can't reveal his identity." She snaps the case shut. "Why not ask Paul?"

Jeff's dad. It's so obvious. "Duh. Why didn't I think of that?"

"Cuz you're a moron?" I punch her on the shoulder. She punches me back.

Every time I visit my mother's freak show of a house, I feel the urge to straighten up the inside of my car. This time I need to also organize all that camping crap. I pile everything neatly, stacking things in the copy paper boxes I retrieved from school. I wish I could lock the car. One of these days I am going to come out and everything I own will be gone. Maybe that's not a bad thing.

I clean up the car also so it doesn't look like I live in it. If Paul knew I was living in the car, who knows what he would do? Jeff keeps threatening to tell his dad so I can move into the basement with him, but I won't let him. His stepmother Dee Dee is not my biggest fan.

I always knew Jeff was part of a different tribe that did not include Annie or me, but it hit hard when Paul started taking my brother away on weekends and holidays. Paul returned to Rooster after he and my mother split up, and he was now married to Dee Dee. When they started having their own kids, Jeff moved back in with us for awhile. Dee Dee didn't warm up to Jeff right away, but Paul took him back when Mom's house got too bad a couple years ago. I don't think Dee Dee likes it much; she doesn't like to be reminded of Paul's previous life of drinking and pot smoking, but Jeff says she treats him okay. Jeff's hardly ever home anymore now that he works.

I park the Blue Whale in front of Paul's garage. It's sort of a combination repair shop and junkyard, and Jeff and I come here a lot for our car parts.

Two Dobermans bark as I open the gate and let myself in. I extend my hand, they sniff, and remember me.

"Hey, Flynn." Paul steps outside the trailer that acts as his office. He looks like an older, balder version of Jeff. "How's the beast running?"

"Guzzling gas likes it's Kool-Aid," I say.

He laughs. He glances at my tires. "I can give you a set of retreads pretty cheap," he says. "We have a total in the lot same model as yours that has good tires on it."

"How much?"

"Fifty, for all four."

"That is a sweet deal," I say. "I don't have any money right now, though."

He waves it off. "You can owe me."

"Thanks." I can't really afford it, but it's too good to pass up. Maybe I can sell something. Like the iPod. "I get paid Friday. I'll pay you back then." Dee Dee would shit kittens if she knew Paul does favors like this for me. She reminds him often he is not my father and owes me nothing. But he did kind of raise me for a year or so, and I am Jeff's half-brother.

"Pull her inside and we'll jack her up."

As he works, the questions I want to ask spindle inside my head. Finally, I just ask, "How long did you know my mom before you married her?"

"We go way back," he says. "She and I went to middle school together. Dated off and on in high school." He heaves off my left rear tire. "Jesus, you were running on slicks."

He hands me the tire and tells me to stack it out back with the others. When I come back inside, I ask, "So did you stay together after high school even though she was pregnant with me?"

He loosens the nuts on the rear right tire. "Yeah. Your mom and I moved to Columbus right outta school." He places the tire in my arms. "I got a job working at Firestone on Broad Street, and she wanted to get out of Rooster."

"So I was born in Columbus?" He nods. I ditch the next tire and ask, "And you married her before I was born?"

He yanks at the nuts on my left front wheel. "We never actually got married. Not that I didn't ask every single day." He stopped and thought for a second. "We lived together just long enough for me to see Jeff come into the world."

"So that's why you aren't listed as my father on my birth certificate."

He hands me the next tire. "Yep."

"Did you know my dad?"

"Why do you ask?"

"I'm trying to find my real father."

He wipes some grease from his hands on the rag dangling from his belt. "What makes you think he wants to be found?"

"Did you know him?"

Paul ratchets the rest of the nuts off the tire and sets it on the ground. "You don't want to go there, son."

"What do you mean?"

He looks at me. "What has she told you?"

"Nothing," I say. "She won't talk about it."

He nods. "Yeah, she's cagey that way. Never told me much either." He hoists the tire at me and goes back to the final wheel. "And to answer your first question, I know she didn't declare me as the father on your birth certificate. It was sort of a sticky point for us."

"What do you mean?"

"It's like she wouldn't let me inside. Wouldn't marry me, wouldn't let me be a father to you. Even after . . . well . . . she just liked to keep things at arm's length. Granted, I was no prince back then," he says. "I was either high or drunk, so your mother was smart not to marry me." He shrugs. "We were both a couple of fucked-up kids."

"Why does she get so freaky about it when I ask?"

He sets down his tools and wipes his hands again. "I'm sorry, Michael," he says. "Maybe she doesn't want to be reminded of that time in her life." He pats me on the shoulder. "We all have crap in our lives we wish we could forget."

"I know how she made a living for awhile. Before Bob, there were a lot of men in the house."

He nods. "Before that, her life was always a bit of a train wreck. I knew something was dark in her home life. Enough for her to take off with me the week after graduation."

"Was that when her brother died?"

"Yeah. And after that she couldn't wait to move to Columbus and never look back."

"But she did come back."

"She ran out of options." Paul rolls a couple retreads over to my car. "Your mother always had these walls around her. I loved her, but she always kept me and everyone else outside her circle." He grabs the lug wrench and glances at me. "I think she still does, doesn't she?"

"Yeah, kind of."

"I tried to deal with my own ghosts with drugs and alcohol," he says.

"But you got better."

"Yeah. I got help. The first step is admitting you have a problem in the first place. Your mother?" He shook his head.

"So she had some issues when she was a kid?"

"Ha! Who didn't?" He sets the first tire on the rear right wheel. He waves me over. "Hold this while I tighten the nuts." We set the tire on the rim and he starts to mount it.

"She never tells us about the past," I say. "Always changes the subject, or invents a story."

"Yeah, she was like that." He sighs. "She was always . . . a little lost. I think that was what attracted me, you know? We men like to think we can fix whatever is wrong. Be the hero in the story."

I feel like that with Shelly. Like she has this deep hollow space I want to fill up so she doesn't fall in.

"Anyway, I knew your mom was a little damaged even back in school, but I loved her. I thought that was enough to protect both of us." He shrugs. "But I couldn't really help her either. I had my own messes to clean up."

He and I mount the next tire. I hold the third tire in place as he tightens the nuts on it. "I'm not sure anybody can."

"Bob was good for her, though," I say. "She seemed happy with him."

Paul nods. "Yeah, he was a good guy. Losing him was like she lost her last good shot at a true life."

"Yeah. It was around then stuff changed for all of us."

"So how bad is it?" he asks.

"The house?" I shake my head. "It's bad." I don't tell him Annie is sleeping on the porch and I'm living in my car. If he knew, he'd probably insist she and I both move into their basement with Jeff.

"You know why she does it, don't you?" he says. "All that crap is a cocoon. It's like a layer of protection from whatever scares the hell out of her. I couldn't be the man to slay the dragons for her."

We work on the last tire. "I haven't seen it since Jeff moved in with us."

"It's to the point where only the bathroom and kitchen are half usable, and that's only because Annie won't let Mom put any more crap in there. She's worried the week she's at band camp that Mom will trash the house even more."

"And there will be no stopping her."

"I can't stand being there," I say.

"Well, if you hadn't screwed up your life you'd be done with school now." He chuckles. "One more year and you'll be on your own. Maybe you and Jeff can get a place together."

"Are you booting him out when he turns eighteen?"

He snorts. "Nah. Jeff's a dream kid," he says. "He's the easiest of the bunch. Appreciates everything we do for him."

"Probably because before you took him in, his life was a mess too."

"Literally and figuratively. But he wants to live on his own after school. Kind of like the old man." Paul releases the lift and my car floats down to the garage floor. "Almost good as new," he says.

"I really appreciate this, Paul. You've been a good ex-stepfather."

"Even though she never would marry me."

I shrug. "Yeah. What reasons did she give for turning you down?"

"She would never give me even one."

I shake his hand, thank him for the tires, and turn to leave. "Paul? Why did my mother leave my father's name blank on my birth certificate?"

He sighs. "She had her reasons.

I cruise by Shelly's house, but I park across the street and just look at the house. I wonder what made her take off and live on her own. "Having a pool isn't reason enough to stay," she had said. Can we all suffocate even in splendor? Her parents are Hollywood handsome and they seem nice enough, yet they treat Shelly like a polite stranger. Are they afraid she will take off again?

Underneath the expensive exterior are ragged bones, gristle, and meat. Under the skin we all share the stench of our own madness, our wild urges. My mother buys things. My sister hides behind a trumpet. I live in my car. God, we're all freaking weird.

What drives Shelly?

I punch up Shelly's number on my phone.

"My homeless Romeo," she says.

I smile. "Shall I stand under your window and recite some Shakespeare?"

She laughs. "Probably not."

"What are you doing?"

"I could lie and say I'm creating a masterpiece, but all I am doing is painting my toenails."

"I'm sitting outside your house."

"Like a stalker?"

"Yeah, kind of."

"Cool," she says. "Never had a stalker before."

"I could hide in the bushes like a paparazzi and take pictures with my phone while I talk to you."

She laughs again. Her laugh is gold flecks in my crappy day. "I would invite you in but my folks have dinner guests. Some people from Dad's office."

"That's okay," I say. "I just wanted to hear your voice, and I just wanted to tell you . . ."

"What?"

"I talked to Paul. Jeff's dad?"

"Yeah?"

"He claims he doesn't know who my father is, either." I say.

"Shit."

"Yeah. It's all shit." I say. "I could be anybody. Maybe I am an Amish alien."

I drive to my mom's and park in front of her townhouse. I hardly ever sleep here because the streetlights are too bright, but for some reason I need to be in proximity of people who care about me. I notice the living room light is on by the strip of light at the top of the window. The bottom part of the open blinds is blocked by stuff. But the sliver of light provides some comfort, knowing someone is awake, probably watching TV. I set the timer on my phone to wake me early so I can be at school when Shelly arrives.

CHAPTER ELEVEN

I wake at six, before the alarm, and drive over to the school for another run before Shelly gets there. I set my pace with a free song I downloaded from an iTunes card I found on the floor near the Starbucks inside Kroger: The Dave Matthews Band's "If Only." It's the one decent song now on the iPod so far, so I sing along. I rarely sing out loud because I sound like a howler monkey in heat, but I figure nobody is up at this hour to hear me. Singing as I run helps me know I won't have a heart attack by the end of the trail. Coach makes us run in pairs and talk to train our breath, but I am alone so the song is my companion. By the third play, I have memorized the lyrics.

Most of the time I run without music, but today the music helps provide a soundtrack where I imagine the camera above panning the shot of me in the woods, zooming in for my close-up. Music also blocks out the noise inside my head screaming, *Who the fuck am I?*

I replay the song four times before I take the earbuds out and listen to my footfalls, the steady clomp, clomp, clomp of rubber against earth, the whisk of my body against tree branches. I started running around the same time my mom started hoarding. It doesn't take a genius to see the connection.

After about four miles, I slow down and lean over to breathe. I need to lay off the donuts and fries. And I should have brought some water. The cross-country trail is five miles total, so I walk/jog the last mile back to school.

I guzzle a bottle of water and collapse onto the open tailgate of my car, wiping my face with yesterday's shirt. When Earl pulls up beside me, I sit up. He hands me a donut and a cup of coffee.

"Thanks," I say. "How did you know I'd be here?"

He snorts. "Kid, you're always here."

"I'm waiting for Shelly," I say. "We go out for breakfast."

"Uh-huh." I can tell from his tone he doesn't believe me. He glances at the boxes in the back of my car. Shit. He knows.

"Just be careful, kid."

"With Shelly?"

"With everything." He smacks me on the back. "See you inside, kid." He shuffles back to his truck. I hold up the coffee, and yell, "Thanks."

I take a shower, head back to my car, and inhale the donut as I wait for Shelly. Just the sight of her loping toward me makes my insides smile. She sees me watching her, and takes giant steps, swinging her arms like a gorilla. There is no one in the world like her.

"The gorilla of my heart," I say. When she reaches me, I pull her close and we kiss.

"You have donut breath," she says.

"Earl brought me a donut."

"How did he know you'd be here?"

"I think he knows."

"Oh shit."

"Tell me about it."

"Yeah, he's no dummy." She kisses me again. "Let's really walk on the wild side today," she says. "Starbucks." She flashes a gift card. "My mom gave me a $25 gift card she won at the club. She hates their coffee."

"Okay." I'm no fan of Starbucks coffee either, so Shelly tells me to order a mocha latte. "It tastes like hot chocolate," she says. We also get breakfast sandwiches and bananas. Shelly ends up with only a couple bucks left on the gift card. "No wonder I never come here," I say. "That's half my paycheck."

Shelly hands me a card for another free song. This one is for a tune called "Everybody's Hurting" by Jakob Dylan. "Good," I say. "Now I'll have two decent songs on my iPod."

We sit down, and Shelly asks, "So how was your visit with your sister yesterday?"

"Good," I say. I take a sip of the latte. It does taste like hot chocolate. "I also spent some time with my ex-stepfather. Separately, of course."

"Anything interesting going on?"

"My sister is headed for band camp," I say. "Oh yeah. Remind me to pick her up before we go back to school." I nosh on the banana. "Oh, and the good news is we are less likely to die in my car."

She raises her eyebrows at me. "Why's that?"

"Jeff's dad put some new tires on my car. They're retreads, but new to me. He's only charging me fifty bucks for all four."

"That was nice of him."

"He's a good guy."

"It's too bad he doesn't know who your real dad is."

I set my sandwich down. "The thing is, I think he does, but he doesn't want to betray a trust. I think he believes it's something my mom should tell me."

Shelly leans in and says, "Did your mom ever keep a journal or a diary?"

"Maybe. I remember her writing a lot late at night when I was a kid. But that was when Bob was still alive. I think her writing died when he did."

"By the way, I have something for you." She reaches into her purse and hands me an Indiana driver's license with my picture on it. It's the picture she took of me the other day wearing one of her brother's shirts. "What's this?"

"You are now Michael Neruda of Terre Haute, Indiana," she says. "You are a twenty-one-year-old biology major at Indiana State with a minor in literature."

I chuckle. "Thanks. But why do I need a fake ID?"

"It will come in handy when you take me to Bar None in a couple weeks to hear Cello Madness."

"Okay?" She may as well be speaking Greek, but I will find out more when the time comes. I slide the card in my wallet.

"I was going to get one for me with the name Michelle Kerouac, but that name might raise some eyebrows."

"You could be Kara Wack," I say.

"Ha ha."

I hold one of her hands in mine. "I hope this doesn't sound dorky, but I'm really glad I know you," I say.

"Thanks," she says. "You're not too bad either, for an Amish alien."

"Wouldn't it be weird if my father was Amish? Like if he and my mom hooked up on his Rumspringa?"

"Wouldn't it be funny if your name actually is Neruda?" Shelly says. "Like he's your illegitimate grandfather or something."

I laugh, and am about to shove the last of my sandwich in my mouth when I look up and see my ex-best-friend Rick and my ex-girlfriend Ashley sit down at the table behind us. Rick glances at me and does a double take when he notices Shelly. Ashley has not yet seen me.

I set the rest of my breakfast sandwich down. My appetite is blown. Rick and I have not spoken since the hearing after I tried to detonate his car.

"You okay?" Shelly asks.

"Yeah. I'm just full."

She gives me a quizzical look. "This isn't like you, Neruda."

Ashley turns and glances our way. "Michael," she says. She waves timidly. "How are you?"

"Great," I say. "I'm better than great. Stupendous."

Shelly crosses her eyes and puts a finger in her mouth to feign gagging. It makes me half smile in spite of the uncomfortable moment.

"How is your summer going?" Ashley says. Her buttery hair falls across her shoulder, but it no longer sets my engines running.

"Miraculous," I glance at Shelly. "Ready to go, hon?"

"Sure, sweetie," she says.

We slide out of our seats. I take Shelly's hand and we saunter toward the door.

"Hey, Michael," Rick says from behind me. "Can we talk?"

"I think we've done our share of talking," I say.

He glances at Shelly, who waves her cigarette pack and heads out the door.

"Seriously, man," Rick says. "I need to talk to you." His voice is anxious.

"So you can apologize for ripping my heart out and obliterating our friendship?"

"No. I mean yeah, I do feel bad about that." He looks at the door. Shelly is outside, lighting up. Rick steers me away from the door.

"Listen, what's your relationship with her?" he asks.

"Are you shitting me? You already have Ashley."

"No, it's not that," he says.

"My relationship with Shelly is . . . well, it's none of your business."

"Listen, man. We've known each other a long time, and I think you know I always have your back."

"Yeah, just like you did on prom night," I say.

"Yeah, I screwed up. But so did you."

"What? By trusting you with my girlfriend?"

"By not really being there for Ashley."

"You're freaking kidding me."

"No?" he says. "How many times did she ask you to do things? Important things, like go see her in *The Wizard of Oz* or take her to the prom? And you always used work as an excuse."

"It wasn't an excuse," I say. "Unlike you, I have to work."

"I know that, but still. She never felt you made much of an effort," he says. "It's almost like you outsourced her to me."

"I don't have to listen to your crap." I step toward the door, but he grabs my arm.

"How much do you know about Shelly?" he asks.

I flip his hand away. "Whatever you think you know, it doesn't matter. I like her."

"How long have you known her?"

"I've known her long enough to know she's the best person I have ever met."

"So you know she ran away last year?" he says.

I had kind of guessed at that. "Yeah, sure."

"And she told you about her getting arrested."

My expression reveals I don't. He stuffs his hands in his pockets. "Jesus, Flynnstone, everyone knows it."

Everyone but me.

"She was living in California with some guy," Rick says. "She was high, and she rammed a car into a row of cars at sixty miles an hour."

That explains why she's not allowed behind the wheel. "So? We all do stupid things when we're drunk," I say.

"It wasn't an accident."

The breakfast sandwich leapfrogs inside my stomach. I recall the remark she made about not caring if I drove her father's car into a wall.

He puts a hand on my shoulder. "I'm sorry, Flynn. I know we have our issues, and I was wrong. But just be careful is all I'm saying. She's got a history. Ask her. It's common knowledge."

I want to punch him, yell that he's a liar, but Rick doesn't lie. Deep inside a kernel of truth exists there. Other than the Ashley debacle, Rick always did have my back. He always accepted everything about me. And he's the only person I have ever allowed to mangle my name. Flynnstone, or Mikester. Everyone else calls me Michael. Except Shelly, who now calls me Neruda. Rick may be a scumbag girlfriend thief, but he is not a liar, nor is he a gossip, so whatever he knows about Shelly just might be true. Still, I feel the need to defend Shelly. "Listen, asshole, I don't know what your deal is, and what kind of gossip you heard, but I think you've done enough damage to my life."

Shelly is leaning up against the rear quarter panel of my car. I don't know how to look at her. She hasn't lied to me that I know of, nor has she told me the truth. I've always sensed a dark secret about her, but it didn't seem to matter.

"What did he want?" she asks.

"Nothing."

"Are you two friends again?"

"Doubtful." I dig for my keys. "Let's go."

I drive down Rocket Road, headed toward school. Shelly rolls down the window and lets the wind whip through her hair. She is one freaking ass mystery.

"He and I were friends for six years," I say, "and I miss him every day, but I don't think we can ever be friends again."

She sighs. "It's hard when your friends abandon you."

We're a few minutes late getting to school, but Earl doesn't mention it.

"Oh crap," I say. "I forgot to pick up my sister."

Earl has no problem with me going to pick up Annie. I offer to stay late but he waves it off.

***

Earl and I are set to clean the other art room today. When I get back from collecting my sister, I hear Earl grumbling loudly inside the art room. I am shocked when I go inside; the classroom almost looks like my mother's living room. The counters are littered with stacks of drawings, paintings, ceramic projects, and art. Mounds of drawing paper, watercolor paper, canvases, and art books cover the tabletops. Teachers were supposed to have everything packed up for summer, but Mrs. Davis's room looks like a tornado had hit.

"Damn it all," Earl says. "We gotta pack all this crap up before we can clean." He looks at me. "Go get Hess and Shelly. And bring some boxes."

I return carrying an armload of flattened boxes and notice Shelly standing in the center of the room, breathing in the waxy paint smell. She expels her breath and smiles.

"The smell of joy," she says.

"I take it art is your favorite class."

"Not so much the class, but the act of creating art."

We start to construct the boxes. Earl grumbles under his breath, "You send out the e-mail, telling teachers to clear all the crap from their rooms." He shakes his head and picks up a stack of drawing paper. Half of it slides onto the floor. "Damn it to hell!" He dumps another load of papers onto the floor and storms out of the room. He comes back into the room with a large wheeled container.

"Change of plans." Earl crosses his arms and scowls. "Throw it all out."

"Really?" Hess asks. "Won't you catch hell?"

"Probably. But I'll give her my brand of hell right back." He waves at Shelly and me. "Go get two more trash bins."

We wheel in two more containers. They're big enough to hold a couple people. "Where do we start?" I ask.

"You two kids take the counter on this side, and Hess and I will begin with the window ledges."

"Do we keep anything at all?" Shelly asks.

"Only keep unopened paint, paper still in wrappers, and clean brushes." He picks up a stack of loose papers and heaves it inside his bin. "Otherwise, it goes in the trash."

At first I feel kind of bad throwing away perfectly good art supplies. We toss out brushes, sketchpads, half-jars of paint, and student projects. After awhile, though, it feels good to toss things out. I wish I could do this at my mother's house.

When I drive Shelly home, she invites me to come in, but I tell her I have some business to attend to.

"Do you want me to come with you?"

"No. Some things I have do on my own," I say. I lie and tell her I am going to confront my mom again. "My mom's likely to be pissed. I don't want the first time you meet her to see her yelling at me." Shelly kisses me and tells me to call her later. I promise I will.

Since running into Rick, I feel odd about Shelly now, and I need to talk to someone about it. Ironically, Shelly is the person I can talk to when shit bugs me, but I can't talk to her about this yet. If I ask her outright, it may just scare her off. She will tell me when she thinks I need to know.

But mystery and uncertainty rattle around in my head like old bones.

Who else can I talk to? Jeff. He's sane.

I text him.

-Wuz up?

-At TH

-How late do you work?

-5:30

-Can I come by?

-OK. Have a break in 15.

I drive over to Tim Hortons, buy a cup of coffee, and sit in the corner booth, trying to wrap my head around the day. Just a few hours ago I was an ordinary guy, living in his car and dating the best girl he has ever known. Now I'm the detritus of an unnatural disaster.

Jeff sits down across from me and slides me a bag of goodies. I open up the bag and see a bran muffin and a cake donut. "Thanks," I say.

"What's up, big bro?" he asks. "Hard day?"

"What can you tell me about Shelly Miller?"

"Why? What do you want to know?"

"Rick tried to warn me off her."

"You and Rick are talking again?"

"Not exactly." I shove a large chunk of bran muffin in my mouth. "We ran into him at Starbucks this morning, and he kind of ambushed me with this wild story about Shelly."

"Oh."

I reach into the bag and bite into the donut. Cinnamon-coated cake. Yum. "Listen, I really care about this girl, and whatever she has done I'm pretty sure I can get past it. I mean, look at me. Am I the poster boy for fabulous?"

He laughs. "Hardly. More like the poster boy for Homeless Guys Illustrated." Jeff slurps his pop. "She came back to school second semester, a few weeks before they booted you out," he says. "She stood out for two reasons. One, her appearance. Before she took off she was a blonde and kind of preppy looking. Now she had this haunted, black hair vibe, and she was anorexic skinny. I mean, she wasn't fat before, but she had a few extra pounds on her."

"That's why she looked familiar the first day I met her," I say. "*Michelle* Miller. Wasn't she a cheerleader and hung around a bunch of preps?"

Jeff nods. "But she didn't come back to school until near the end of the year. Shortly before they flung your sorry ass out the door." He steals the rest of my bran muffin and noshes on it. "All these rumors about her started flying," Jeff says. "You know I don't gossip, but I heard stuff at lunch and in study hall. People claimed she was a heroin addict or had cancer or had joined a cult."

"So what is the truth?"

He shrugs. "Nobody but Shelly really knows all of it," he says. He glances at the clock. "Hey, my break's almost over. Stop by the house in a couple hours and we can talk some more."

"Okay. I have to pay Paul for my new tires anyway." I remember the camping gear. "Can I stow some camping stuff in your basement until winter? Mom gave me a tent and sleeping bag so I won't freeze to death, but it's kind of taking up a lot of room in my house."

Jeff chuckles. "Sure." He hands me his car keys and says, "Just put it in the trunk, and I'll take care of it."

I kill the next couple hours by checking my work schedule, shooting the shit with Mitch, and taking a sponge bath in the men's room at the mall.

Paul has his head under the hood of a '96 Taurus when I pull up. They live in a slightly run-down house not far from the school. One of those three-bedroom houses that look like all the others on the street. What distinguishes their house is the scattering of toys in the yard. They live in the kind of neighborhood where the neighbors don't complain about messy yards. Kind of like my mom's neighborhood, except here the people own their homes instead of rent. Their driveway is littered with oil stains so I pull the Blue Whale onto the pavement. Paul always has several cars in the driveway and on the curb. "I like to bring my work home with me," he likes to joke. He keeps threatening to black top their yard, but his wife insists they need a yard for the kids.

Paul clatters around and looks up when he hears me slam my car door.

"Jeff home yet?"

"He's in the shower," Paul says. "Washing the donut smell off. Hey, go grab me a beer. Help yourself if you want."

I step inside the house. It's cluttered, but not stuffed to the gills like Mom's. One good vacuuming and dusting and the place would look fine. Their mess is from four kids and two adults living in a place meant for a couple with one kid or a dog. It's family mess, not the insane clutter of my mother's house. Their dog, Buster, greets me and licks my hand. He chuffs and barks once. Dee Dee, who is standing in the kitchen at the stove, turns to see who came in. She's short and plump but has a pretty face.

"Hi Dee Dee." I move to the fridge.

She glances at me as she stirs something. "Hey," she says, but not in a welcoming tone. Things have never been smooth between us, and they've been more tense since my arrest. I guess I wouldn't want my kids around a would-be arsonist, either.

"Paul wants a beer." I hold two cans in my hand. "He said for me to help myself." She nods and keeps stirring something fragrant, like homemade spaghetti sauce. "Smells good."

I'd love to be invited to stay to eat, but I know I won't be. I hold up the two beers and mutter, "Thanks." I join Paul in the driveway and hand him his beer. He crams his rag in his jeans and pops open the can. We lean against the quarter panel of the Taurus.

"You seem troubled by something," he says.

I take a gulp of beer and let its salty bitterness soothe my tension. "Yeah. Kind of."

"Spill it."

"What do you do when you find out something bad about a person you care about? Something that may or may not be true, but most likely is?"

"Can you give me little more detail?"

"There's this girl I like."

"Women," he says. "They always spell trouble."

I smile. We clink our cans together. "Go on," he says.

He knows about the whole Rick problem, so I don't have to remind him of that. "I ran into Rick and Ashley today at Starbucks. I was with this new girl," I say. "I've been seeing her the past couple of weeks. And things are going well with us." I take another swig. "But Rick stops me on my way out the door. At first I think he wants to apologize for being a shithead, which he sort of does. But what he really wants to do is to tell me something bad about Shelly, my new girl."

"How bad?"

I gulp down the rest of the beer and wipe my mouth with the back of my hand. "Bad."

"Is it true?"

"I don't know. Some of it is, I guess. I'm hoping Jeff can fill me in. He knows her, and he was at school when Shelly came back from her long, mysterious absence."

Paul slaps me on the back. "Hope you get this worked out. Just remember, gossip is often just idle jealousy."

I nod. "It's just that Rick has never steered me wrong before. I mean, yeah, he stole Ashley, but before that, he always had my back."

"Do you like this girl?"

"Yeah. I like her a lot."

"You're screwed," he says.

The screen door slaps and Jeff comes out wearing jeans and an orange-and-black Rooster High T-shirt. His hair is still wet from the shower. "Hey, bro," he says.

"Hey. Wanna go for a ride?" I ask.

"Okay." He sees the beer can. "I think I'll drive, though."

I smirk. "One beer doesn't make me drunk." I crumple the beer can and hand him my keys anyway. I slide in the passenger side and fasten the seatbelt. "It's weird being on this side of my own car. I'm used to seeing the world from the left side."

Jeff adjusts his seat and backs out of the driveway. "This may change your whole outlook on life," he says. We swing by McDonald's and get fries and Cokes. As we pull away from the drive-thru, Jeff says, "What's up, bro? Is Mom okay?"

"Yeah. I mean, no. She's still a nut bag."

"How's about Annie?"

"She just left for band camp today."

"Good," he says. "She deserves a break." He keeps his eyes on the road and chews on his bottom lip. He always chews on his lip when he stews over something. He makes a lousy poker player because when he has a bad hand, he sucks in his bottom lip so much it looks like he's wearing dentures.

"Shit, Jeff, what do you know?"

He changes lanes and heads east from Rocket Road, away from the traffic. "It's not so much what I know, for sure. Nobody knows all the facts. But I was surprised when I saw you with her earlier this summer. But then I remembered you were cleaning the school over the summer, and I figured she was too. I didn't know you were dating her, though."

"It didn't start out that way," I say. "We've gotten to know each other. I thought pretty well. But then Rick dropped a bomb on me earlier today." I summarize what happened at the restaurant and what Rick told me.

"Well, he's not entirely wrong," Jeff says. "You missed the last few weeks of school, so you don't know the whole story."

"I didn't even know her before this summer. I mean she looked sort of familiar, but we never traveled in the same social circles before."

"I kind of knew her because we were lab partners in biology together sophomore year. And she was okay. Some cheerleaders are stuck up and don't talk to those of us lower on the social strata, but she was nice enough."

"So why didn't I see her at school last year?"

"She took off before school started, and came back around the time you got the boot. And when she did come back she looked totally different," he says.

"There were a bunch of stories in the paper about a major drug bust in Columbus and car theft and how a local teen was involved. Shelly's name was never mentioned because she's under eighteen, but people at school kind of put two and two together. The dates of her arrest and her disappearance kind of meshed. And former friends sort of corroborated the story."

"Former?"

"Yeah. She used to hang with a group of rich bitch country club preps, but most of them dropped her. The only one I know for sure who sort of hung in there as a friend is Maggie Alter."

"Shelly never mentions anyone," I say.

"Maybe other kids' parents forbid them to hang with Shelly."

"She seems friendly enough with you."

"Hell, man. I don't judge her," Jeff says. "Who are any of us to judge? Aren't we all freaks under the skin? Even the most normal person has some shadow lurking under the bed."

I remember how I used to scare him and Annie by telling him there were shadow monsters under the bed. Because I was the eldest they always believed me. To a point. Eventually they figured out I was full of shit.

"How do I get Shelly to talk to me about it? How do I let her know I don't care what she did?"

"Just say that. Say, 'Shelly, I don't care why you got arrested. We're here, and this is now, and whatever you did before is history.'"

I nod. "Yeah. That makes sense. But what about the rumor she meant to kill herself behind the wheel? How do I approach that?"

"How do you feel about it?"

"I don't know. I don't get a suicidal vibe from her. I mean yeah, occasional sadness, but . . . Rick said she was really high."

"Yeah, maybe. People do weird shit when they're high. Stuff they wouldn't normally do."

I watch cornfields and soybean fields whooshing by. "Why wouldn't she be upfront about this?"

"Why would she, dude? First off, she probably thinks you already know. Everyone else does." Jeff hangs his arm out the window as he drives. "Does it matter?"

"What do you mean?"

"Does it matter why she got busted? I mean, you knew she had some trouble. So did you. So if you like her, does it matter why she's in trouble?"

I sit back and let the wind blow over my face and close my eyes. "I guess not."

"Did you share your troubles?"

"She already knew about me. She calls me the Unabomber."

He laughs. I open my eyes and look at my brother. "And she knows I live in my car."

"Holy shit," he says. "That's big."

"She doesn't know why, though. I told her Mom threw me out after the Rick debacle."

"What did she tell you about why she's working at school all summer?"

"She said she got busted for smoking."

Jeff laughs. "That's sort of true. She got five days out for smoking in the girls' restroom."

Jeff and I are quiet for awhile. The rumble of the tires on pavement soothes me.

"So do you like her?" he asks.

"Yeah," I say. "I like her a lot."

"More than Ashley?"

"A whole lot more. I hate to admit this, but Rick's right. He and Ashley are better suited for one another. They both have that artsy music thing going on."

"What do you like best about Shelly?"

"She's brave," I say. "And generous and funny, and she kicks my ass."

"Good for her."

"But there's this wall around her."

"Don't you think it's because she's been burned?"

"Yeah, maybe. Now that I know what she was up against."

"So what are you going to do next?" Jeff asks.

I lean back against the headrest. Sometimes it's a relief to let someone else take the wheel. I am suddenly tired from worrying about my mother, my sister, Shelly's secrets, and my own crappy life. "Sleep."

When Jeff pulls in front of his house, Paul is in the front yard dangling his son Danny from his feet. The six-year-old squeaks in delight and tries to wriggle away. Jeff won the lotto with dads.

Dee Dee comes to the door and says, "Clean up guys, it's dinnertime." She spears me with a look, and I know I'm not invited to stay. She has to accept Jeff, but I'm not Paul's son. There is something off about me. Sometimes *I* don't want to be near me.

Paul tries to insist I stay and eat, but I claim I have to work. I get back in my car and notice Jeff has left a $10 bill on the dashboard. Good thing, since we used up most of my gas. I wave the ten at my brother and yell thanks.

I forage for some donuts behind Dan's and find two jelly-filled and a chocolate cake. After I eat, I go to Graham Park and sit on a bench and read from a battered copy of *The Call of the Wild*, one of the books Earl let me keep from locker cleanup. At first I think I'll pass on it because the main character is a dog and it's usually assigned in middle school, but I quickly get into the book. Near the end of chapter two I recognize myself in Buck, the dog.

> *"This first theft marked Buck as fit to survive in the hostile Northland environment. It marked his adaptability, his capacity to adjust himself to changing conditions, the lack of which would have meant swift and terrible death. It marked, further, the decay or going to pieces of his moral nature, a vain thing and a handicap in the ruthless struggle for existence. . . . his development or regression was rapid. His muscles became hard as iron, and he grew callous to all ordinary pain. He achieved an internal as well as external economy. He could eat anything, no matter how loathsome or indigestible, and, once eaten, the juices of his stomach extracted the last least particle of nutriment; and his blood carried it into the roughest and stoutest of tissues."*

I flip the book over to the back cover and study the author's picture. A handsome young guy wearing a leather bomber jacket. He died when he was only forty, in 1916. I wonder why he died so young. My mother's age. I make a note to check on it in the library at school tomorrow.

By the time I'm beginning chapter five, it grows too dark to read, so I drive around to find a place to sleep tonight. Since Earl is suspicious now, I park in front of my mom's again. I set my alarm for 6:15 so I can run again. Training season for cross-country begins in a couple weeks and I want to be ready. I'm hoping Coach Baker takes me back on the team, even with my criminal record.

I try to sleep, but my mind buzzes with too much information. I almost wish my life was like that guy's in *Memento*, where every day he wakes up and doesn't recall yesterday. But my life is not a movie.

CHAPTER TWELVE

"Hey, you," Shelly says. She climbs into my car next to me and we kiss.

"Hey you yourself." She is wearing a pink top and blue shorts and barely resembles the Goth creature I first met. She still has the black hair, but there is something else different about her, and I can't figure it out. Maybe it's the sandals.

"God, you smell good," she says. After a morning run, I showered and swabbed another cologne sample all over myself. "What is that you're wearing?"

"Montblanc Legend."

"That's like $70 a bottle," she says. "How can a homeless guy afford it?"

"Maybe I'm only pretending to be homeless," I say. "Maybe I'm just an actor researching a role for a film."

She narrows her eyes at me. "Seriously?"

I sigh. "Unfortunately, no. I am truly a resident of anywhere I can find a safe parking spot."

"How do you always manage to smell good? Even before I gave you that bottle of Blue, you never smelled like a vagabond."

I laugh. "*Esquire, Sports Illustrated, People*," I say.

"Reading makes you smell good?"

"Every time I find magazines or check one out of the library, I steal the cologne sample pages."

"Very resourceful," she says. "You should write a book called *How to Be Homeless, Yet Live Like a Rich Guy.*"

I laugh. "It helps to have friends whose fathers bleed money." It must be her earrings. That's what's different. They're small, gold buds, not the dangly ones she usually wears.

"Have you asked your mom any more about your dad?" she asks.

"No. She gets mad every time I bring it up." I glance at Shelly again, trying to figure out what's new. Her eyes seem bigger, but it's not her makeup.

"Well, we know you're not Asian or black since you have Caucasian features and hair," she says. She squints at me. "You could be Greek or Middle Eastern. You do have that beaky nose."

"Thanks a lot." I study her face. "Bangs! You got bangs."

"Took you long enough to notice, Neruda."

"I noticed. I mean, I knew something was different, but I couldn't figure it out."

She feigns a British accent. "So what do you think? Do you like my fringes?"

"It's hot," I say. "Very hot." I'd like to blow off our day at school and go make out with her somewhere. I wrap an arm around her, and she rests against me. I like the feel of a soft, warm girl against my chest. For a second I remember what it was like to have Ashley in my arms. She was affectionate, yet I don't pine for her anymore. Shelly is so not Ashley. Ash would never have dared to use a fake ID to get booze in Kroger or have taken me on a fake birthday adventure.

Maybe Rick is right; maybe I never loved Ashley. Casting me aside for Rick was no doubt hard for her. She never liked hurting anyone's feelings. Once at her house last fall, early in our relationship, while watching a movie in her basement, Ashley noticed a huge wood spider crawling across the floor. Kind of a mean-looking creature, big, black, and hairy. I stood up ready to flatten it with my boot, and Ashley said, "Oh, don't kill it."

"Huh?"

"Let's scoop it up and set it free. Let it take its chances outside." She handed me a *People* magazine. My instinct was to roll up the magazine and whack the ugly creature, but I let the eight-legged thing crawl onboard and rushed it to the family room door before it had a chance to crawl up my arm. I flung the magazine and the spider into her backyard in the pouring rain.

"Now wasn't it better to save it rather than squish it?"

I shrugged. "I guess. But I killed your magazine."

"That's okay."

As gentle and lovely as Ashley was, I never told her about my mother's hoarding obsession. I told her I wasn't allowed to bring friends home because my mother worked a lot of nights and needed rest. Not a total lie. Sometimes Mom does work swing shifts, but she sleeps with a box fan on high that drowns out most of the noise. My sister and I just agree not to let anyone in on our living conditions. Children's Services would have a field day.

Ashley didn't know I started living in my car, so in a way, besides my immediate family, Shelly is the person who knows the most about me. But even Shelly doesn't know all of it.

My memories of Ashley are blurry now. To think I almost landed in jail over a girl who can't measure up. I kiss the top of Shelly's head and hug her tighter. Whatever the truth about her is, I like her a lot.

"I'm glad I met you," I tell her.

She nods. "Yeah. I am pretty amazing." She pulls out a fresh twenty. "Let's go eat."

We make it back to school in time, but Shelly wants to smoke a quick cigarette before we go in the building. "It's too nice to be indoors today."

"Too bad we can't blow off this place and go for a drive," I say. "Crash another family reunion."

Earl and Hess are laughing in the staff lounge where a plate of snickerdoodles sits. Earl looks up. "Enjoy your smoke?" he asks.

Shelly plops down and grabs a cookie. "We did. It's way too nice outside to make us work. We should get a good weather day today."

Earl laughs. "Nice try, kid."

"We could have them pull weeds out front if they want to be outside," Hess says. "It's supposed to rain the next couple days, so today might be the only day to do it."

Earl raises an eyebrow and looks us over. "Yeah. You could be right."

Shelly and I wheel a trash tub out to the school's entrance. Each of us carries gardening gloves and these tiny shovels. "Do you know how to pull weeds?" I ask.

She laughs. "It's not that hard."

"But how do I know which are weeds and which are supposed to be plants?"

She shakes her head. "You really are . . ."

"What?"

"Nothing," she says. "Just follow my lead."

"You were going to call me an idiot, weren't you?"

"No."

"Listen, I can't help it that I wasn't born with platinum or silver dangling out of my butt. There's a lot of shit I don't know." I toss my gloves and shovel to the ground.

"I'm sorry," she says. "You're right. I can sometimes be a condescending bitch."

"You think?"

She kneels in front of the flowerbeds and waves me down next to her. "We'll start here," she says. "See these spiny looking things?" I nod. "Those are thistles. They're weeds. So we need to take our spades and loosen the soil, then grab them and pull them up by their roots and toss them in the can. Also, we need to pull up dandelions. You do know what dandelions look like, don't you?"

"Yes." I grab for a thistle and draw my hand back. "Ow! That stings."

"That's why we have gloves." She waves mine at me, and I glower at her before I slide them on.

She and I sit side by side, pulling thistles and dandelions. This side of the building is hotter because we are in the sun, but it still feels good to be outside. Shelly tells me not to move too fast. "We don't want Earl and Hess to find more work for us to do."

That's kind of the way she and I have worked this summer anyway. In fact, Earl and Hess never seem to hurry. Earl told me once summertime was his favorite season to work. "I don't have all you kids and teachers messing up my work right after I'm done fixing or scrubbing something," he said.

"I feel bad about the other day," Shelly says.

"What do you mean?" Knowing exactly what she means.

"You know, when we were kissing and I . . ."

"It's okay," I say. I wave a gloved hand at her. "We don't have to rush into anything. What do I have to offer you, anyway? A thirty-year-old station wagon and lots of laundry."

She stops and looks at me. "I like you a lot, Michael Flynn Neruda, no matter where you live. And I think it's time you heard my story, the real story, and not the fiction that's being spread around town about me."

CHAPTER THIRTEEN

Shelly stabs at the soil. "It was last summer," she says. "The first thing I did was dye my hair black."

"Why?"

"I had suddenly become a new person, and I needed to look different."

"Why black?"

"I don't know. At a slumber party in middle school I once colored it dark, and I liked it. Besides, it made me look older."

"Why did you need to look older," I ask.

She studies me for a second, and says, "Because of Theo."

"Who is Theo?"

"He's part of why I left. But we're getting ahead of the story." I raise my hands in an apologetic gesture, and she continues. "So I dyed my hair."

"What did your parents say about it?"

She glares at me, and says evenly. "They didn't know."

"Okay. I won't interrupt anymore."

She grins at me. "Yes you will. *Anyway*, nobody was home that day. My parents were golfing at the country club and my brother and his girlfriend drove to Kings Island. They all knew I wouldn't be home when they got back because I lied and said I was spending the night at Amelia Preston's house."

"But you had already left. Where did you go?"

"I'll get to that," she says. "I had to pack light, so I crammed a couple pairs of jeans, some shorts and tops and underwear in a tote bag, along with a carton of unfiltered Camels."

"But you smoke Marlboros," I say.

She tosses a weed in the trash bin. "I was changing everything about myself, erasing the ditzy blonde cheerleader, including what I smoked."

"Yeah, I've been meaning to ask you about that," I say. "How did you get away with smoking as a cheerleader? Most athletes don't smoke."

She laughs. "First of all, most people don't consider cheerleaders athletes, even though it requires strength and agility. Second, cheerleaders get away with a lot. Parents and teachers would be shocked to learn several of Rooster High's varsity cheerleading squad smoke things a lot stronger than cigarettes on a regular basis." She scoops up a bunch of weeds and dumps them in the canister.

"So what else did you pack?"

She sits back down, and starts digging again. "Well, I couldn't take my phone or Kindle because Big Brother knows who you're talking to and what you're reading. But I had planned ahead and bought a Tracfone with tons of minutes and took about 3,000 bucks out of my savings."

"You had *$3,000* in savings?"

"Actually, I had more, but I didn't want the bank to alert my dad if I took it all out." She glances at me, detecting my envy. "I'm not going to apologize for having rich parents," she says. "It's the card I was dealt."

I yank a large thistle out of the ground and slam it into the trashcan. "I know. Sorry. I just wonder how with everything you have you'd want to run away."

She is quiet for a couple minutes, and I wonder if I've pissed her off. Then she says, "I've always felt I was playacting the role of Michelle Miller, the prep princess cheerleader who got decent grades and never caused trouble. But deep inside I knew this was a myth, and if you flayed me open, the feral beast would emerge. But how do you break out of your fictional shell and become who you want to be in Rooster, Ohio? Especially if you don't know who that is?" She smooths the soil over the hole I left in the ground where the thistle had been. "I blame it all on Mrs. Silver."

"The English teacher?"

"Yeah. Before Sophomore CP English I wasn't much of a reader. But the first book she assigned was *The Catcher in the Rye*. Most of my friends hated it, but I related to Holden Caulfield."

I nod. "He's kind of a raggedy guy." I had read the book and thought Holden was kind of a jerk, but I don't want to spoil her memory of it.

"You know what my favorite scene is?" she asks. "When Holden wanted to erase all the 'fuck yous' scrawled on walls so his sister and all little children wouldn't have to wonder what the expression means."

I liked that scene too. I dread every day when Annie finds out more ugly truths about the world, when kids call her racist names or refuse to make eye contact. Maybe *The Catcher in the Rye* is a better book than I remember.

"Anyway, I didn't know I could disappear for awhile, even if it's inside someone else's head. So in a lot of ways Mrs. Silver ruined my life."

I laugh. "How?"

"By feeding us stories that make you question everything, where you wake up and find you've been turned into a cockroach, or you choose to kill your own child rather than allow her to get taken onto slavery."

I nod, knowing exactly what she means. "Literature doesn't ruin your life, it expands it."

"God, you sound like Mrs. Silver."

I shrug. "I'm a book nerd."

"Well, I never was until she got her mitts on me."

"So how many books did you take with you?"

She sighs. "I could only fit four in my bag."

"So you took *The Catcher in the Rye*," I say.

"Obviously. Holden Caulfield started it all."

"What else?"

She sits up and brushes the dust off her butt and moves down to the next patch of weeds. I stand up and wheel the trashcan to follow her. We plunk down and start digging again. "Well, I also wasn't a big fan of poetry before her class because it was always the old dead guys like Keats and Milton or Shakespeare. But Mrs. Silver introduced us to Pablo Neruda, and everything I took for granted before like watermelons, which he called the green whale of summer, or tomatoes that have sex with onions and flood the streets." She stops and takes a deep breath. "It was like I'd been living in the dark and suddenly been granted a window."

"So you took a Neruda book."

"Duh."

"Which one?"

"It was a toss-up between the *100 Love Sonnets* or *Neruda: Selected Poems*. I liked the picture of him on the cover of the selected poems." She placed a hand on her heart. "Did you know he was like a rock star? Theo and I watched a film about Neruda. He wasn't good-looking. Kind of short and chubby, but he had Paul McCartney eyes. And his poems made people all over the world worship him."

I think of the poems Shelly had bought me for my non-birthday and Neruda's amazing sequence of words, ordinary words, but when combined they say things like "your house sounds like a train at noon." I guess if I were running away I'd take a Neruda book too. "What else did you take?"

"*Fahrenheit 451* is a small book with big ideas," she says, "and it's scary too because a lot of what Bradbury wrote about all those years ago is kind of happening now, like how people are all into reality TV and they don't read anymore. And that character named

Faber pointed out how we all have the potential to be happy, but we just aren't."

I pull up a cluster of dandelions and wave them at Shelly. "And the last book you packed was *On the Road*."

"How did you know?"

"You mentioned it in the bookstore that day."

"Oh yeah, I guess I did." She smacks me with the thistle she has in her hand. "I kind of had to take it since Kerouac was the catalyst for the journey. Have you read it?" I shake my head. "Basically it's a road trip where two close friends drive back and forth across the country. But there's so much more that happens."

"Did you read it for class too?"

"Oh no," Shelly says. "Mrs. Silver told us she'd lose her job if she had us reading it because it's full of sex and profanity."

I stand up and dust myself off. "Where are you going?" she asks.

"To buy a copy of the book right now."

She laughs and pulls me back down. "*Anyway*, Mrs. Silver read us a few passages from it." Shelly closes her eyes and recites, "'Soon it got dusk, a grapy dusk, a purple dusk over tangerine groves and long melon fields; the sun the color of pressed grapes, slashed with burgundy red, the fields the color of love and Spanish mysteries." She opens her eyes. "Isn't that wonderful?" I nod. "And then," she lifts her hands, and says, "'Marijuana floating in the air, together with the chili beans and beer. That grand wild sound of bop floated from beer parlors; it mixed medleys with every kind of cowboy and boogie woogie in the American night.'" Her voice catches a little, and she looks at me. "I wanted to live inside those boogie woogie nights and discover their Spanish mysteries, you know?"

"I get that," I say. "So is that the reason you ran away?"

She scrunches her face. "Not entirely. I mean, I got hooked on Kerouac and read all his books. But then I had a chance to go across the country with a friend of sorts."

"What do you mean by 'of sorts'?"

She sighs. "I found a Jack Kerouac web page on Facebook. It was originated by this guy named Theo. He posted quotes and interesting stuff about Kerouac and the other beat writers sometimes. One of my favorites is, '"It was drizzling and mysterious at the beginning of our journey. I could see that it was all going to be one big saga of the mist.' Isn't that great?" I nod. "Theo also posted puns like, 'a will is a dead giveaway, or a bicycle can't stand alone because it's two tired.'"

He sounds like a tool, but I say, "Clever."

She nods. "I started commenting on his posts, and we began sort of an online relationship."

"Oh, shit." I feel something gnaw inside me.

"It's not what you think," she says. "He's not a perv or anything. Theo's a grad student working on his PhD in American literature. His dissertation is about Kerouac and the social significance of the Beats as a comparative modern literary renaissance of Classical literature."

"That sounds . . ." I was about to say it sounds like a load of crap, but I want her to continue her story, and I don't want to piss her off. "Cool. Go on."

"He told me he and a buddy were planning to recreate Kerouac and Cassady's trips across the country, and he invited me to come along."

"Yeah, it's always a good decision to get in a car with strange men."

Shelly smacks me in the leg with her trowel. "Fuck you!"

"Ow!" I rub my shin, where she left an anvil-shaped mark. "But you have to admit . . ." Shelly gave me murderous look. "Okay, tell me the rest of your story," I say.

She vigorously dug out another weed. "Not if you're going to judge me."

"I won't. I promise. I want to hear the rest," I say. "And who the hell am I to judge? So what did you do next? Did you leave a note?"

She looks at me from the corner of her eye. "Yeah. I said something like 'By the time you get this I'll be long gone because after all that happened I couldn't stay here anymore.'"

"So besides this Theo guy, what happened to make you want to leave?"

"I found out the truth about myself." She pauses. "I grew up thinking my family was fairly normal: two parents, two kids, one family dog. We lived in nice houses and took regular family vacations. On the surface my family is the American dream.

"Yet as I said, I always knew something was off-kilter, like when Mason Lee came out freshman year, he told me he'd spent his whole life pretending to be straight because being different bothers people. I knew I wasn't *gay*, but there was *something* alien about me. I just couldn't figure out what. Then last summer, after I learned the truth about my myth, it was like the lid blew off and I was free to just go."

She was scaring me a bit. "What did you find out?"

She stopped digging. "Last June I started applying for scholarships. I know most people wait until they're seniors, but there are some early scholarships for juniors. And this particular one required a photocopy of my birth certificate, so I went out to ask my dad about the documents.

"He was sitting by the pool with his leg propped up, drinking a margarita. He had broken his ankle playing tennis when he tripped on a tennis ball.

"My dad was always cagey about letting my brother and me look at the details of our lives. Maybe it's the lawyer in him, but he didn't like for Josh and me to be in his office unless he was there.

He'd always say there were too many confidential documents in there, and he didn't want to compromise anyone's information.

"But that day, maybe he had drunk one too many margaritas, or taken too many painkillers. I don't know, but something blurred his judgment, and my mom wasn't home to stop him since she was teaching a yoga class. So my normally cautious dad handed me the keys to his office and told me my folder was in the bottom drawer of his desk. He asked me to go get it, and said he would finish the application for me."

Shelly dusts her elbows and continues. "I loved the leather and polished wood smell of my father's office. As a kid I often played on the Persian rug in front of his massive desk where he worked on legal briefs. It was like being in the President's office. I'd sit there and eavesdrop on his phone conversations where he used big words like *legerdemain* and *pari delicto*. I liked that my father was smart. Anyway, I opened the drawer and noticed two thick, clear plastic envelopes, one labeled with my brother's name and one with mine.

"I pulled mine out. I knew it held my passport, medical records, and other important documents. Some of them I'd seen, but I'd never seen my birth certificate, so I pulled it out. I was kind of amazed how tiny my hands and feet had been. And then I read the parental information and the name on the certificate. It wasn't mine.

"I ran outside and handed the birth certificate to my father and asked, 'What does this mean?' He set down his drink and took the paper. His expression told me he'd been caught in a big fat lie.

"I pointed to the name on the certificate, and said, 'Who the hell is Valentine Falls?' My father sighed, and said, 'We meant to tell you.' 'So I'm adopted?' I said. 'Sort of,' he replied. 'How does someone sort of get adopted?' I asked. He explained that my mother had cervical cancer, and it was discovered when she was pregnant with Josh. After he was born she also had her cervix removed, and they couldn't have more kids. Then my mother's sister Karen showed up with her baby, but she was a drug addict and unable to take care of me, so she left me with the Millers."

I feel something pressing against my chest. "So your parents are actually your aunt and uncle?"

"Yeah."

"And your name is really Valentine?"

"It was, but they changed it to Michelle when they adopted me," she says.

"How old were you when this happened?"

"I was just a baby, so I don't remember." She tamps down some loose soil. "As far as I knew until that day by the pool I was always a Miller."

I lean against one of the pillars in front of the building and let out a big breath. Shelly and I have more in common than I realized. "I'm sorry you had to find out that way," I say. She shrugs, and does more digging. "Have you met your real parents?"

"My father OD'd on coke before I was born," she says, "but I found out where my mother was. Or at least where she headed after she abandoned me: San Francisco. So when Theo asked me to go on this trip, which included San Francisco, I thought, yeah, I can go meet her."

"So you ran away with this guy you met on Facebook."

She leans forward and her hair hides her face. "I know, it sounds dumb and dangerous now, but he turned out to be a really nice guy."

"Did you fall in love with him?"

"I don't think so. He was a lot older for one. Twenty-four. And I was only sixteen."

"Did he know you were underage?"

She brushes the hair away from her face with the back of her hand. "No. He thought I was a sophomore in college." She stands up and moves down to the next bunch of weeds. "And I had a fake ID."

"Jesus," I say. I start digging again. "How did you get there?"

"We had to take my car because Theo didn't have a car, and his friend Dale, who came with us, drove a piece of junk worse than your car. We stopped at a few of the places Kerouac wrote about, like Denver, Phoenix, and L.A., and met with some of their friends. They were all interesting people, like poets and artists and lit majors, and we stayed with some of them. And some places along the way were scary and beautiful."

"In what ways?"

"We took turns driving all day and night. When we hit Kansas, we were in the middle of nowhere, and it was spooky. Like the three of us and the guy in the store were the last people on earth. And it was sunrise, which in Kansas, because it's so flat, surrounds you in all directions. I wondered how Kerouac would describe it. I can picture him saying something like 'the iridescent flat dawn of Kansas surrounded us as its itchy fingers pulled up the sun.'"

"Nice," I say.

"And in Arizona, we stopped and slept outside one night, which was also kind of scary and wonderful. We pulled off the freeway into a campground near the Petrified Forest, and took a side road to this remote place. Even though it was only a few miles from the highway it felt like we were on another planet with its dusty red earth and cerulean sky. And even though it was hot, it's true what they say about dry heat. It's not as bad as the sticky heat we get here. But it gets cold at night in the desert, so Theo built a fire and it was like being in the Old West. We lay on our backs in sleeping bags where it was quiet and scary and exhilarating, with stars so bright. Other than our fire, it was totally dark. I ended up sleeping in the car, though, after Dale mentioned we could get eaten by coyotes."

I snicker, and she continues. "We stopped in L.A. for a couple days and swam in the ocean, then ended up in San Francisco, and it was exciting and fun."

"What kinds of things did you guys do?" I ask.

"We went to coffee shops and bookstores to hear jazz and readings. Did you know City Lights Books has a whole floor of just poetry? Anyway, we also saw free concerts in parks, walked around the city, went to pubs, and met a lot of cool people."

"How did you get into bars?"

"Fake ID, remember?"

"Oh yeah." I crack a smile.

She sighs. "It was great until the money ran out. San Francisco is astronomically expensive, and even though we lived in crappy hotels, it didn't take long to burn through our money."

"Where did you live?"

"At first we stayed with a friend of Theo's, then found a fairly cheap hotel in the Sunset District. It was in walking distance to the beach, and just walking along listening to the waves is nothing short of awesome. But it's cold there in summer, and Theo and I had to buy winter jackets at a thrift store. Then Theo discovered bed bugs in our room, so we had to move. And this place was more expensive, plus my car got broken into. But I still loved San Francisco. I ended up selling the car because there's nowhere to park and you can get a trolley or a bus to anywhere there. Since I didn't have the title, the shady guy we sold it to didn't give me much for it.

"And even though we lived in a terrible room in the Mission District and survived on bread, fruit, and the McDonald's Dollar Menu, every day felt like an adventure.

"But soon the money issue got critical. Theo took a part-time job at the docks, partly to duplicate Kerouac's experience, and partly for the cash. Since I was a runaway with a fake ID, I couldn't exactly get a regular job. And I was afraid to tell Theo the truth because I was afraid he'd send me back to Ohio. So I got a job in a laundry that hired illegals and paid cash. It was horrible work, but we both earned enough to survive. The only luxuries I allowed myself were an occasional latte and hair dye.

"But when my hands got too raw from washing hotel sheets and table linens, I started to panhandle. I hung out near trolley stations on Union Square and looked for tourists. All the while I looked for Karen, my mother. Sometimes Theo helped. Karen's last address was Haight-Ashbury, and she could have been one of the thousands of street people who slumped inside doorways or begged on street corners. But we didn't find her there.

"We walked around the Mission District, Castro, Sunset, and Golden Gate Park and asked people if they knew Karen. All I had was a twenty-year-old picture I had stolen from my mom's photo album. Nobody seemed to know her, but the people we asked were mostly high and wanted money.

"One evening I showed Karen's picture to a toothless woman sitting on the ground in Sunset near the Bed Bug Motel. She glanced at the photo, and said, "Most likely she be dead, honey. We don't live too long out here. Myself, I got another year or so before I'll either be dead or in jail."

"So you didn't find your mother?"

Shelly's shoulders sag and she shakes her head. Her voice grows thinner. "No. And after three months of being broke and cold the charm started to wear off. I felt ragged and missed my family, and was actually relieved when I got arrested for panhandling outside Powell Street Station."

She leans against me and I wrap my arms around her. My hands are coated in dirt but she doesn't seem to mind when I stroke her hair and kiss the top of her head. I'm glad Earl hasn't come outside to check on us. "Did you ever find out what happened to your mother?"

She shakes her head and wipes her face. "But other than upsetting my family, I still don't regret my journey."

"So how did your parents deal with it?"

She pulls away and moves to the last clump of weeds. "After their relief of finding out I wasn't dead, my parents wanted to kill me, but my father contacted an attorney friend there to get me out of jail, and they still sent me a plane ticket."

"What happened to Theo?" I ask.

"He's in Seattle now, working in a coffee shop," she says. "Still working on his dissertation."

"He didn't get arrested for kidnapping or harboring a minor?"

"I never ratted him out to my parents. He didn't know I was underage, and if he had, he never would have taken me with him."

"But nothing flamed between you two."

She gives me a wistful look. "No, I guess not." She shakes her head. "I still love him as a friend, though. We took care of one another. He convinced me to come back home and finish school."

"How come you waited until spring to go back to school?"

She tosses a handful of weeds in the garbage can. "I was just done with everything and everybody, so I did online classes."

I notice the garbage can is starting to overflow. I stand up and tamp it down with my foot. "But you came back to school second semester." I dump some more weeds inside and sit down to battle my last thistle.

She plops onto the ground next to me and rests her head on my shoulder. "I got lonely. I thought coming back would make me feel normal, but I wasn't the same. The whole high school drama shit is so trivial. Who gives a crap if someone looks at you funny, or someone else is wearing the same skirt as you? There are so many more important things to get pissed off about, like people out there starving and living on bus benches. My friends kind of dropped me because I stopped going places with anyone. But their lives were so shallow."

"So you never stole a car and rammed a bunch of parked cars while high on drugs?"

She laughs. "Well, I did steal a car."

"Is that why your parents still don't let you drive?"

"Yeah," she says. "I not only stole one of their cars, which was worth about 16,000 bucks, I sold it for 800 bucks."

"Did your parents press charges?"

"No. They threatened to, but they couldn't bring themselves to do it. But they did want me to suffer a little."

"Which is why you're helping me clean the high school all summer."

She laughs. "It was either this or paint restrooms and outhouses in state parks."

I put my arm around her. "I'm glad you chose to clean the school."

She punches me lightly. "Me too." She looks at me. "That first day I recognized you as someone from my planet."

"And which planet is that?" I ask.

"The Planet of Damaged Souls. We're both looking for lost pieces of ourselves, the image missing in the mirror," she says.

"My mirror is shattered."

"Maybe, maybe not."

"What do you mean?"

"I found out my real father is dead and couldn't find my mother," she says, "but let's seriously see if we can find your father."

"What if we don't?"

"Then you'll be no worse off than you are now."

CHAPTER FOURTEEN

The next few days it does rain, so we do more cleaning inside the building. It rains so much it feels clammy inside even with the AC running full blast. "I think we can breed mosquitoes in here," Earl says, as he and I traipse through the boys' locker area. It's always kind of dank in here anyway, but it's even worse with the football players steaming it up every afternoon for showers after practice. Today we're here because the coach had told Earl the water in one of the showers wouldn't shut off.

"These damn automatic faucets waste more water than the old-fashioned kind," he mutters. "But people are too damn lazy or stupid to turn water off and on and flush their own toilets these days."

I'm dying to take a shower myself. It's been a couple of days, but now that I know Earl is suspicious of my living arrangements, I don't mention it.

After that, we finish cleaning the art room, and it takes all morning to scrub the counters and set up the tables and chairs. By lunchtime the sky has cleared and it turns out to be a nice day. Earl tells us to take a full hour for lunch. "You kids should be able to enjoy a little bit of summer."

I hold Shelly's hand as we walk to my car. "He really is a good guy," I say.

"Yeah, but don't let that be common knowledge, or he'll grind you into little pieces. He likes that kids are scared of him."

I laugh and nod. "Let's do a picnic somewhere," I say.

Shelly and I order a drive-thru lunch at Wendy's and drive over to Graham Park. We find a vacant picnic table in the shade, and

I guide her to the bench. We sit next to each other, our bare legs touching as we unwrap our chicken sandwiches and french fries.

"If every day were like this we'd be a happier species," she says.

I nod as I chew. I close my eyes and notice a fresh, loamy fragrance, the epitome of summer where the world is an okay place. Winter seems a million years off in the future. "It's a good day to be alive."

It doesn't take us long to eat, so we move to a spot in the sun and lie in the grass. The sun is like a warm hand on my face. Shelly rests against me and I stroke her hair, sun-warmed and vanilla-scented.

My phone buzzes. I want to ignore it and enjoy my moment with Shelly, but it's my sister. I never ignore Annie's phone calls. "What's up? How was band camp?"

"Great." she says. "Wish I could go back. But that's not why I called. I was scrounging around in my room for a book to read and found a box marked 'Michael'."

I sit up. "Really? What's in it?"

"It looks like a bunch of papers and some old pictures," she says. "It smells kind of rank, so I have it all on the back porch to dry out."

Everything in my mother's house has an odor. Even if Annie found "clean" clothes, she'd have to air them out.

"I'll stop over after school." After I hang up, I tell Shelly, "Annie found a box of papers in the house with my name on it. There may be clues to my existence inside. I'm stopping by after school to pick it up."

"Can I go with you? I'd love to see what's in the box."

I pretend I don't hear her and say we need to head back to school. I stand up and help Shelly to her feet. As we walk to the car, she says, "Okay, so what's up with your house? Why are you so cagey every time I ask about going to your house?"

"Uh . . ."

"This is the part of your story you're withholding from me, isn't it?"

I sigh. "Yes." I guess now it's my turn to reveal my dirty truth. We stop at my car, and I take her hands in mine. "Before you agree to go there with me, there's something I have to tell you," I say.

"About what?"

"My darkest, grisliest secret," I say. "And what I have to tell you may change how you feel about me. It might . . ."

Shit. I don't think I have ever said the words 'my mother is a hoarder' out loud to anyone. But I want Shelly by my side when I discover what Annie found. Besides, I kind of owe her the rest of my story now.

"Are there bodies buried in the basement?"

"I wish that was all."

"Is there something grotesque about your mom?" she says. "Is she a circus freak with two noses? A nudist? Are there wild animals in the house?"

There may be dead animals under all the piles. I study Shelly's face and replay all our conversations in my head, only in fast forward. Has she ever said anything judgmental? I don't think so. She accepts things as they are. And she lived in places with bed bugs.

"My house . . . shit," I say. "This is hard."

"Say it!"

"My mother is . . . she's the reason I live in my car. I didn't get thrown out of the house after I got expelled. I chose to leave long before then." I open her car door, walk to my side of the car, and slide in.

"Wait. You lived in your car in the winter?"

"Yeah. And believe me, it wasn't easy. Every once in a while if the temperature dropped below zero, I'd spend the night at Jeff's. I'd text him and he would sneak me into his basement since his stepmom doesn't like me. Or I'd go to the bus station or the waiting room of the ER." I shrug. "There are infinite ways to survive."

"Yeah. Tell me about it." She says, "So why did you move out?"

I take a deep breath. "Remember that day we were at your house watching *The Big Hoard*?" She nods. "The reason I got up and left the room wasn't because I'm squeamish. It was too hard to watch because my mother is a hoarder." It burns to say those words aloud.

"Oh," she says, as if she's disappointed. "Okay."

"She lives in disgusting filth," I say. "From the outside it looks like normal people live there, but inside." I shake my head. "The stench is indescribable, and the stacks and stacks of junk are . . . suffocating. You can only get the front door open about a quarter of the way." I snap my seatbelt. "I never take people to my house because I don't want anyone to see it."

"But it's not your fault."

"Yeah, but shit. It's my address. It's where I'm from."

"Do you worry her hoarding might be contagious?"

"Maybe. I mean, look at how I live now. I trash pick and never turn down free castoffs."

"But that's out of necessity," she says. "You have to survive."

I run my hands through my hair, start the engine, and pull out of the parking lot. "The house is a giant mess inside. You know how Earl grumbled about all the crap in the art room? That was minimalism compared to what is inside my mother's house. Hell, my sister has moved out to the back porch. She only goes inside to use the bathroom or the kitchen."

"Where will she live in the winter?"

"I may have a roommate in the Blue Whale."

"Oh my God," Shelly says.

"Yeah, a couple years ago Jeff's dad finally talked his wife into letting them take Jeff in after it got so bad."

"That's so sad, Michael. I'm sad for you and your family."

"Yeah, but you can't tell anybody. I'm eighteen now, so I don't matter, but if Children's Services knew, Annie would be screwed and probably be living in foster care. And I don't think that . . ."

After a beat, Shelly asks, "What?"

"I think if Annie got taken away, it would send Mom over the edge. She loves us in her weird, whacked out way."

"Your mother needs help, though, doesn't she?"

"Yeah, but she doesn't see it," I say. "She's aware she has too much stuff, but Mom always justifies it with, 'I can fix that and give it to so and so' or 'that will be worth a lot of money someday.' And if you try to throw anything out, she goes ape shit."

"If she has so much, how does she notice?"

"I don't know, but believe me, she notices if something is missing. Annie and I have to dispose of shit carefully when she's at work. Like one or two things at a time. Stuff buried underneath."

"Why do you think she does it?"

"I don't know. I think after Bob got shot, she just sort of snapped."

Shelly closes her eyes and listens, and I continue. "She got married again when I was in sixth grade and we moved into the townhouse where she still lives. After Tomas moved out, she started holding onto things. People at her job started giving her things. They felt sorry for the single mom, and they'd give her castoffs of clothes or furniture, then she'd make almost daily trips to Goodwill or go trash picking. At first, it was cool. We had lots of not too terrible toys and clothes that we got for free. But then crap started to accumulate. And even when we outgrew things, Mom freaked when we tried to throw them out." I cringe at the memory as I turn the corner to the school driveway. "Within two years the house was a total mess."

"So you moved out," Shelly says.

"Yeah. Living in my mom's house is like living inside a Ziploc bag with rotting fruit," I say. "It's dark and stinky and totally unlivable. I only go there occasionally to use the shower and to try to find a shirt or something."

Shelly caresses my face. "I am so sad for you, Michael."

I feel myself getting all fragile inside, like I am scratched glass. One tap and I will shatter. "The thing is," I say, "I love my mom a lot. And I know she loves me. She tries to buy me crap, and sometimes it's stuff I can use, like that camping gear. That gear will probably help me survive this winter, but most of what she gives me, I toss out. It's either too battered, or I don't have room for it."

We pull up in front of the school building and I park the Blue Whale. "My mother appears normal, and she's had the same job for years. Strangers can barely tell there's something off about her."

I shut off the car. "I just wonder about the dark mysteries that linger from her past, and why Paul feels so guarded about it. He's known her most of their lives, and he always knew something was wrong, but she functioned. Like now, she functions. She goes to work, pays her bills, drives her car. Outside her house, you'd barely detect my mom is freaking nuts."

"Does she date?"

"Sort of, but now she always meets guys out in public. She doesn't bring them home anymore."

"Kind of like you."

"What are you talking about?" I say. "You're in my home every day."

She smiles. "Oh yeah. The car."

We walk to the entrance of the building. "I guess my mom taught me how to survive by forcing me to discover it for myself."

"So are you going to let me go home with you?" Shelly asks.

"You're such a pain in the ass," I say.

She nudges against me. "Yeah, but you like me anyway."

After school, we stop at Rite Aid and I buy some Vicks VapoRub, gloves, paper masks, and matches. When we get back to the car, Shelly asks if I plan to burn the place down.

"Someday, maybe. The matches are for the odor. I learned in science class that the sulfur dioxide from the flame masks the odor."

"What's the VapoRub for?"

"The eucalyptus also masks the odor if you put some under your nose." I pull up to the row of townhouses. "Ours is the end unit," I say.

"You're right," she says. "It looks fairly normal."

"It's all a façade," I say.

My mom's car is not there, and I'm never sure if that's good or bad. She could be working, or she may be at Goodwill or dumpster diving. Annie hears my car and comes around from the back as Shelly and I are walking across the lawn. My sister looks concerned that I have brought someone here. "Hey, Annie," I say. "This is Shelly."

"I've heard a lot about you," Shelly says, as they shake hands.

Annie's eyes display surprise. "He has said absolutely nothing about you."

"Your brother is a funny creature," Shelly says.

"That he is," Annie nods. We walk to the back porch and Annie glances at Shelly.

"She knows," I say.

Annie nods. "I took stuff out of the box and laid it on a tarp in the sun," she says. "To get the stink out."

It's a sea of small white papers, photos turned over to protect their surfaces. Annie has anchored some of them with stones. "You're a treasure," I say.

I kneel down and turn over one of the photos. The boy in the photo looks familiar, yet he's also a stranger. This kid is free of worry, as if he's the happiest kid in the world. I don't recall having such unguarded moments of joy. I was six years old in this snapshot, before Bob died and life was carefree and fun. It's taken in Whetstone Park, and I'm surrounded by golden leaves, running at the photographer, most likely Bob or my mother. My hands are stuffed with leaves, and I have shoved leaves inside my sweater like the scarecrow in *The Wizard of Oz*.

Shelly kneels next to me. "Is that you?" I nod. "You were so cute. What happened, Neruda?"

"My life."

I turn over another. It's a snapshot from the same day, and two boys smiling with an ineffable happiness stand on the dirt trail in the park, surrounded by trees. The boys are dressed in flannel shirts and jeans and hiking boots. They look clean and new, well cared for, even if their hair is a little ragged. The bigger boy, me, has his arms around a tow-headed Jeff.

"God, is that Jeff?" Annie says. "His hair was so white."

"He still kind of looks like that," I say. "He still has that cheesy, senseless happiness."

"Aw. Who is this little monkey?" Shelly says, as she picks up a photo of a toddler with static cling hair. My hair looks like I've been electrocuted.

I laugh. "I look like an orangutan in that one. I'm lucky I was cute."

I scan the other papers on the tarp and look for official-looking documents.

"I didn't see anything that identifies your father in the box," Annie says. "But you still might want some of this stuff."

Old grade cards from elementary school. Homemade birthday cards, a drawing I made of a ship. "I don't even remember doing this."

"I think she kept something from every day of our childhoods," Annie says.

"Did you find an Annie box?"

She shakes her head. "Everything is an Annie box."

"Sorry," I say. I squeeze her into me.

"I'll keep looking for more of your stuff, though."

"Where do you think Mom would keep anything with information about me?"

Annie shrugs. "There has to be something."

"So you can't ask your mom directly?" Shelly asks.

"No," Annie and I say in unison.

"She's odd about her past," Annie says.

"What about your grandmother?"

"We never see her," Annie says.

"But would she turn you away if you stopped for a visit?"

"Probably not," I say.

"But she's odd too," Annie says. "She won't talk about things either."

"Is your grandfather still alive?" Shelly asks.

"We don't know. Neither of them will talk about him."

"Do you have any aunts and uncles?"

"Mom had a brother who died in a motorcycle accident when she was in high school," I say. "Paul said it changed her."

"Wait!" Shelly looks like an alarm bell went off in her head. "Maybe we're looking in the wrong place. Maybe your dad was another student at high school."

The three of us stop, as if the world stops spinning. "But Paul claims he doesn't know him."

"Paul might be lying," she says. "You said he tries to protect your mom's secrets."

"So what are you proposing?"

"We find a means to look through old yearbooks," Shelly says. "We might see pictures of her with a guy other than Paul."

Annie, Shelly, and I gather the pictures and papers up and carefully place them in a Kroger bag. They still bear a sour odor, but I think I can tolerate it.

Shelly and I drive to Wendy's, order Cokes and fries, and sit in a corner table. "I'm just glad you didn't see the inside," I say.

"Maybe next time," she says.

"Maybe never," I say. "I like you well enough to never take you inside."

I drop Shelly off at her house, and go to work at the theater. After I get off, I am tempted to park somewhere in her neighborhood, but my crappy car might attract attention, so I take my usual parking space near the stadium. Sleep comes easily, partly because I can lock the doors from the inside and only crack the windows. Cool nights are best, nights when I can wrap myself in a blanket. And now that Shelly knows my worst, and has not judged me, I feel lighter.

CHAPTER FIFTEEN

As I walk toward my car fresh out of the shower, Shelly sniffs me. "Mmm. You're wearing L'Homme Libre," she says. "Where did you get that one?"

"*GQ* left in the teacher's lounge."

By lunchtime, my fancy cologne smell has vanished. Earl has us waxing the floors. But first we have to strip off the old layer by dissolving it with what smells like embalming fluid. We all reek like dissected animals by the time we go to lunch.

When Shelly pulls out a cigarette, I say, "Aren't you afraid you're flammable right now?"

"Yeah, you may be right. Loan me a shirt."

I find a couple clean shirts in one of my boxes.

"Turn around," she says. I quickly change my own shirt, and turn back around just in time to see her smooth my Jim Morrison shirt over her hips. The shirt is so long she looks naked underneath. "Nice dress," I say.

We eat a quick Wendy's lunch in the parking lot since we're too stinky to go inside anywhere, and then head back to work detail.

After a day of stripping floors, Shelly and I slog to my car around two, drenched in sweat. My phone buzzes. "I hope this isn't work," I groan and look at the text. "It's Annie."

-Mom is working today. Do you have to work after school?

-No.

-You have 8 hours to snoop through boxes. If you can stand it.

-Might bring Shelly.

-Let me tidy the house.

-Ha ha

I tell Shelly I'm going to look through boxes at my mom's. "Wanna come along?"

"Are you sure you want me to?"

"No, but the more people we have searching, the quicker we can find out how futile this will be."

"Okay. Let me text my mom."

"Wear ratty clothes," I say. "Something you'd be willing to throw away."

She looks at her shorts, and she is still wearing my T-shirt. "I'm not tossing Jim Morrison," I say.

"I'll wear what I had on earlier," she says.

"We should probably stop by your house and pick up something you can change into afterwards."

I park in front of Shelly's house. She opens her door. "Aren't you coming in?"

"No," I say. "I smell so bad I'm emitting fumes." She shakes her head and walks up the driveway. "Put on shoes other than flip-flops," I yell from the open window. "Her floors are treacherous. And can you get a couple trash bags?"

She nods and continues toward her house. She comes back a couple minutes later with a sack of clothes, a wad of white trash bags, and two bananas. She hands me one.

Annie sits on the back porch reading *Catching Fire*. She is halfway through it.

"I love that series," Shelly says.

"This one is even better than the first." She stands up and stretches her legs. She looks Shelly over. "Are you sure you're ready for this?" Shelly nods.

I tell Shelly to leave her extra clothes on the porch. I open the bag of supplies I bought yesterday. I smear VapoRub under my nose and hand the jar off to Shelly. The three of us wear masks and gloves.

"We look like a hazmat team," Shelly says.

"Believe me, we should be wearing hazmat suits," I say.

I grasp a trash bag and open the door. It's been weeks since I've been inside my mother's house. I adjust my mask, but the odor still permeates the gauzy filter as soon as I step through the back door. Shelly follows me in and stops to gaze around.

"What are you thinking?" I ask.

"That this is surreal." Her voice is muffled through the mask.

The kitchen floor is fairly clear due to Annie's insistence, but the counters are heaped with the clutter of dishes, pots and pans, and open food containers. The dead mouse smell lingers, along with mold and rotten fruit.

"Are you okay?" I ask Shelly.

She nods.

"Watch your step," I say as we move into the living room. Odd name for a room where life can barely happen. Shelly and I climb on top of stuff that sometimes slips under our feet. "Damn," I say. "I forgot the matches."

"Seems to be a pattern with you," Shelly says.

"Maybe I should have tried to blow up this place instead of Rick's car."

"Why do you have matches?" Annie says. "Are you planning to have a bonfire?"

"Wouldn't be a bad idea." I stop and scan the mountain in front of us. "I really don't know where to start. Annie, do you have any ideas?"

"How about over by that desk?"

"What desk?"

"The one in that corner." Annie points to a spot near the picture window.

The boxes and objects are stacked up to the light fixture. "Oh yeah, we do have a desk."

I remember when we first moved in all three of us kids would sit and color or do homework at the desk, and sometimes Mom would read or pay bills there. I step forward and hear something snap under my feet. I look down. It's a plastic doohickey now broken under my feet. I open a trash bag and toss it in.

"Will your mom notice?" Shelly asks.

"Probably. She remembers everything."

I tread carefully toward the corner. "I'm going to move some of this shit by handing it to you guys. See if you can find a spot for it."

"Wait!" Annie says. "Do you have a camera phone on you?" she asks Shelly.

"Yes. Why?"

"So we can take a picture and move everything back the way it was."

"Good idea." Shelly hands me her phone, and I snap a few shots of the corner. I give her back the phone. I reach up and slide the board games off the top of the pile and hand them to Shelly, who passes them on to Annie.

"I remember playing Candy Land," she says. "I wondered what happened to the game."

There must be twenty boxed games. "We never played any of these," I say. I cough as dust spumes around me. "She must have gotten them free somewhere."

"Why would she accumulate kids' games?" Shelly asks.

"Her logic would be some day our children would play them," Annie says.

"My children will never set foot inside this house," I say.

It takes about twenty minutes, but enough space is cleared that I can reach the stacks of boxes resting on the desktop. I open the first box; it's full of cancelled checks from several years ago. I hand it off. Shelly reaches to place it somewhere and slips. A pile of detritus loosens and pummels her on the head. "Ouch."

"Are you okay?"

"I think so."

"Let me know when this gets to be too much," I say.

"I'm fine," she says.

After moving several boxes of checks, I finally unbury the desk. I pull on the top drawer. "It's stuck," I say. "Is there a heavy object around here I can use to bang on it?"

Shelly and my sister rummage through a couple piles. "I found a brass lamp base," Shelly says. "Is it valuable?"

"Nothing's valuable," I say.

The lamp has no bulb or shade. Or even a plug. Just the base. I grab it from her hand and whack the drawer until it pops loose. I set the brass lamp aside. I'd throw it away, but it may come in handy again. I slide the drawer open. Part of why it was stuck is it's overfilled. I reach in and pull out crumpled paper, ripping it as I go. It's an old grocery list. I wad it up and place it in the trash bag. Inside the drawer are hundreds of pens. "Good God, look at all these dried up old pens." I toss those in the bag as well. I grab at everything in the drawer and stuff it inside the bag, clawing until the drawer is empty. I sigh and rest myself against a stack of crap.

"What?" Shelly says.

"It's all so pointless," I say. "I emptied one drawer, but it's like cleaning one tile at a time in a cathedral. This could take years," I want to throw out everything in sight. "How the *hell* did it get like this?" I yell. "Damn it! Damn it! Damn it! It's a needle in a fucking haystack. It's insane." I'm angry at the amount of stuff, and that I did nothing to stop it from accumulating.

Shelly places a gloved hand on my back. "Keep going," she says. Her voice calms me.

I open the next drawer. "More goddamned pens!" I trash all of them. The next drawer is crammed full of paperclips, which I also throw out.

I whack the bottom drawer with the lamp base to open it and find what looks like a ledger book with pink flower decals pasted on the cover. I pull this out and open it. Instead of numbers, it contains pages of writing. My heart starts thumping. "It could be nothing, but I may have found a diary." I set the trash bag down and thumb through it. "Shit, it *is* a diary." I look at Shelly and Annie. "Should I take it?"

"Duh. Yeah," Shelly says. "It may have some answers."

"What if she goes looking for it?"

"It's been in there like a hundred years," Annie says. "You couldn't even get the drawer open. Mom's not going to go looking for it now."

"You can sneak it back later," Shelly says.

I nod and hand the book off to Shelly, who passes it to my sister. Annie takes the book and sets it on a semi-clear space on the floor. The rest of the drawer is just more paperclips, and a set of keys. I stash those back in and shut the drawer.

"One more drawer," I say. I grip the top of the desk and lean down to the lowest drawer. Inside is a bulging white envelope. I pull it out and peek inside. "More pictures," I say. I hand these off to the girls. I start coughing and sit down. "I can't do any more," I say. "Let's put the games and other crap back where they were."

It takes us awhile to reassemble the mess so it looks undisturbed. Shelly grabs the pictures and ledger, and I drag the trash bag on the way out. As soon as I step outside I whip off the mask and gloves and add them to the garbage. The others follow suit.

"Wow, you filled a bag." Annie says. "Good job."

"Yeah, a whole bag," I say. "It's useless, though."

Shelly holds up the book and envelope. "These might give you a clue to your identity, though."

"Maybe, but not likely." I go out to my car and change into Josh's borrowed shirt and shorts as the girls change their clothes on the back porch. I also find my flip-flops. I can't throw away my shoes, but I can air them out before I wear them again. I won't reuse the socks, though. As I approach the porch, I open a new trash bag and dump my stinky clothes inside. After the girls dress they, too, trash their old clothes. I pick up both bags to hurl them in the trash bin, but Shelly stops me.

"Leave the bags," she says.

"Why? We can't wear them again."

"I have an idea."

"I don't want them stinking up my car," I say.

She ties each bag extra tight. "They won't."

I shrug. "Now what?"

"Let's go somewhere where the air is pure as sunshine," Shelly says.

"McDonald's?" Annie says.

We pull into McDonald's, and I reach into the backseat for the envelope and book. We go inside to order Cokes. I can't eat right now, but Shelly orders a sandwich and fries.

I sip the cola, and the aroma of Shelly's food wafts my way. Those fries do smell good. Maybe a couple won't hurt, so I steal a few and munch on them.

"So you don't feel the need to rush home and take a shower?" I ask.

She shrugs. She dips a fry in ketchup and swirls it around. "My hair kind of stinks, but like I said, I've been in some crappy places."

I carefully pull the pictures out of the envelope. Their odor knocks me back. "I think we need to air these out too." I slide them back in the envelope and clasp it tightly.

"Okay, but first we need to do something," Shelly says.

Annie and I glance at each other and shrug. "She's the boss," I say.

Shelly guides me to Graham Park and tells me to park near a cluster of picnic tables. "Do you still have the matches?"

"In the backseat."

"Bring the McDonald's wrappers and bags too." Shelly grabs the trash bags and marches to a metal dumpster. She dumps the garbage inside the canister. "This is a symbol of your past," she says to my sister and me. "And what you will let go of. All the crap that has happened to you and what you have no control over, and what you can't blame yourselves for." She takes the white paper bags and strikes a match until the bag is a torch. She tosses it on top of the trash. She adds other papers she found on the ground until the canister is aflame. Shelly stokes the fire with a nearby stick. The three of us watch as the stinky shirts and old, dried-up pens sizzle and pop.

"I feel like we should say a prayer or something," Annie says.

"Let's observe a moment of silence for . . . what?" Shelly says.

"Finding out who Michael is," Annie says.

I raise my drink cup. "I'll drink to that."

We bump pop cups, drink, and drizzle the rest of our sodas over the embers to put out the fire.

"So who's up for a swim at my house?" Shelly says.

Shelly loans me Josh's trunks again, and she tells my sister she has a million and one bathing suits. She and Annie go to Shelly's room to change. I lie in a lounge chair and enjoy the sun.

Shelly walks out followed by my kid sister, who, wearing one of Shelly's bikinis, no longer looks like a kid. My sister is beautiful, and this thought both delights and disturbs me. Annie is not the kind of beautiful girl who flaunts it, yet her attractiveness will make her the target of men. We're awful creatures, really. We see girls and women and immediately assess their do-ability. Even nerdy guys like me who take AP classes and live in their cars.

Shelly sets a stack of towels on one of the lounge chairs beside the pool. She goes into the house and comes back a couple minutes later carrying a basket of clothespins and a wooden contraption that she unfolds.

"What's that?" I ask.

"It's for drying hand-washable stuff. I thought we could clip the pictures on here so they can air out while we swim."

"You're a genius," I say.

Annie sets a towel on the ground and dumps the contents of the white envelope on it. An array of people in color and black-and-white photos gazes up at us. "Some of these are really old," she says.

I glance at each as we clip the edges to the dryer rack with clothespins. I recognize my mother, younger and less skinny. "Mom was really pretty," Annie says.

I recognize a younger version of my grandmother, standing next to a man I have never met, and a teenaged guy who resembles my mom. "This must be our uncle," I say. I pass the photo to Annie.

"Wow, they all look so young." She hands the picture back to me and sneezes. "Sorry. These things are pretty rank."

We quickly clip them all onto the contraption.

"Those pictures hanging there remind me of that time Rick and Ashley and I pasted Post-it notes all over your car," Annie says.

"Right after Paul gave me the car," I tell Shelly, "the three of them littered it with hundreds of yellow Post-its. I wasn't living in it then."

"Some of the notes had messages on them, like 'Cool car for a dork like you' and 'convenient if you plan to raise a family of whales,'" Annie says.

"That's how she got named the Blue Whale," I say.

Shelly laughs. "When I was a cheerleader we used to do that to some of the football players' cars."

I open the book halfway and let it sit in the sun as well.

"We need music," Shelly says. She runs back into the house, and suddenly we are surrounded by sound.

"They have an outdoor speaker system?" Annie says. "This is so cool."

"I know," I say. "I keep asking Shelly if her parents will adopt me."

"And I keep reminding him my parents don't like the children they have." Shelly points to an outdoor shower. "We're all pretty gross. Let's rinse off before we jump in the pool."

After the cold shower, the three of us dive into the pool, where I immediately splash my sister, who splashes me back. I recall a time when Annie and I were last in a pool together. So long ago, back when Bob was still alive. One of his colleagues had a pool, and I remember going to this guy's house for a party. Annie was small, and Mom had to hold onto her in the shallow end while Jeff and I splashed around and played. Annie was fearless, even then. We swooshed water all over her, and she laughed her baby laugh.

Shelly's pool is bean shaped, so it's not good for laps, but I still manage to do some breast strokes. I notice Annie and Shelly chatting as they linger at the shallow end. They crawl under the water, knees bent, looking like frogs.

"What are you guys talking about?" I say as I swim up.

"Boys and sex," Shelly says. She dunks my head underwater. I pop up.

"My sister is not allowed to have sex until she's at least thirty," I say.

They laugh. Annie dunks me.

We play in the water until our skin starts to shrivel. Each of us steps out to dry off. I spread my towel over the lounge chair, lie back, and close my eyes. "This is the life," I say. "A perfect day."

"Made exceptionally fine by your companions," Shelly says.

"Absolutely."

"You guys thirsty?" Shelly asks. "I'll go get us some iced tea."

"Want some help?" my sister asks. The two girls go back into the house. The music has stopped, so I close my eyes and listen to the sounds of summer, thinking how long it has been since I have had a moment of stillness like this, a moment where I can turn off the world and tune into just being alive.

I hear two sets of flip-flops slapping on the brick patio and shade my eyes from the sun to see Annie and Shelly walking toward me. Shelly holds a tray of iced tea and three glasses of ice, and Annie grasps a giant bag of potato chips and a bag of oranges.

Each of us pours tea over the ice and snatches an orange. As I peel mine, Annie offers me the bag of chips. I grab a handful and set the chips on my damp towel.

"I should have brought out some plates," Shelly says.

"Those won't be there long," I say. I set the orange peelings on the tray.

The three of us eat in companionable silence.

"Should we find out what's in the book?" Annie says. All three of us glance at the journal, its pages curling in the sun.

"I'm kind of afraid to," I say.

"I'll do it," Shelly stands up and walks to the book. She reaches down and stops. She turns and hands it to me. "No. Neruda, I think you should be the one to read it."

"Why do you call him Neruda?" Annie asks.

"It's my fake ID surname." I lean back and open the cover when my phone buzzes. I glance at the screen. It's Mitch.

"Ignore it." Shelly says.

"I can't," I say. "I need the money."

CHAPTER SIXTEEN

Around midnight, I pull up to the dumpster behind Olive Garden to see if I might hit the jackpot again. It's Friday night, and the restaurant will have been busy. My door squawks as I get out of the car. I keep forgetting to ask Jeff to loan me some WD-40. I step over to the trash bin, and I hear rustling. Jesus. Are there rats in there? A head pops up; it's an older guy wearing a tattered knit cap. We stare at one another for a long second.

"What do you want?" he growls.

"Apparently the same thing you do," I say.

"I was here first," he barks. "Get lost."

I notice the rolling cart next to the dumpster. Inside is a paper bag filled to the rim with empty pop cans. I realize there are different levels of homelessness. At least I have a car and a job, and have not yet resorted to collecting cans. "Okay buddy. You win." I get back in my car and drive off. Plan B. Maybe Dan's Donuts has a fresh stash in their dumpster.

I find a bag of stale peanut butter cookies in the trash at Dan's Donuts. The best of many worlds! Sugar and protein wrapped in a wonderful tasting package, and free at that.

I sit on the tailgate using the streetlight to read. I crack open the journal. Its pages are weathered and curled, as if they got wet and dried, but the pen markings are still legible. My mother's handwriting is smooth and juvenile, not birdlike and scratchy as it is now. It hadn't occurred to me our handwriting can change. I wonder how my own will evolve. It's pretty bad now.

August 25, 1993

Senior year! I am almost DONE with this place. I am sad and happy at the same time. But more happy than sad because high school overall kind of sucks. Maybe the popular kids feel different, but for girls like me who live "on the wrong side of the tracks," we have a hard time getting noticed. Even a lot of teachers don't see us. We are kids in the middle. Not bad enough to go to prison, but not good enough to go to college. We are kids who get by.

I think I can do more than what everyone else thinks, but I don't know how. So far I pass with a C average, except I get As in art and choir, but if you do the work and show up in those classes, how can you not get As? Like Mrs. Beasely, the art teacher (some of the kids call her Mrs. Beastley, but I like her) says I am talented and should think about being an artist and go to this art school. What does an artist do, though? I mean, for money?

Bill Nye makes science look fun. But I get terrible grades in science. But if I had the brains I would be a mad scientist. One of those people who discovers volcanoes or cures for things. Like in this movie we saw in science class. James Bond (the actor, not the character) lives in this jungle and found plants that cure diseases and people tried to kill him over it. But wouldn't that be cool to discover something so rare that people want to kill you?

Not that I want someone to kill me. But I want to be admired, and maybe have people jealous of me.

Nobody is jealous of me. Except maybe Monica Deal, but that's because she's chubby and says she "just looks at food and gains five pounds." I am tall and thin, and I can eat anything. It just doesn't stick to me. So even though Monica and I are friends, I think she secretly hates me because I'm thin and she's fat. But we hang together because we are both from the wrong *side of town and ride the same bus. She's pretty too and she actually has nicer hair. Hers is thick and dark and wavy, so I hate her a little too since mine is straight as a poker.*

Monica is also smart and gets good grades and will probably head to Ohio State or OU because she can get scholarships if she wants. They don't give money to kids with a 2.0 grade point like me.

But nobody else is jealous of me. I'm sort of not noticed. You know? And who would be jealous of a girl who lives in a trailer with no heat or hot water?

I don't think too many people know. Paul, of course, since he lives down the road, and sometimes in winter I go there to take showers and his mom also lets me run a load of laundry. Otherwise Mom and I hand wash stuff in cold water in the kitchen sink and it takes three days to air dry sometimes when it's cold.

This summer the cold showers felt good, and even now, it's still fairly warm out, so a chilly shower is sort of refreshing. But it's hard to soap up my hair.

I set my mother's journal down. Jesus. Is history repeating itself? Is survival my inheritance? I'm not sure I should read more. It's like I'm invading my mother's privacy. Yet I can't stop myself. I reach into the bag and eat another peanut butter cookie. I read the next entry.

August 28

My brother moved out. He moved in with Ginny, his girlfriend. They live in a battered-looking house just on the edge of town. The front porch is falling off, so they have to use the back door, but the rent is cheap. Ginny says I can shower over there now if I want to.

Before he left, Gil fixed me up with a car so I can drive back and forth to Burger King after school. I'm working three or four nights a week plus weekends. I started there in July. Paul stops in a lot, and I have to tell him not to hang out so I don't get in trouble. The manager is funny about us having boyfriends hanging around. Even though Paul is just my friend. Sort of.

I hate my uniform. Orange and brown polyester. Ugh! I look like a Cleveland Browns fan. Yuck. Steelers, baby! I should get a job at the roller rink. They wear black shirts with yellow stripes. But I don't know how to skate. Do you have to know how to skate to work there? Anyway, this job sucks too. I smell like french fries at the end of each shift, so I have been stopping by Ginny and Gil's every night to take a shower and change clothes before I go home. Sometimes I just sleep on their couch. It has a giant gap in the middle where their dog chewed the stuffing out, but if I stuff a towel in the hole I'm able to get half comfortable. I should just move in with them, but the house is real small. It only has the one bedroom. So when I stay over I am up and out the door before they even wake up. They like to party at night when Gil isn't working. He works second shift at Corning. He says he can help get me on there when school is done. Probably not the factory, but maybe I can work reception or filing. But like I said, I want to get OUT of Rooster. I'm afraid if I start working at Corning I will never leave. I'll marry Paul and pop out sixteen kids and work until I am buried here.

I think I want kids. But I don't want to raise them like I have been. I want us to have a big house and a nice yard. With flowers. Not like where I live, the yard littered with beer cans and crappy car parts. Tree branches that never get cleaned up after storms. When I was a kid I stuck plastic flowers in the yard to make things look nicer. My mom ran them over with her car.

It's a good thing we live outside the city and nobody sees how we live.

I want the kind of house I see on Days of Our Lives. They all have nice homes, with pretty furniture and paintings on the walls. Except for Patch. He reminds me of my brother, except Gil doesn't wear a patch. But he looks like him with the blond hair and motorcycle jacket.

September 5

Senior year kind of sucks. Nothing interesting happened this week. I have a feeling it's going to be a long ass year.

September 16

I think I told you I like science class. But that was biology. This year I have Physical Science II which is like chemistry and physics together and its soooooo hard. I am barely passing, and I won't graduate if I don't pass it. I talked to Mr. Long about it, and he said I could get peer tutoring. This is where they have a smart kid help you in the library during your study hall periods. They get Service Learning credit for helping the dumb kids like me. But I want to pass science, so I said sure, so today I go to the library and find out I am matched up with and it's ~~%$#@*!T*&^Me&~~!!!

The name is scratched out. I flip through the pages and notice all throughout the next few pages of my mother's diary this name is obliterated. Interesting. I continue reading.

So I sit down next to him in the back of the library and introduce myself.

I know who you are he says.

Really? I'm one of those invisible girls. I say. Nobody knows me.

He laughs. You're not as invisible as you think you are ~~%$#@*!~~ tells me. I feel a little jolt of electricity run through me. Even though I am dating Paul, I have always liked ~~%$#@!~~. He is sooooo good-looking, and smart and his family has shitloads money. They own half the town and live near the country club on a lake. They have a yacht and things. Wayyyyy out of my league. And he is dating ~~C%$@SW#!(*&~~ so I wonder how in the world ~~%$#@*!~~ would bother to notice me.*

Anyway, he asks me what I need help with. I show him my last test paper with the big 26 percent on it. Sometimes Mr. Long talks so fast I don't get what he says, I say. It's like Mr. Long speaks a different language.

I expect ~~%$#@!~~ to laugh and shake his head at me, the hopeless idiot. But he nods. Yeah, I know what you mean, he says. Let's look at the ones you missed and see if I can explain this better.*

And he kind of does. Like one question about the difference between an element and a compound

Elements are the basic structures, he says. Like hydrogen, and oxygen. Compounds are when you combine them to form a new substance. Kind of like when you use flour in cakes, and pizza, but each of those has other ingredients that make them unique.

That makes sense, I say. I wonder why Mr. Long didn't just say it that way. Maybe you should teach chemistry instead of Mr. Long.

~~%$#@!~~ laughs and shrugs. He glances over my test paper and says, it looks like you missed all the formulas too.*

Yeah I don't get those at all. Like what's the difference between an atom and a molecule?

Atoms are the tiny, tiny particles that make up things. They're so small we can't even see them with the naked eye. Yet not all atoms are created equal. The atoms of the different elements are different. For example, Hydrogen and oxygen are both invisible gases, but hydrogen is lighter in weight, so it reacts with other elements differently.

But why do they both have H and O but are different chemicals? All those letters with the numbers after them don't make any sense.

Atoms can only hookup a certain way, creating molecules. It's like the sun appears every day, but it rises in the east and sets in the west. So depending on the number of atoms you string together, they have to go the same direction. H_2O and H_2O_2 look similar on paper and in a glass, but they are totally different. Make sense?

Um . . . Yeah?

You understand how H_2O equals two hydrogen atoms and one oxygen atom to form water, right?

I nod.

Well, it's the same principle with these others. Say you're baking an ether cake. Your recipe is going to need 6 cups of carbon. Add 10 cups of hydrogen, and one measly unit of oxygen. Your formula becomes $C_6H_{10}O$.

And he draws a little picture of it and it clicks in my head.

But you can't have 16H and 4O atoms. There is an order to things.

The period ends too quickly. I tell ~~%$#@*!~~. *Thank you.*

And he smiles and says, Anytime. He has the best teeth, gleaming and straight, like perfectly laid tile. And his eyes kind of look over me in a way that makes me feel tingly inside. Oh my. They are the prettiest blue-green. Like a swimming pool. And he has long lashes. Why do boys always get the best eyelashes?

September 22

Over the next few days I meet ~~96$#@*!~~. in the library again, and by the end of the week we don't talk much science anymore. He asks me how long I have been going out with Paul.

Forever, I say. And that's sort of true. I have known Paul forever. I mean like we played in the sandbox together, where we sat in our underwear and blew sand off one another's skin. And now we still breathe on each other's skin but this time in a different way, a way that feels good, like what no six-year-old can imagine. It's like when you go to the movies and the screen lights up with lovely colors and rainbows. I guess kissing and sex are the imaginary worlds we pictured as kids, but did not have the images to complete the picture. But for some reason I also tell ~~96$#@*!~~. I don't plan to marry Paul or anything. (I know he's dating ~~C96$@S W#!(*&~~ yet I think I want to leave the door open in case he breaks up with ~~C96$@S W#!(*&~~ Like I have a chance. Ha ha.

~~96$#@*!~~. laughs, and says let's hope not. You're too young to get married.

September 23

I stayed after school to help on the homecoming committee and my car would not start and I would have been late for work, but lucky for me ~~96$#@*!~~ stayed after school too for football practice and he offered me a ride. And I'm kind of surprised ~~C96$@S~~ isn't with him, and I say so. He sneers, and says they sort of had a fight. This shouldn't make any difference to me, but it makes me feel good. Even though I tell him I'm sorry.

Don't be, he says. I think we're near the end of our run.

I'm glad I am not wearing my skanky Browns fan Burger King uniform. I have it in a bag in the trunk of the car. I *grab all my stuff and get in the passenger side of his car. I tell* ~~%$#@*!~~ *to drop me off at the mall, which is close to Burger King. I don't know why, but I don't want him to know I work at Burger King. I'd rather he think I work in a place where I don't wear a uniform.*

September 28

Homecoming is my favorite dance because the weather is still nice in early October and it rarely rains. So you don't have to worry about your hair getting wet or that you'll have goose bumps from wearing a sleeveless dress. This year my dress is light cat-eye green. What they call tea length. And it's sort of chiffon-like with a full skirt. Even though I bought it secondhand, I still love it. It fits like it was made for me. It makes me look like a Barbie Doll, and I found some pretty white pumps to go with it. I asked Paul to wear a light green shirt so we sort of match. He doesn't get to wear jeans. Poor guy. He hates to dress up, but it's not like it's prom where you have to wear a tux, I told him. He only has to wear dress pants and a green shirt.

So like an army work shirt? he asks.

NO. I told him. A dress shirt.

Paul gets all MAD because he hates to dress up, so I tell him, FINE. Then stay home.

FINE, he says. I will.

October 4 Dance Night

Paul takes me to the dance, but acts like his clothes itch. At first things are okay. We sit with Monica and her date. Some guy from another school. She says she met him through her church. He seems nice and he and Monica spend most of the time on the dance floor.

But Paul refuses to dance with me. Claims to have two left feet, which he kind of does, but still. I look all pretty, and he should make the exception tonight. He says he needs a few beers in him, so I get mad and run out of the gym to get some fresh air and I notice %$#@*! standing outside the building. He gives me a look of shock at first because he is smoking a joint, but then relief when he sees it's me. He looks me over with those pretty eyes, and without even thinking, I blurt out, Hey, my dress matches your eyes!

He laughs. Maybe because he was stoned, but still, I liked that he laughed.

Where's C%$@S W#!(*&? I ask.

He shakes his head. Mad because I wasn't nominated for Homecoming King so we won't be crowned together.

She's the queen?

She thinks she is. He shakes his head. They won't announce it until near the end of the dance.

Oh, I say. I don't keep up with such things. I'll never be queen of nothing.

He smiles at me and asks where Paul is, and I tell him we had a fight because he wouldn't dance, and I ran out on him.

%$#@*! holds the joint out to me. Want a hit?

Sure, I say. And I take a long toke. Paul and I smoke every once in awhile, so I know my way around weed. %$#@*! and I finish the joint. While we smoke we talk about music and how his favorite is jazz and blues.

I'm not sure I've ever heard that kind of music, I tell him.

He hums a tune and I tell him it sounds nice. And it does. Kind of slow and soothing.

It's called "So What?" by Miles Davis, he says.

%$#@*! takes my hand and we go behind the school in a dark spot and we lean into one another and start kissing and it feels natural, as if we have been dating for a long time. All

the times I had kissed Paul NEVER felt this good. ~~%6$#@*!~~'s lips on me felt like fireworks exploding every time he ran his hands over my skin and put his lips on me. He kisses my neck and my bare arms. Then ~~%6$#@*!~~ reaches under my dress and starts to . . .

I stop reading. I can't read about some guy reaching under my mother's skirt. It's weird enough to read she smoked pot in high school. I set the journal aside and run my hands through my hair. I glance at my phone to see how much charge I have left. Maybe half an hour's worth. I lie down and close my eyes and try to sleep, but my mother's diary gnaws at me. Shit. I grab it and turn on my flashlight.

I wanted to, but something in me stopped. I tell him I didn't want to do anything on the side of a building all stoned.

That's cool he said. We kissed some more then some of his friends came outside. Football-type guys and their cheerleader girlfriends. They all were wasted too and the girls kind of look at me like what the hell am I doing with ~~%6$#@*!~~. I feel uncomfortable and tell ~~%6$#@*!~~ goodnight and go back inside the dance. I find Paul, who says he's been looking for me.

Let's leave, I tell him. He doesn't argue.

October 20

~~%6$#@*!~~ *is still helping me with science, even though it feels kind of weird now. I like him and I think he likes me, but even though she didn't get queen, ~~C%6$@S W#!(*&~~ is sort of back in the picture. So it's a good thing I didn't let things get too far, but something has changed. I like spending time with ~~%6$#@*!~~ . And I think it's mutual. We meet every day, and we rarely talk about science.*

When ~~%$#@*!~~ sees me in the hallway he says *Hi* if he's alone, but if he is with any of his jock friends or ~~C%$@S W#!(*&~~ he barely acknowledges that he knows me. He'll just nod his head or smile or raise his eyebrows.

He apologized to me the other day for that.

I get it, I told him. And I do. He's from a different social class, and we aren't exactly friends. But I think we are. Sort of. He talks to me. He says I'm a good listener.

Like the other day we talked about what we want to do out of high school. He told me he doesn't want to go to college in the fall. *Maybe never*, he said.

But you're so smart.

He shrugs. *All my life I've felt pressure to be the best, and I'm tired of being what everybody thinks I am.* He shakes his head. *But my dad expects me to take over one of his businesses.*

What do you want to do? I ask.

Maybe be a beach bum.

I laugh. *You're good-looking enough to be an actor or a model.*

All I know is I don't want to waste my whole life in this town, he tells me

Me either, I say.

And he asks me my plans.

Nothing special.

Tell me, he says.

I shrug. I almost rattle off how Paul thinks he and I are going to get married and settle here, and I love Paul, but I don't think I love him enough. And I feel kind of bad about that. He's such a good guy, but I'm not sure he's the ONE, you know? He represents HERE, and I think the first chance I get I am getting out of HERE too. Somewhere BETTER. Somewhere BIGGER. Like Columbus or Cincinnati, a place where I might get a good job and meet people who have been *to other countries and drink fancy wines, and maybe someday I can go to Hollywood and you will see me on TV and you will say, Hey isn't that the girl who lived in a trailer? The one we all kind of made fun of because yeah, she was pretty, but she had a hick accent and wore used clothes and always stank like smoke. Yeah, wow, she cleans up nice! That's my dream.*

But all I tell %$#@*! is, Well, I want to do something exciting, something where I travel to other countries and stuff.

Like an airline hostess? he asks.

I think for a minute. Maybe. But I have never flown before, I say.

He laughs. You don't have to fly the plane! You only have to serve coffee and stuff to people on airplanes. And herd them toward the exits if the plane crashes.

I don't like the idea of crashing, but the rest of it kind of sounds cool. And that would get me around the world. I could do that, I say.

So I guess %$#@*! and I are friends. We just can't tell anyone.

November 15

Sorry. I've been too busy to write!!!

My grades in science are so much better now. I'm not making As, but I get Cs on almost every test and homework. When %$#@*! and I sit in the library our thighs touch. It feels like electricity burbling through me, and even though I have not been alone with him since that night at the dance I would love to just kiss him right here.

We write notes to each other too. When I sit down he hands me one. Like today he wrote, "The trees are full of glowing colors that remind me of you." And it's funny how nobody suspects anything because he and I are both seeing

other people, and we never see each other outside of school.
Like we are hiding in plain sight.

December 1

%$#@*! came into Burger King tonight with C%$@
SW#!(*é and I felt my heart shatter into a million pieces. I
KNOW he has a girlfriend, and I'm with Paul, but there is
something about him, about us together that feels right. Seeing
%$#@*! with her, I wanted to bolt into the back room, but I
didn't know they were standing there until I looked up. I had
my back turned while straightening up the cups and when I
heard the door open. I turned, and there they were, together. I
looked at him and his eyes grew wide, almost in panic.

I jumped in surprise and dropped the row of cups in my
hands. My manager came over and snarled at me for being
so clumsy. I'll clean this up, he barked. Just take care of your
customers!

I know my face was tomato red. "Hey," I said to %$#@*!.
He nodded, and said hey, Susan. I saw C%$@S W#!(*é
shoot him a look. How may I help you? I asked.

He ordered for both of them. 2 double cheeseburgers, one
with extra pickles, 2 fries, and one large Coke, one large Diet
Coke. I rang it up and took his money. As I got their drinks
I heard her say How do you know HER? She said HER as if
she was holding her nose in the air.

She's in choir class with me, he tells her. Which is true. It's
just he's on the other side of the room with the tenors and I'm
with the sopranos. Funny how he didn't mention the tutoring.

I heard her mumble something to him, and he said, Can
we get that to go?

C%$@S W#!(*é glared at him. I thought we were eating
here! I hate eating in the car!

I think the line at the theater will be long, he said.

She crossed her arms and rolled her eyes. WhatEVER.

I was relieved when they left, but still bothered too. Did he know I worked here? Did he bring her here on purpose? But he looked surprised to see me. What movie did they go see? And the biggest thing that bothered me is what did they do afterwards?

December 4

At school today when I meet ~~%$#@*!~~ *in the library, he says, I'm really sorry about Saturday. I would never have come there if I knew that's where you worked. Under the table he squeezes my hand. My skin is warm from his fingers and sparks flutter inside me. His fingers loop around mine and we keep them clasped together under the table the rest of period as he tries to explain the Doppler effect.*

January 5

I can't believe it's been a month since I wrote in this. So much has happened.

~~%$#@*!~~ *and I meet secretly at school. We still go to the library every day during study hall, where we sometimes talk about physics. But during lunch, when* ~~C%$@S W#!(*é~~ *has a different lunch period every other day, he and I meet in one of the storerooms underneath the stage where they store sets and props for school plays and concerts. He discovered the door is never locked. I don't ask how he found this out.*

Anyway, ~~%$#@*!~~ *meets me there. The first time was right after we got back from Christmas break. He and* ~~C%$@S W#!(*é~~ *had sort of broken up again, and during study hall he seemed upset. I asked if he wanted to talk. The librarian, Mrs. Simpson, was eyeing us from the front desk. I think she's suspicious of us anyway.*

Not here, he said. I know a place, he whispered. Then he scrawled out a note that read MEET ME UNDER THE STAGE DURING LUNCH. We both have fifth period lunch. He knows that because he sees me every day but has to pretend he doesn't.

I stand outside the prop room and wait for %$#@*!. *He shows up a couple minutes later, book bag slung over one shoulder, looking AWEsome. He turns the knob and guides me into the dark room. He reaches up and pulls on a light. The room is cluttered and comfortable, like a very crowded living room with couches and lamps and props they use in the plays.*

I notice a red velvet cape draped over a screen. I lift it off and cover myself with it. I feel like a queen. I swing the cape back and forth. %$#@*! *laughs. This place is cool, I say. It's like my imagination can go wild in here.*

I knew you'd like it.

I glance through all the stuff. I notice a box overflowing with necklaces and bracelets. %$#@*! *reaches inside the box and pulls out a crown. He places it on my head.*

All I need is a throne, I say.

Hold on. He climbs to the back of the room and rummages around. He comes back with a giant wicker chair. Your throne, my lady.

I sit and cover myself in velvet. Send in my royal subjects! I say in a demanding tone.

He grins at me and kneels. I beg of thee, my lady, do not send me to the gallows.

I find a plastic sword and tap each of his shoulders. I anoint you Sir %$#@*! *of Rooster, Ohio.*

He stands and kisses my hand. Thank you, your highness. Your wish is my command.

I blush, and say, my wish is for you to kiss me.

I set the journal down and text Shelly.

-U still up?

-Yeeesss

-Need to call you.

-K.

"Hey," I say, when she answers.

"Wuz up?"

"I think I found out who my father is," I say.

"Shit."

"Yeah." I run my hand over the cover of my mother's pink-flowered diary. "Not his name, but . . . can I read it to you?" I say.

"Over the phone?"

"Something like this is better in person."

"Do you want to come over?"

"Now? Won't your parents get mad at me coming over so late?"

"They sleep like mummies," she says. "Meet me out by the pool. I'll leave the back gate open for you."

CHAPTER SEVENTEEN

I set the journal on the passenger seat and back out of my space under the streetlamp. As I drive, I think about how I am digging up secrets she doesn't want me to know. But they are my secrets too.

I park in front of the house next to Shelly's so her parents won't see my car in case they have heard my getting-louder-each-day muffler. I grab the book and skulk across their lawn, and as Shelly promised, the gate hangs open. Two lounge chairs are pushed together. Shelly is reclining in one. She sits up when she notices me and waves me over. I plunk down on the other chair with the book on my lap. She hands me a flashlight.

"So, do you want to start from the beginning?" she says.

I recline next to her and open the journal. The candles on the table produce just enough light for me to read the cursive writing on the pages. I begin to read. "August 25. Senior year! I am almost DONE with this place. I am sad and happy at the same time . . ."

February 5

I LOVE fifth period every other day. It's the best part of my week when ~~%6$#@*!~~ and me snuggle together under the stage. Sometimes we hear footsteps above us when people walk across. I know we're taking a chance especially now with the Valentine Concert coming up. The band rehearses during fifth. In fact one time ~~%6$#@!~~ and I had to hide quickly under some props because we heard someone coming into the room.*

I love this room. It's like a giant sandbox full of toys. Every day ~~%6$#@!~~ and I find new stuff to play with and we* *pretend. Like today we found costumes from West Side Story. I pretended I was Maria and wore a dark wig. He found a leather jacket and said he was Tony of the Jets. We pretended we were at the school dance.*

Valentine's Day

Today ~~%$#@*!~~ and I did IT for the first time. He and I have been messing around some since our first time in the prop room, but never all the way. This morning when I woke up I sensed today something would turn in our relationship.

I made him some lemon bars and he kissed me deeply as a thank you. He brought me one of those little heart-shaped boxes of chocolates with a bear on it. I tried not to think about HER.

And I soon forgot after ~~%$#@*!~~ laid me down on a mattress and started to unwrap me from my clothes. Time stopped and he just looked at me naked. You're so beautiful, he said to me. Like a sculpture. Then he stood up and took off all his clothes and laid down next to me. Feeling his skin on mine felt like nothing I ever felt before. With Paul we never really got naked all the way. A lot of times we just did it in his pickup. But here I was skin to skin with ~~%$#@*!~~ and he was warm and smelled so clean. And we started kissing and he rolled himself on top of me. I wanted my body to melt inside his. I have protection, he said. And he put on a rubber, and then he slipped himself inside me and we rocked until I felt the Fourth of July just explode inside me.

February 20

I think someone else is using our room for the same reasons as me and ~~%$#@*!~~. We started finding used condoms among some of the props.

But so far nobody has caught us.

March 1

Happy Birthday to me.

Mom and I had a HUGE fight today because the first thing she says to me this morning is, You're 18 now. Get out of my house! See, now that I am of age, Mom can't get any support money on me. All Gil and I have ever been is welfare money to her. Checks she can use to buy booze and shit. She did the same to Gil when he turned 18. So it's not like I'm surprised. But still. Can't she wait a couple months until school is out? I'm never tossing my own kids out just because they turn 18. I plan to love my children.

March 12

I knew ~~%$#@*!~~ was into sports, but I didn't know he did pole-vaulting. I found out when he was trying to explain trajectory to me. I had a problem where I was supposed to predict a trajectory of tossing a softball???? Who thinks about this kind of stuff?

It's like in pole-vaulting, he said. I have to mentally calculate how much speed and how many steps down the runway to achieve maximum speed and initiate my takeoff at the end of the approach. I also need to figure out the angle to hold my pole. At the beginning my pole is upright, and as I run, I lower the degrees gradually as I get closer to the landing pit. The pole acts as a lever to vault me over the bar.

I nod. Kind of like in the Middle Ages and they used catapults to throw boulders over castle walls?

Yeah, exactly, he said. I'm like a human catapult.

But how do you know where you will land?

Part of it's luck, but mainly it's simple physics. I kind of make a mental movie of it before I start. I count my steps backwards from the starting point to the box. But I have to calculate my stride length and speed together, only counting *the steps taken with my right foot, until the last three steps, which are faster, are counted as three, two, one. The goal here is to use the kinetic energy, or K, from the approach and to use the potential energy of the pole, or P, to jump off the ground and obtain vertical lift.*

But how do you get all the way over the bar once you're up in the air? Doesn't gravity make you fall?

Yes, but I use my body to defy gravity for a split second. I raise my arms above my head, beginning with my left arm, since I'm left-handed, and extend my right arm perpendicular to the pole so my body forms a T, so when I drop the pole into the box, the whole thing pulls me up and forward at the same time. But this is where I have to be careful to keep my legs straight.

Why?

It's like having a spoiler on a car for speed. You have to hold your trail leg just right.

What happens if you don't?

The trajectory is wrong, and I knock the bar off.

He makes a sketch of the bar and a stick figure holding a pole.

Imagine this is a triangle. I draw a mental picture of this triangle before I run, and my goal is to make my body part of this triangle. But once you're over you're not home yet because you have to twist yourself on an imaginary axis while releasing the pole so it falls away from you before you hit the mats.

Is there a certain way you're supposed to land?

Face up. Otherwise you can break your nose because your trajectory is still pretty fast. I tend to land on my back with bent knees.

Wow, everything is physics, isn't it?

Yeah, pretty much. You should come watch me sometime.

Maybe I will, I told him. I'm pretty sure I won't because ~~C%$@S W#!(*&~~ *will be there. I wonder what he sees in her. She's such a snot and I know she makes fun of me. I went to the second floor girls' restroom the other day when she was in there with some of her homecoming court cheerleader friends. They were all at the mirror teasing and spraying their hair, and they stopped talking when I came in. After I walked out I could hear them through the door laughing, and* ~~C%$@S W#!(*&~~ *saying I was Most Likely to Grow up and Work in a Donut Shop.*

So no, I don't think I will ever go watch ~~%$#@*!~~ *pole-vault.*

March 14

I had to move in with Gil and Ginny. I guess it's okay because now I am closer to work. And they love me and I love them right back. Ginny is teaching me how to ride a motorcycle. Gil's is way too big and heavy for me.

Oh well. Other than Gil and his friends staying up too late a lot of nights, I like living there. The only bad thing is my period is late. I hope this doesn't mean anything.

March 20

I'm so confused. I meet ~~%$#@*!~~ *in the prop room almost every day now, and we have the most amazing time. Sometimes we just talk. Other times we spend the whole time kissing and stuff even though I am still dating Paul and he has* ~~%C$@S W#!(*&~~ *and it's not like this can go anywhere. We both have other plans. And we're not in love. I don't think we are. But I dread the thought of not seeing him every day once we graduate.*

We didn't make love right away because both of us see other people. But you know how when kissing gets hot and heavy and you sometimes just can't help yourself? Well, that happened to us a couple of weeks after the first time we went there. So now we are both kind of comfortable with it. Except sometimes he forgets to bring condoms. So we have to be careful. I push him away when I think he's about to come. But not always. It just feels too good to have him inside me and we're breathing together, and we become like we're one person, almost breathing for each other.

March 25

I got my period, so I'm okay. WHEW! I had a scare for a minute. I bought a box of condoms and stashed them inside a drawer in the prop room so we always have them. Hopefully the other people using the room don't find them.

I'm not worried about getting AIDS or STDs because %$#@*! *says* C%$@S W#!(*& *won't do it all the way with him. She's sort of religious in her bitchy mean girl way. I wonder if girls like that have a special place between heaven and hell.*

But still, %$#@*! *and I need to be more careful.*

April Spring Break

I usually LOVE spring break, but I miss %$#@*! *so much I'm dying. Paul and I sort of broke up a couple of weeks ago. He knows there's something different about me. I don't think he suspects me and* %$#@*! *getting together. But he knows SOMEthing's up.*

AND. I crashed Ginny's bike. Messed it up really bad. Kind of hurt myself a little too, but not as bad as the bike. I have some bruises and scrapes. But I wasn't going all that fast, and I did wear a helmet. But the bike is bad. The whole front end of it is bent, and it will need a new front wheel and some mechanic-y things that make the bike run. Paul says he can get parts for it but it's going to cost about $300!!! I promised *to pay for it. Lucky I'm not hurt so bad I can't work. I asked for extra shifts this week to get more cash and keep my mind off my crappy life.*

Meanwhile, Gil and Ginny have to ride on his, or I give her rides in my car. I think I'm more upset about it than she is. "This way I get to keep an eye on my man," she says to me. Ginny's so cool. I love her like a sister.

May 12

It's prom this week but I am not going. I don't have a date (Paul and I are still broken up) and I have to work that night anyway. Besides, it costs WAY too much money for a dress and all that. I'm still trying to scrape together enough money to fix Ginny's bike. I'm about a hundred bucks short. And as much as I would like to see ~~%$#@*!~~ *it would KILL me to see* ~~%$#@*!~~ *with HER.*

May 18

I had the flu today and stayed home even though that means no ~~%$#@*!~~ *today. I wonder if* ~~%$#@*!~~ *missed me. Of course I couldn't tell him ahead of time I wouldn't be there. I think he figured it out when I didn't show up at the library. But I miss him. Did he miss me?*

May 20

I had the flu again today so I stayed home from school. I felt better in the afternoon so I went to work. I almost have enough $$ to pay for the bike repairs.

May 23

Glad to be back at school. ~~%$#@*!~~ *said he missed me. I brought him some homemade cookies as a thank-you gift because it's finals week and I might even get a C in the class! I* *make awesome peanut butter chocolate chip cookies. He loved the cookies and ate half of them while we were sitting in the library. He had to sneak eat them every time the librarian looked away.*

May 29

I AM pregnant. It's not Paul's. How do I tell ~~%$#@*!~~*? We graduate this weekend and I may never see him again after this week.*

I close the journal.

"That's it?" Shelly says.

"I searched through the whole thing, but that was the last thing my mother wrote."

"Holy shit," she says. "Crossed-out-name-guy is your dad."

I turn off the flashlight and set it on the ground. "But she crossed out his name because Mom didn't want anyone to know."

"But maybe she did," Shelly says. "She didn't destroy the book. Maybe she hoped someday you'd find it."

"Maybe." I page through to the last entry again. I sit up straight. "Shit, shit, shit!" I say.

"What?"

"This is dated May 29. When was Memorial Day that year?"

Shelly grabs her smartphone and Googles the date on her phone. "Memorial Day, 1995. May 30."

"Oh man," I say. "She figured out she was pregnant with me the day before my uncle and Ginny got killed." I slump back. "And I'll bet she blames herself for Ginny's death since she had to ride with Gil everywhere." I run my hands over the tacky surface of my mother's journal. Sorrow burns a hole inside me. "Oh, Mom." Shelly reaches out and touches my arm. "No wonder she cracked," I say. I sit back and take a deep breath.

Shelly takes my hand. "I'm so sorry, Michael."

I try to respond but I find I can't speak. Shelly curls up closer to me and strokes my face. The sadness comes like ice, and Shelly places her fingers on my eyes. She kisses my eyes, licks the tears from my face. The ice softens, and our bodies are sand and surf, infinite and immediate, twining night with sorrow and joy. Her touch thaws the snow inside me, melts this anguish I've carried inside me most of my life.

The world drops away, and there, by the pool in the fading candlelight, we shed our skins. We forget the moon and the blooming honeysuckle and only know the salt and wheat of our skin. We devour one another like starving beasts, savoring the bread and wine of our bodies, two thorny weeds, savage undergrowth, pulling one another from a smoky labyrinth and breaking into blossom.

We lie together afterwards, with our clothes randomly reassembled, her head resting against my chest. "That was unexpected," I say.

"Unexpected and wonderful."

I tighten my hold on her. "Yet I feel like this is the part of the story where one of us suddenly dies." And a thought occurs to me. "Or gets pregnant."

"I'm on the pill," she says, "so you won't repeat your parents' tale."

"That's a relief," I say. "But why do I still feel sad?"

"That inability to enjoy life is our inheritance," she says. "We don't know how to just roll with it because it can get ripped away at any second."

I think about how the uneven landscape of my life has prepared me to be cautious. I think I am in love with Shelly, and want to say it to her, but I don't want to kill the moment. Instead I say, "My first memory is upheaval. I remember being wrenched from the backseat of a car by a policeman. My mother screaming Jeff's and my names as they separated us."

"Was your mom being arrested?"

"Yeah, I think so. This is just one of several jumbled memories of being passed through unfamiliar hands."

"Wow," Shelly says. "At least my memories are all pretty good. I mean, my mother abandoned me, but to people who love me." She snuggles against me. "So I think my mother did me a favor by leaving me."

I stroke Shelly's hair, and listen to the murmur of the pool filter. "My grandmother told me my mom didn't leave the house for two weeks after Gil died," I say. "Didn't even go to graduation. Then Paul came over one day and said he was moving to Columbus and asked her to join him. My mother packed a bag and left."

"So her life was also sort of ripped apart," Shelly says.

"Yeah."

Shelly sits up and looks at me. "I'll bet your dad doesn't even know he *is* your dad."

"Probably not."

"Then we need to find him!"

"How? I don't even know his name," I say.

"But we have enough details from your mother's journal."

"Maybe," I say.

"There's no maybe about it. Crossed-out-name-guy is your father, and we're going to find him."

CHAPTER EIGHTEEN

Shelly and I stand in the back room of the library, or as always Rick called it, the vault. "It's where old documents go to die," he said to me when we were middle school library aides. "You know, like in *The Adventures of Indiana Jones*." It always reminds me of the Cemetery of Forgotten Books. Earlier this morning I told Earl my mom went to school here and asked if I could look in the library storage to find her yearbook picture.

"Sure, kid," he said. "Knock yourself out."

During our lunch break, he opens the storeroom for Shelly and me in the library. "Don't leave a mess or Mrs. Morgan will have my hide."

"We won't," Shelly says.

"What year did your mom and Paul graduate?" Shelly asks.

"I think '94 or '95."

She grabs for the 1994 and 1995 books. We sit down and open the 1995 yearbook. The cover is tacky from humidity and all the pictures are in black-and-white. "God, look at the hairstyles," Shelly says. "Those bangs look like a bird crashed into their foreheads."

We scan the pages of the seniors. My mother's picture stands out because she is one of the few girls whose hair doesn't look like it exploded. Like she does now, she wore her hair long and straight with a center part. She does not smile in the photograph. She looks at the photographer as if she's thinking, "I'm only getting this picture taken because someone made me."

"Your mom was so pretty," Shelly says.

"She still is, sort of. Just a little more rough around the edges."
I thumb through the book and find my stepfather. "Look at Paul!"
I say. "He had a mullet!"

Shelly looks at Paul's picture. "Oh my God," she says.

"He looks better now that he's bald."

Shelly studies several of the senior boy pictures. "Didn't your
mom say what's-his-name had dark hair and greenish eyes?"

"Yeah."

"So we're looking for a clean, intelligent-looking version of
you."

"Shut up!" I nudge her with my shoulder.

"Hey, if the truth fits." We comb though the pictures and
narrow our target down to six guys who might fit that description.
"It's hard to tell eye color in black-and-white."

"Wait," Shelly says. "Didn't your mom say the guy's dad owned
half of Rooster?" I nod. She flips to the back pages. "I'll bet a guy
like that bought full-page ads. Or at least half a page."

We scan the advertisements. Coffman Shoes had a half-page,
and McNabb Funeral Services boasted a whole page. "Here's
one for Meadows Motors," I say. "And another for Meadows
Appliances & TV, and one for Meadows Sporting Goods."

"I've never heard of any of them," she says.

"Me neither. But looks like this Meadows guy did own Rooster
back then." I flip back to the seniors and find Meadows, Ashton.
I feel the molecules in my body percolate and I stop breathing for
a second. Thick, dark, longish hair with a slight wave. Like mine.
Similar brow. Prominent cheekbones. Like me. He's one of the few
guys not smiling in his picture, so I see he has the same misshapen
lips where one side turns up and the other slightly frowns. "Holy
shit," I say. "I think I found him."

Shelly leans over the book. "Jesus, Joseph, and Mary," she says,
looking from me to him and back again. "It's like looking in a
black-and-white mirror, isn't it?"

We glance through the index and find four more pictures of Ashton Meadows in the yearbook. "My God," Shelly says. "He even stands like you."

The picture she points to labeled "Ashton Meadows" shows a lanky guy standing with a group from an intramural basketball team. He wears a T-shirt and cargo pants, and his hands are shoved in the pockets. He stares right at the camera, unsmiling. Shelly dog-ears the page and flips to the next picture of him.

This photo shows him at the prom with a perky blonde named Ellie West. She has one of those birdcage hairstyles. Ashton and Ellie stand on the dance floor in a slow dance, but he looks like he would rather be anywhere but there.

"Oh my God, Neruda. I've seen that look on your face."

We glance through the 1994 yearbook and find four more pictures of Ashton Meadows from his junior year. He was in choir and basketball. "OMG," Shelly says. "He was on the track team. It's like you're this guy's clone."

Shelly flips to the index. "Didn't your mom say he liked to pole-vault? Look at this photo." The picture captures the moment the guy flies though the air. It's a great shot. Meadows is suspended mid-air, three-quarters of his body just over the pole. His hands grip the vaulting pole as his body almost clears the bar. Beneath the photo the caption reads: Ashton Meadows, master of the pole.

Again, he doesn't smile in the team picture. "He doesn't seem like a happy guy, does he?" I say. "Makes me wonder what he's thinking at that moment."

"Yet your mom said she made him laugh."

"My mother can be spectacularly funny," I say. "Like when Jeff and I were kids, Mom used to try to scare us by claiming she was an alien. She'd wait until dark, and come into our room with a flashlight and a towel over her head. She altered her voice to sound like Darth Vader. 'I'm a hungry alien, and I feed on little children. Are there any children here?' And I would yell,

'No! Go away,' clinging to Jeff. And she'd roar. 'Children! Yummy yummy children!' My brother and I would squeal and screech as she lunged for us."

"That is funny."

"She used to do stuff like that all the time, back when we were all happy."

Shelly grabs the yearbooks and walks to the front of the library where the copier sits. She plugs it in and waits for it to warm up. "We're going to copy every picture we can find of him and your mom," she says.

We put the yearbooks back and Shelly and I walk down to the staff lounge. "Find what you were looking for?" Earl says.

"Yeah," I say. I hold out the two pictures of my mother, one each from her junior and senior years.

"I remember her," Earl says. "Pretty little thing. Dated Paul Nolan."

"Yeah, that's my mom." I glance at Shelly, who has stashed the copies of Ashton Meadows in her giant handbag. I look back at Earl. "Do you remember a kid named Ashton Meadows?" I ask.

Earl sighs one of those sighs that means he has bad news. "Oh yeah."

I'm terrified to ask, but I do anyway. "What happened to him?"

"Not so much to him, but his family," Earl says. "Big scandal with his dad. They lived in a big place over on Silver Lake. Had its own boat dock and everything. I think it's a restaurant now."

"Smoky's Ribs?" Shelly says.

"Yeah, that's the place. The kid's dad was a bigwig here. The kids were okay, but Brock Meadows was a prick. Acted like he owned the school. Hell, he kind of did, I guess. He paid for the new gym, the tennis courts, and the track. So he made damn sure his kids played whatever sports they wanted whether they were any good or not."

"What about the family?" Shelly asks.

"Like I said, his kids were okay."

"But you said something bad happened to them?" I say.

Earl stuffs a cud of chewing tobacco in his mouth and sucks on it for a bit. "Yeah. Brock Meadows lived big. Big house, big cars, big businesses. But it all caught up with him. He also owed big taxes, and had big-ass gambling debts. Turned out he was worth more dead than alive, so he even died big. Took one of his cars, I think it was an Alfa Romeo, and drove it right into Silver Lake." Earl shakes his head. "The family lost everything."

"That's so sad," Shelly says.

"So what happened to the kids?" I ask.

Earl shrugs. "Happened a long time ago. They all left town I think." Earl stands up. "Okay, slaves," he says. "Back to work."

After our shift at school, Shelly and I pick my sister up and the three of us head to Shelly's house. We spread the photocopies out on the floor of Shelly's room. "You look just like this guy," Annie says. "He has to be your dad."

"But where do I find him?" I ask.

"That's what the Internet is for, dummy." Shelly sits at her desk and opens her MacBook. She pulls up her browser and types in "Meadows Motors." Annie and I stand behind her. The screen fills with listings for a place in New Jersey, two in Michigan, and one in Seattle. We scan each website to see if one of these is owned by Ashton Meadows. No dice.

"Type in Meadows Motors AND Rooster, Ohio," Annie says.

Shelly types it in. Google shows a link to a news article in the Rooster Call archive.

"Crap," I say. "It says we have to pay for access."

Shelly rolls her eyes at me. "My dad's a lawyer. You think we don't have access?" She logs in and links to the article titled LOCAL BUSINESS LEADER DIES.

The article pretty much summarizes what Earl told us.

Shelly then pulls up her Facebook page. "Let's look under Ashton Meadows and see what we come up with," she says.

We scan through several guys with variations of the name. Ash Meadows. A. Meadows. No Ashton Meadows. "Maybe he has a LinkedIn account."

"Just Google him," Annie says. Shelly types in the name in the Google bar.

The first Ashton Meadows has a blog called "The View Down Under." She clicks on it. There's a photo of the blog author, an American economics professor living in Australia. He looks to be about sixty and has a beard.

"He's too old," I say. "My dad will be around forty."

We go back to the Google page and click on a number of pages that highlight Ashton or Meadows, but no matches.

"Didn't your mom write that he liked science?" Shelly asks.

"Yeah. Maybe he's on a science database somewhere," Annie says.

We look at Google science and click on science news. She types in his name on the search bar." Nothing by or about Ashton Meadows."

"Try Ash Meadows," I say.

"Fifteen matches!" she says. We scan the titles and all are related to marine life.

The most recent shows Ash Meadows as one of several authors for an article about sea turtles. She clicks on the article. In the author's note it says Dr. Ash Meadows is a marine biologist who splits his time between Hawaii and Seattle. "I think we may be getting somewhere," Shelly mutters.

Shelly looks at the University of Washington site. "Bingo," She says. "Ash Meadows is a professor in the biology department." She moves the screen so I can see it better. "He stole your Hawaiian shirt," she says.

The photo next to his name shows a good-looking man with longish hair wearing a short-sleeved flowered shirt. The biggest difference between this guy and the one in the yearbook is, besides being twenty years older, in this picture, he is smiling.

She loads her printer with photo paper and prints a 9" × 12" picture. We hold it next to the ones we photocopied in the library. The eyes are the same, as is his face shape. His dark hair is now streaked with silver, but it's the same guy.

Annie jumps up. "We found your father!"

"Yeah," I say. "It seems surreal." I sit there, staring at the photo of my biological father, the guy I have been looking for my entire life. It's almost too much to process.

"Funny how Mom always picks smart guys to father her children," Annie says. "I mean, Jeff's dad isn't a college professor like ours, but Paul's smart in other ways."

I nod.

Shelly studies me. "You found your dad."

"Yeah," I say quietly. I sit on her bed, holding the photos.

Shelly sits next to me. "You seem kind of bummed."

"I'm not sure how I'm supposed to feel," I say.

"Is it because the mystery is solved?" Annie says.

"That may be part of it," I say. "But now that I have a genetic blueprint I can track down, what do I do with the information? It's not like I can call or e-mail this Ash Meadows guy and say, 'Hey dude, I'm your long lost son. Be my daddy.'"

"True," Shelly says. "He might have a wife and kids."

"Go to Seattle and meet him!" Annie says.

"Yeah, right. Let me just go through those millions I have stashed under the front seat of my car and buy a plane ticket to Seattle."

"Wait," Shelly says. "Annie may be on to something."

"What do you mean?"

"Why not apply to colleges in Washington?"

After getting expelled, I hadn't even considered college as my next step. I figured I toasted my future by my stupidity. "I wasn't planning on going to college."

"Why not?"

"First of all, I don't have the money."

"How did you do on your ACTs?"

I shrug. "I did okay. I got 36 in writing and reading, but I tanked science and math."

"What's your comp score?"

"Thirty-two, I think."

"Um, duh! A 32 is pretty damn good, you idiot," Shelly says.

"Oh."

"He got a Five on his AP English junior year," Annie says.

Shelly wrinkles her brow at me. "Jesus, Neruda. How can such a smart guy be such a moron? Write a bang-up essay describing your plight and you'll be flooded with scholarships."

"You mean tell them I live in my car?"

"Yeah," Shelly says. "And tell them why. Colleges like quirky people."

"I got expelled from school for a semester," I say. "That alone is a red flag. They might question my mental stability."

Shelly wraps an arm around me. "Your psychosis is part of your unique charm."

"Play up the hoarding mother and the poverty-stricken-half-orphan thing," Annie says.

"Yeah," Shelly says. "You'll have financial aid departments falling over themselves to send you money."

Shelly scrolls through the University of Washington website. "Look, they emphasize cultural diversity," Shelly says. She scans the course listings. "You could learn Urdu!"

I chuckle, yet I feel a fist forming in my stomach. My family is here. Shelly is here. Yet the man I've been looking for my whole life is there.

CHAPTER NINETEEN

It's late when I leave Shelly's house. I drop Annie off and find my usual parking spot on the school grounds. Just as I settle in, I get a text from Shelly.

-You okay?

-Yeah. I think so.

-Will you tell your mom?

-Don't know. Today was hard. Lots to process.

-Want me to sing you to sleep?

-Hell NO

-Yer loss. ☺ Sleep well

-Yeah right.

My future has always been a clean slate. I live day to day, amazed to find I have survived yet another one. Yet as wonky as my life is, it's workable.

In my English class last year, Mrs. Tucker had us write a narrative essay where we had to do something outside our comfort zones. This was near the beginning of the year when the weather was still fairly warm. I had just begun living in the Blue Whale, and it hit me my life was one giant leap outside of my normal comfort zone. But I wasn't going to write about any of it.

The teacher gave us a list of things we could choose from, such as wear a style of clothes we wouldn't normally wear, or shop in an unusual store. "You guys might want to try Victoria's Secret," she said. Just the thought of that made me cringe. Another item on the list was to talk to someone you don't know. "This could be a new kid, or someone outside your social circle," the teacher had said.

I had been the new kid before, and my best friend was someone new I had talked to. At the time of the assignment Rick and I were still good. At lunch that day, I showed Rick the assignment. "Talking to the new kids is not out of my comfort zone," I said. "I talked to you."

He grinned. "And look how splendidly that turned out."

"Yeah, it almost got me killed." I recalled the near beat-down at recess that day.

"You're pretty brave, though," he said. He glanced at the list of possible risky tasks. "You have no style, so the clothing thing is moot."

"Asshole."

He read aloud from the list. "Be silent for a day, using only gestures or notes." He studied me. "I've seen you use plenty of gestures."

I flipped him the bird. "See? That's in your wheelhouse." Rick looked at the list again and gazed around the cafeteria. He pointed out the pretty blonde I had mentioned to him a week ago. "I'll bet it's out of your comfort zone to talk to her."

"Well, yeah," I said. "Because she's about 10,000 light years out of my league."

He handed me back the project sheet. "There's your assignment, then." And that was how I started my relationship with Ashley Anders. And look how well that turned out.

So if I chuck it all and move to Seattle to look for a guy who may or may not know I exist, or may not want to be reminded I exist, how will that enrich my life?

Yeah, this is way out of my comfort zone. And I really wish I could talk to Rick about it.

***

I hear my name repeated like a mantra. "Michael. Michael. Michael. Michael!" I am startled awake to find Shelly hovering over my head. "My God," she says, "You sleep like a block of cheese."

I roll over and groan. I pull the blanket over my head like a mummy. "I think I only slept a couple hours." I bury my face against my pillow. "What time is it?"

"Seven." She snuggles next to me and throws an arm over my mummified self. "I'd offer to go get us something to eat so you can sleep longer, but I'm not allowed to drive."

"You're useless," I say.

"Yeah, but you like me anyway."

I am almost asleep again when I hear Shelly say, "Oh, hey." She pokes me.

I unwrap my head. Earl is standing at the open tailgate, leaning into the car.

"Morning, sunshine," he says.

"Oh shit," I mutter.

"It's not what you think," Shelly says. "I just got here."

Earl pulls a pack of Red Chief tobacco from his pants pocket and unrolls it. He stuffs a wad in his mouth. "Then why don't you tell me what this is?" he asks.

I sit up. "I, uh, had to work really late last night and didn't want to be late to school."

Earl leans in and scans the detritus scattered in the back of my station wagon. "What I mean is, why don't you tell me why you're living in this wreck of a car?"

Shelly and I glance at each other.

"Tell you what," Earl says. "Go get cleaned up and meet me in the lounge." He eyes Shelly. "Both of you."

We watch Earl saunter toward the building. Once he's out of earshot, I mutter, "Shit. I'm screwed."

Earl is sitting with his elbows on one of the lounge tables when Shelly and I walk in. "Where's Hess?" she asks.

"I sent him out for coffee and donuts," Earl says. He motions for the two of us to sit. "So how long have you been living in your car?"

I clear my throat. No sense in lying about it now. "A few months."

"So you've been homeless for awhile."

"Technically I still have an address," I say, "so I'm not homeless. I choose to live on my own."

"Interesting."

"I get along fine with my mom." I glance at Shelly, and continue. "But I'm eighteen. I can live anywhere."

Earl leans back in his chair and studies me. "You'd rather live in your car than in a house?"

"I thought it would help my mom to have one less person to feed."

"So if I call your mother, she will say she did not throw you out? That you left on your own accord?"

"Yeah," I say. "But please don't call her."

"Why not?"

I shoot Shelly a look. She gives me a slight nod. "My mother . . ." This is where I usually fabricate some lie, like my mother doesn't speak English, or she's out of town, but I know I can't bullshit Earl. "My mother is a hoarder." This time saying it out loud does not fracture me. "I can't breathe there," I say. "The amount of junk inside her house is . . . indescribable."

"What about your siblings?"

"Annie still lives there. Jeff lives with his dad."

"I see."

He looks at Shelly. "And you knew about this?" She nods. Earl wraps his hands behind his head and rocks back in his chair.

I'd love to know what's spinning inside his head. *Please don't call Children's Services.*

He eyes me. "What about when it starts to get cold out? Where are you planning to live then?"

"I . . . uh . . ."

Hess rescues me by strolling in with a box of donuts from Dan's and four cups of coffee. "Breakfast!" Hess announces and sets the grub on the table.

We each take a cup of coffee. I choose a chocolate-covered cake donut.

"So, is this a staff meeting?" Hess says.

Earl wipes powdered sugar from his lip and points at me. "Kid's been living in his car for several months."

"Whoa," Hess says. "That's different."

"Says he'd rather live in that blue wreck than in his mom's house."

"Really?" Hess chomps for a few seconds. "So it's kind of like you're camping all the time." He swigs some coffee. "Could get old, though."

I am immobilized. My donut sits untouched on the napkin. Shelly, who is munching mindlessly, has been no help at all.

"Don't you have any other family you could stay with?" Earl says.

"I might move in with Jeff's family when it starts to get cold," I say.

"No you won't," Earl says. I flush. How does he know I'm lying? "Our kids are grown. We have this big rambling house. We got room." He grabs for a second donut. "Plenty of room for you there."

I am about to fall out of my chair.

Shelly and I exchange glances. Living with Earl? "Have you asked your wife?" I say.

"Dot and I talked about you at great length," he says. "Told her what I suspected about your living arrangements a few weeks ago. It's her idea."

"One thing for sure," Hess says. "You'll eat well. Dot's the best."

"Since you're over eighteen," Hess says, "We won't have to mess with courts or anything."

"I'd rather not have Children's Services involved," I say "I'm afraid my mom could get in trouble."

"Michael, what about Annie?" Shelly says. "She can't live on your mom's back porch forever."

Earl looks like he may explode. "Your sister is living on the back porch?"

I nod.

He stands and wipes his mouth with a paper towel. "Get up. You're taking me to your mother's place now."

It's bad enough Shelly had to see the horrors inside my house, but I don't know Earl well enough to gauge his reaction when he sees it. "Uh . . . it's pretty horrible," I say.

"Kid, nothing I see at your house is gonna horrify me. I did a tour in Nam."

"My mom might be sleeping," I say.

"Then we'll wake her up."

I am silent inside Earl's pickup truck as he follows the directions I give him. He leans his arm out the window and chews on a cud, his eyes on the road.

I breathe a small sigh of relief to see my mother's car is not parked out front. A confrontation between her and Earl would not go well. Hopefully she's still at work and not shopping.

Earl and I get out of the truck and he walks up the steps to the front door. Earl is not as heavy as Hess, but he's big enough. I don't think he will fit inside the door. "We should probably go through the back," I say. "It's easier to get in that way."

He shrugs and follows me out back. He halts when he sees Annie. My sleeping sister is spread out on the lawn chair, wrapped in a battered quilt. She is surrounded by a dresser, a nightstand with a kerosene lamp on top, and the screen, as if Annie were a character onstage and this was her set.

"Jesus Christ!" he mutters.

We tiptoe carefully up the steps so as not to wake Annie, but the screech of the storm door rouses her. She half opens her eyes. "Hey, Michael." She sits up abruptly when she notices Earl behind me.

"He figured out I was living in my car," I say. "I had to explain why."

I shove the back door open and the wretched odor hits me. I glance at Earl, who has followed me in. I wish I had thought to bring masks.

He scans the kitchen, taking in the stacks of dirty dishes, opened boxes of food, and pillars of junk. "That's some smell," he says. He yanks the refrigerator door open where there is more black mold than food. "Jesus," he mutters and slams it shut. He lifts his boot. "Is the floor always this wet?"

"Not that I know of." The fridge is surrounded by a half-inch-deep moat.

"Well, something's sprung a leak." He stamps his boot free of water. "Fire hazard." He reaches behind and unplugs the fridge. Earl heads toward the living room, holding his hands close to his body. His eyes travel around the room as if he's studying cathedral walls. "Are all the rooms like this one?" he asks.

"Yeah, pretty much."

"How long has it been like this?"

"It started getting unlivable a couple years ago."

"That when your brother moved out?" Earl asks. I nod.

Earl pulls out his cell phone, one of those old-fashioned types you have to flip open. He punches in a number. "Dot? Get two rooms ready. He has a younger sister. Okay. Bye." He shoves the phone back in his pocket and eyes me. "Let's get the hell out of here."

Annie is dressed and has stowed the lawn chair when Earl and I come back outside.

"Pack your bags, kid," Earl says to her. "You're coming home with us."

CHAPTER TWENTY

Dot sets enough food on the table for dinner to feed a small planet: a whole chicken, mashed potatoes, gravy, green beans, corn, biscuits, and butter.

"Eat up, kids," Dot says, as we sit around the food-laden table.

Annie and I fill our plates and chew quietly, listening to Earl tell his wife about our workday. "So we have a whole string of running toilets in the boys' locker room," he says. "Damn things are self-flushers, and half the time they go ape shit and won't stop." He gnaws at a drumstick and sets it back on his plate, wipes his mouth with the napkin, and continues. "How stupid are people now that they can't flush their own toilets?" He shakes his head. "A big damned waste of water if you ask me."

After Earl had loaded my sister's bags in his truck he brought her back to school with us. Annie worked with Hess and Shelly scouring the girls' locker room, and Earl and I cleaned the boys'. He muttered under his breath the whole time. I kept my mouth shut.

When Shelly, Annie, and I went out for lunch, Annie said, "How are we going to tell Mom?"

"I don't know."

"Do you think she'll be pissed?"

"Maybe," I said, "but Earl's pretty persuasive."

At home, Earl is still Earl, but a softer version. Dot just nods and smiles when he sputters his opinions. They've been married since dinosaurs roamed the earth, so I guess she's used to him.

Annie and I carry our plates to the kitchen and offer to do dishes.

"That's what the dishwasher is for," Dot says. "Go sit on the porch and I'll bring you each a dish of ice cream."

Earl lives in a big old house with an enormous front porch. The house is only about ten minutes from school, but it feels like we are out in the country.

I sit in one of the rocking chairs and scan the green acreage around us. Annie rocks in the chair next to mine. "I never want to leave here," she says. "But I'm going to worry about Mom."

"Yeah," I say. "Me too."

We rock in unison for a bit. "I feel like we've been dropped into an episode of *The Waltons*," I say. Our mom loved that show and used to make us watch reruns of it when we were kids.

Annie rocks and smiles, but it's a sad, wistful smile, a smile that says she will be making a hard choice if our mother begs her to come home.

"Maybe your leaving will be the catalyst she needs to finally get help," I say.

Annie's eyes fill up. "I hope so."

The painted slats of the porch floor creak under us as we rock. "Do you think she's noticed your absence yet?"

"Hard to tell," my sister says. She wipes her eyes with the back of her hand. "I sometimes wonder if she knows I'm there at all."

Earl steps out onto the porch. He is holding three bowls of ice cream and hands one to each of us. "Homemade peach," he says.

Annie takes a bite. "This is awesome."

"Like eating bites of heaven," I say.

Earl snickers. "Dot knows a way to a man's heart is through his stomach," he says. "Had a heck of a time getting our kids to move out 'cause of Dot's cooking."

"He tried to get me to stop feeding them," Dot says, as she steps outside. Dot pats Earl's back and sits on the porch swing.

Earl sits down next to her. "They lost their usefulness when they started high school," he says. "Dating, jobs, and all that. It was like pulling teeth to get them to do their chores."

"And you miss them terribly every day," Dot says.

Earl shrugs and shovels some more ice cream in his mouth.

"Foster still lives nearby, and they bring their kids out every Sunday," Dot says. "They have two boys." She looks at Annie. "You might know Conner. He's a freshman too."

Annie thinks for a second. "Oh, yeah," she says. "I hadn't made the connection."

Dot and Earl swing slowly. "Most of this damned town is related," Earl says. "About half the teachers and kids at school are relatives of one or both of us."

"Earl and I were high school sweethearts," Dot says.

Earl puts his arm around his wife. "And we're still sweethearts."

Dot rests her head on Earl's shoulder.

***

Annie's and my rooms are next to one another with a shared bathroom. Annie cried when she first sat on her new bed and surveyed the sparkling, feminine space. "This was our daughter Jane's room," Dot had said. "But you rearrange it however you like, hon."

My room is their youngest son Foster's old room, and it, too, is clean and inviting. As it starts to get dark, I haul the rest of my stuff upstairs. I hang up a couple shirts and put my clean socks and underwear in the drawers. It's been a long, long time since I have been able to do that.

I hear Annie rattling around in her room, and I knock on her door. She yells for me to come in.

"Hey, how's it going?" I can see she has not changed the arrangement. Only set a couple of her things on the dresser.

She sits on the bed. "It feels weird to actually have a bed again."

I nod. "Do you want me to go talk to Mom tomorrow?" I ask. "Or should we go talk to her together?"

"I'd love it if you came with me," Annie says. She runs her hands across the flowered bedspread. "I can't fully enjoy any of this until I know she's okay, you know?"

I nod. "I'll pick you up when I'm done with my shift at school. Get some sleep. "

I saunter back to my own room. It's been at least a decade since I've had a bedroom comfortable enough for restful sleep.

I figure I'll lie awake all night thinking, but I sleep like a mummy. Earl and Dot actually have chickens that act as feathered alarm clocks at 5:30 in the morning. It's weird waking up in a real bed. I stretch my arms up completely over my head. Funny how a simple thing like being able to stretch my arms makes me feel so grateful.

I hear footsteps below, and Earl and Dot's muffled conversation. A few minutes later I smell coffee and bacon.

I get up and pee, brush my teeth, and wash my face. I run into Annie in the hallway; she is holding a towel and a change of clothes. "How'd you sleep?" I ask.

"Great," she says. "At first it felt too quiet, but it was nice not to have to hear raccoons knocking over trashcans."

I sniff the air. I smell eggs and toast along with the bacon. "I think you and I will get fat living here."

She laughs and closes the bathroom door behind her. After I dress, I race downstairs toward the food. Earl sits behind the newspaper with a coffee mug in front of him. Dot stands at the stove, scrambling eggs.

"Smells great in here," I say.

"Breakfast is almost ready," Dot says. "Help yourself to coffee."

I sit down across from Earl with my mug. "Sleep okay, kid?" he asks from behind the paper.

"I did. Thank you."

Earl slides the sports section my way, and we read in comfortable silence until Dot places a plate of breakfast in front of each of us. Earl folds the paper and starts eating. Dot joins us with a plate.

"Annie takes forever to get ready," I say.

"Girls always do," Earl says.

I take a bite. "These are the best eggs I have ever eaten," I say.

"They're fresh from our hens," Dot says. "Nothing beats free-range eggs. Happy chickens produce good eggs."

It occurs to me I will miss breakfast with Shelly. I left my phone upstairs so I can't text her. She knows I'm here, but I hate the thought of her standing around alone outside the building. As if Earl reads my mind, he glances at his watch, and says, "Better finish up so you can meet your girlfriend."

I feel myself blush, and I shovel the food in my mouth. After I thank Dot for breakfast and leave to go upstairs, I hear Earl yell, "Don't be late, kid. Eight A.M.!"

I smile and shake my head.

Shelly stands at the back fence, smoking as usual. She waves as I pull up. When I step out of my car, she says, "Neruda! You don't look like feral car. Sleeping in a house agrees with you."

I chuckle and kiss her. "Good morning to you too."

"So, how is life living with Earl?"

"His wife is real nice," I say. I pat my stomach. "And she's the best cook in the world."

"So you've already eaten?"

"Yeah, but I can take you somewhere. I'll have a cup of coffee."

As we pull away from the school, Shelly asks, "Is Earl any different at home?"

"Not really. He has that gruff exterior, but he's a pussycat underneath."

"He takes in strays," Shelly says, "so he's got a soft spot somewhere." I nod. "How is Annie doing?"

"She really likes it there, but she's worried about our mom."

"How do you think she'll react? Do you think she's noticed Annie's gone?"

I shrug. "Hard to tell. I mean, she barely noticed when I left. Annie left a note, but Mom may not even find it. How could she, with all that stuff?"

"But she will notice eventually, right?"

"Yeah. Hopefully she won't freak out. Annie's worried this could take Mom over the edge."

"Or it could force her to get some help."

"Maybe," I say. "Earl and Dot plan to meet with her and talk her into letting them get custody of Annie." We pull into Steak 'n Shake. "Did you know Earl takes in foster kids?"

"Really?"

"Yeah. Dot says they started fostering kids after their own moved out." I am just about to get out of the car when I notice Rick and Ashley. "Shit!" I slam my door shut and put the key in the ignition.

"What's the matter?" Shelly asks.

"I can't deal with him." I point to Rick sitting in a booth near the window.

"So every time you see him, you're going to get back in your car and drive away?" she says. "You know Rooster is a small town, and you two will run into one another."

I still have my hand on the key ready to turn it. Then I sit back and run my hands through my hair and groan. I hate to admit she's right.

"Neruda, I don't know Rick," Shelly says, "but it seems he's forgiven you. Maybe you haven't forgiven yourself."

"Why would I need to forgive myself?"

"For being an asshat."

"Like he wasn't?"

"Okay, you're both idiots," she says.

"I have nothing to say to him." I glance at her. "And besides, he's spreading lies about you."

She scrunches her face. "Who isn't? I'm over it." She pulls the keys out of the ignition. "I'm hungry, so let's go inside and sit down."

I groan and step out of the car. Shelly and I stroll inside hand in hand as I try not to look in Rick and Ashley's direction. The only free table is a booth near them. Shelly pulls me toward it and we sit.

I hide behind my menu, and Shelly kicks at my feet. "Stop it," I mutter.

"He's looking this way," she whispers. "It's pretty obvious you're ignoring him."

The waitress blocks Rick from view. I take my time looking over the menu even though I have already eaten breakfast. Shelly orders her meal and glares at me. "We don't have all day, Neruda."

I close my menu. "I'll just have a cup of coffee."

After the waitress walks away, Shelly calls me an ass. She slides out of the booth, and before I can stop her, she walks to Rick and Ashley's table. She looks directly at Rick. "Okay, you guys need to kiss and make up because he," she points back at me, "is driving me nuts."

"So is Rick," Ashley says.

I roll my eyes. I can't even get up and leave because Shelly still has my keys. Rick sighs and sets down his fork. He throws up his hands in defeat and strides to my table. He sits across from me as Shelly claims Rick's place at the table across from Ashley.

"Hey," he says.

"Hey."

The waitress, looking confused, sets Shelly's and my coffee down. "Thanks," I say. I glance over at Shelly, but she is deep in conversation with my ex-girlfriend. That can only be a disaster.

Rick taps on the table and looks out the window, and I fumble with the handle on my coffee cup. "You're wrong about Shelly," I say.

"Okay," he says. "I'm sorry. I just went on what I heard."

"Get a hearing aid, Grandpa, because what you heard was a truckload of elephant shit."

He snorts a laugh. "Does this make us even for you trying to kill me?"

"I didn't try to kill you," I say. "I only wanted to blow up your car."

"Yeah, and that turned out well for you."

"You started it."

Rick considers this. "Yes, I did. But you were the inadvertent catalyst in pushing Ashley and I together."

"Ashley and me."

"Fuck you and your AP English grammar."

I smile. He always hated it when I one-upped him. "Words are all I have," I say. "I got expelled from school, I am spending my summer cleaning the school, and until yesterday, I was living in my car."

Rick leans against the back of the booth. "Say what?" he pauses, wrinkles his forehead. "*What?*"

"You know how I never took you to my house these past couple years?" He nods. "There was some truth that my mom slept in the daytime," I say. "She often works nights. But the real reason is she's a hoarder. The house is a total disaster. And it got to where I couldn't stand it, so I moved out and started living in my car last fall."

"Jesus," he says. "You lived in . . . did Ashley know?"

"Nobody knew. Other than Mom, Jeff, and Annie," I say. "And Shelly. She figured it out the first day she met me."

"But where are you living now?"

"With Earl."

"The custodian?"

"Yeah," I say. "He noticed my car was on the school lot before he got there every morning. Once I admitted to Earl I lived in it, he insisted I move in with him and his wife." I take a swallow of coffee. "Annie's there too."

"Holy shit, Flynnstone. You could have moved in with us."

I look down. "I didn't want anybody to know."

He shook his head. "No wonder you went a little crazy."

I shrug. "I was crazier before. But yeah," I say, "the pressure may have exacerbated things. I was often hungry."

Shelly approaches the table, holding a carry-out bag. "So are you two friends again?"

I raise my eyebrows and look at Rick. "I guess," he says.

I smirk. "Someone has to do it."

"Neruda," she says, "we have to get back to school. I've already paid."

Rick and I slide out from behind the booth. "Neruda?" he asks.

"It's his chosen name," Shelly says. "For his fake ID. Michael Neruda."

"Cool."

"Yeah, well, see ya." I say to Rick.

"Shake his hand," Shelly nudges me.

"Okay, but I'm not kissing him." Rick laughs, and he and I shake. "Later, man."

I wave at Ashley as we walk out. Interesting how I feel nothing for her anymore.

Shelly starts nibbling on her breakfast in the car as I pull out onto Rocket Road. "Thanks," I tell her. "I no longer feel like something is poking needles on my innards." She nods and chews. "And it's getting easier to tell people my mom is a hoarder." Shelly takes a long sip on her coffee.

"Maybe I'll put it on a billboard," I say. "Susan Marie Flynn is a Giant Hoarder."

Shelly laughs and takes a big bite of her sandwich.

"You have no idea how much better I feel right now. Like the sun came up after a long, hazy winter," I say.

At the stoplight, I lean over and kiss Shelly. She tastes like eggs and cheese. She leans her head on my shoulder the rest of the way back to school.

CHAPTER TWENTY-ONE

I'm not looking forward to facing my mother with Annie. Earl offers to join us, but I figure he might stoke the fire. "Let me see how she takes it first," I tell him.

As we pull up in front of the townhouse, Annie says, "Let's hope she's in a good mood."

"Or that she hasn't called the cops and filed a missing person report."

We head to the back of the house and walk in through the screen door. Mom is standing by the counter, pouring herself a cup of coffee. Her freshly showered hair hangs in a long braid down her back. "Hey kids," she says. She picks up a cigarette and twists the base before putting it in her mouth. She inhales and expels smoke.

"You didn't light it," Annie says.

"It's called an e-cigarette," Mom says. "It expels mist, but no tobacco smoke." She hands it to us to look at. "I'm trying to quit, and one of my patients gave it to me."

"Cool." I hand it back to her.

Annie clears her throat. "Have you noticed the back porch is clean?"

"Yes," Mom says. "What did you do with it all?"

"I moved."

Our mother raises her eyebrows. "Where?"

"We're both living with Earl, the head custodian at school," I say.

"Earl! Oh my God. He was there when I was in school."

"Yeah," I say, "He said he remembered you."

Mom starts puttering around with stuff on the counter. Annie and I glance at each other. "Mom," Annie says. "Did you hear what I said? I moved."

"Yes, I heard you." Mom pulls a large plastic bowl from a pile of junk on the counter and rinses it off in the sink. She sets the bowl down, turns to us, and says, "I need to go get dressed for work now." She grabs her coffee cup and her e-cigarette, and disappears into the other room.

Annie and I just look at each other. "What was that?" she asks.

"Beats me."

Our mother went on a rampage when Paul picked Jeff up. She threw things at them both as they loaded Paul's truck. When Jeff climbed into the passenger seat, Mom grabbed his sleeve and pleaded with him to stay.

"I'm sorry, Mom," Jeff said. "I can't live here anymore." He gently removed her hand from his shirt and closed the door. As Paul and Jeff drove away, Mom collapsed onto the yard and wailed.

When I left, she helped me load my car. "Now whenever you get cold or need to eat, make sure you come back inside," she said. "Don't be a stranger."

"It's like I don't even exist." Annie storms out the back door.

"Mom!" I follow my mother into the living room.

My mother doesn't notice my presence. She sets down her coffee cup and electronic cigarette and lifts an afghan from the couch. She drapes it around her shoulders like a cape. She closes her eyes and twirls, her lips curled in a wistful smile. And it hits me. The cape—like the one she described the first time she and my father met under the stage. This mess of a house is her prop room. My mother has never left that room.

I back out quietly and go look for my sister. Annie is sitting on the back steps, sobbing. I kneel and wrap my arms around my sister.

"She cares more about all that junk than she does her own children," Annie says between sobs.

"She's confused," I say. "She doesn't know what she cares about anymore." Someday I'll explain to Annie what I figured out, but right now is not the moment to do that.

I drop Annie off at Earl and Dot's and head to work at the theater. On the way, my phone rings.

"So how did your mother take the news of you and Annie living with Earl?" Shelly asks.

"Surprisingly well," I say. "She was creepily calm."

"What do you mean?"

"When Annie told her we moved in with Earl, all she said was she remembered him from when she was in school. Then she went to dress for work," I say. "But I figured out why she hoards."

"Oh?"

"Remember in her diary when she went to the prop room with my father? How she felt comfortable among all the clutter? She's recreated her own prop room."

"That's so sad, Neruda."

"Yeah," I sigh. "It is."

EPILOGUE

Daring Enough to Finish

Face that lights my face, you spin
intelligence into these particles

I am. Your wind shivers my tree.
My mouth tastes sweet with your name

in it. You make my dance daring enough
to finish. No more timidity! Let

fruit fall and wind turn my roots up
in the air, done with patient waiting.

Rumi

Earl and Dot are officially Annie's foster parents, and they have not tossed me out yet. My mother didn't even try to fight giving them custody of my sister, but she went ballistic when Social Services showed up at her house to talk her into cleaning it up. She called me and screamed expletives I didn't even know she knew. And now she's not speaking to me.

I go over every few days to talk to her, but she won't answer her door. Last time Jeff came with me, and I thought she'd come outside since she's not mad at him, but she shouted from her bedroom window, "You people are trespassing. You go away or I'm calling the sheriff."

"I'm not giving up, Mom," I yelled from the lawn. "One of these days you'll come down and talk to me."

"Don't bet on it," she screeched.

Later, Jeff and I talked to Paul about it. "She may end up losing everything," he said. "She doesn't own the property, so if she doesn't clean it up, the landlord can throw her out. She could end up homeless."

Earl went with me once and offered to help her, but she threatened to call the cops on him too. He threw his hands up in the air, and said, "Sorry, kid. You can't help someone who doesn't want to be helped."

One thing I know for certain is I can never tell my mother I found out the truth about her and my father.

At school Earl still treats me like a stray dog, but he only has Shelly and me another week, so he and Hess are getting as much bang for their buck as they can. This week we are painting the hallways. School starts in two weeks.

Rick and I don't hang together like we used to, but we're friends again. The four of us went out for pizza together last weekend. Ashley and Shelly get along surprisingly well.

"You do realize both of us have dated you," Shelly said to me.

Rick laughed. "So both of you have had major lapses in sanity."

I puffed out my chest. "No, it means the women at this table have amazingly good taste in men." Ashley and Shelly both rolled their eyes, and Shelly made a gagging noise.

Maybe someday Rick and I will be tight again, but right now things are still stiff between us. He and Ashley are both headed to college in a few weeks. He's majoring in theatre and music at University of Chicago and she's going to Wright State to major in art. Maybe distance and time will heal all of us. Odd to think I'm still technically in high school for another year.

And I'm looking forward to school this year. I could have taken the GED and been done with high school, but I like the idea of spending senior year with Shelly. We won't even be on the high school campus. The principal and guidance counselor suggested the best option for us odd ducks is to do postsecondary options where we take classes at the local branch of Ohio University. We will avoid the awkward high school drama, get our high school diplomas, and also receive college credit. So in a way, I'm headed to college too.

Since I'm eating real food every day I can lay off the donuts and junk food, and now I easily run five miles without feeling like I need oxygen. I'm not training for anything. Running just keeps the craziness of my life from detonating inside my head. Besides, I need to work off all the food Dot force-feeds me. Best of all, Shelly says I have a rocking body now. "Your abs look like you're made of Legos."

Shelly, Shelly, Shelly. I've never known anyone like her. She is light and wind and thunder and ocean, and I can't imagine I would have survived this summer without her.

Shelly and I are sitting here at Starbucks, drinking lattes, using her laptop to find information on colleges and majors, even though I clearly told her I am not going to college after this year.

"You're going away to college, Neruda," Shelly says. "I'm not going to be associated with a mental midget."

"But I come from nothing."

"So did Lincoln, and he ended up becoming president."

"Maybe I like being nothing," I say. "Maybe my biggest ambition is to manage the theater at the mall."

She sneers at me. "You're going to college."

"Okay, I'll stay here and take classes locally."

"You're getting out of this town. Far away from here, Neruda," she says. "Far, far away."

"But what about us?" Shelly is a big part of my life now, and it makes me sad to imagine not seeing her every day. There are infinite reasons to stay, and only one, selfish reason to leave.

She sighs. "If we are meant to remain us, we'll find a way to make it work."

"I can't leave now," I say.

"Why not?"

"I've never even been to another state."

She rolls her eyes at me.

"And then there's my job. It doesn't pay much, but I'm not totally dependent on Earl and Dot. I can pay my own way." I fidget with the stir stick. "Most of all, I'd be leaving behind the people I love. The idea of not being able to see my brother and sister any time I want punches me in the gut. My family needs me."

She narrows her eyes at me. "Neruda, you can't forfeit your life in order to solve your family's problems."

"But I'm afraid my mom will go off the deep end if I leave."

"She still has Jeff and Annie," Shelly says. "And your sticking around here won't make your mother less screwed up," she says You have to let yourself be the kid, not the parent." She pauses and looks at me. She reaches across the table and takes my hand. "You have to go find what you've been looking for all these years."

"What if I show up in Seattle, and my father turns out to be the biggest asshole in the world?"

"That's not possible," she says. "You're already the biggest asshole."

I raise my middle finger at her. She blows me a kiss.

"Isn't it enough just to know he's out there?" I say. "The option for me to go out there someday exists, but I've earned the right to settle down and be average. Until a few weeks ago my life was a mess, but it's pretty boring now, and I'm kind of okay with that."

She leans back and studies me. "What are you really afraid of, Neruda?"

"You're a pain in the ass," I say. I look away and take a deep breath. Haven't I spent my life looking for him? Yet now that I have a chance to meet my father, I'm paralyzed, like those prisoners trapped in Plato's cave who, after learning they can leave, must be thrust into the light and possibilities outside the cave. I look back at Shelly, and say, "I'm afraid he won't want to know me."

"That's the chance you have to take."

I sigh. "Yeah. Uncertainty sucks."

She looks at something on her screen. "You'll miss me when you head west, but deep down in that weird ass soul you won't be happy unless you take the risk. Besides, I'm not even going to be here in Rooster. I could end up in college in Seattle or wherever myself."

Shelly is applying to colleges and universities all over. On the Common App she applied to thirty different places. The closest one to here is University of Chicago. "You need to go to college and it needs to be in the state of Washington."

"But what would I major in?" I say. "I have no skills."

"You have plenty of skills."

"None of them useful."

"You write," she says.

"Grocery stores and coffee shops are full of English majors. Like Theo. Isn't he working in a coffee shop?"

"He chooses to do menial labor as part of his research."

"I already work a crappy job," I say. "Why torture myself with even more school just to keep working crappy jobs?"

"You could teach classes in survival," Shelly says.

"Is that a major?"

"Maybe." She types on the keyboard and slides her laptop across the table toward me. "Outdoor studies."

I laugh.

She takes her computer back and starts tapping on the keyboard again. "You know, you have a unique advantage," she says. "We both do."

"What do you mean?"

"Our stories make us freaks," Shelly says. "It's almost unfair the advantage you and I have on the 'Describe the Challenges You Have Faced' question."

I nod. "But do you really think any sane university would take a chance on either of us?" I ask. "I mean, you're a car thief and big flight risk, and I might clutter up the dorm."

She crosses her eyes at me and sips her vanilla latte. "Colleges will be recruiting *us* for our fascinating diversity," she says. "Both of us could end up at freaking Harvard or Yale."

"And how would I pay for it?"

"I already told you," she says. "Colleges will be throwing money at you. You're from Appalachia, your mother is nuts, and you have a book-worthy life story."

So I am sitting in Starbucks, drinking a mocha latte, looking at a legal pad containing a list of five colleges where I plan to apply. All of them are in or near Seattle.

ACKNOWLEDGMENTS

Many people have helped bring this book to fruition.

Thanks to David Greenberg, who showed me I had started my draft in the wrong place. Thank you Amy Gibson, Cynthia Rucker, Debbie Hardin Day, Cindy Sterling, Logan Paskell, and Brandi Young, for reading and commenting on early drafts. I'd like to thank Mark Malatesta, Elaine Miller, Les Edgerton, and Krista van Dolzer for their writing tips and encouragement, and Leslie Skoda for giving me Pelee Peugeot. Thank you Deb Stetson and Jackie Mitchard for your editorial insight and encouragement, and Meredith O'Hayre for your eagle-eyed copyediting, Chris Duffy for answering my endless questions, and Peggy Gough at University of Texas Press for help with the permissions process.

Much appreciation goes to Giacomo's Bread & More and Starbucks in Zanesville, Ohio, for supplying me with coffee and sustenance as I sat, tethered to a corner table wearing my headphones, writing and revising this novel. I'd also like to give a shout-out to the Aloha Cafe in Lynnwood, Washington, for feeding me as I worked on my final edits.

I owe a special thank you to Elizabeth Juden Christy, who loves my characters as much as I do and doggedly corrected my numerous typos and inconsistencies.

And, of course, this novel would not have been possible without Pablo Neruda.